# THE
# POOR BOY'S
# GAME

Also by Dennis Tafoya

*The Wolves of Fairmount Park*
*Dope Thief*

# THE
# POOR BOY'S
# GAME

# DENNIS TAFOYA

Minotaur Books
New York

THE POOR BOY'S GAME. Copyright © 2014 by Dennis Tafoya. All rights reserved. Printed in the United States of America. For information, address St. Martin's Press, 175 Fifth Avenue, New York, N.Y. 10010.

www.minotaurbooks.com

Library of Congress Cataloging-in-Publication Data

Tafoya, Dennis.
  The poor boy's game / Dennis Tafoya. — First Edition.
      p. cm.
    ISBN 978-1-250-01953-0 (hardcover)
    ISBN 978-1-250-01954-7 (e-book)
  1. Women detectives—Fiction.  2. Organized crime—Pennsylvania—
Philadelphia—Fiction.  I. Title.
    PS3620.A33P66 2014
    813'.6—dc23

                                                    2013047142

St. Martin's Minotaur books may be purchased for educational, business, or promotional use. For information on bulk purchases, please contact Macmillan Corporate and Premium Sales Department at 1-800-221-7945, extension 5442, or write specialmarkets@macmillan.com.

First Edition: April 2014

10  9  8  7  6  5  4  3  2  1

# ACKNOWLEDGMENTS

What I love most about writing a novel is the opportunity to learn. I got some fantastic lessons while I was writing *The Poor Boy's Game*, about the city and its history, the way crime and punishment works, and the craft of writing. Some of the great and generous folks who helped school me: Megan Abbott, Jim Baker, Anthony Celli, Dan Conaway, Greg Gillespie, Mike Gospodarek, James B. Jacobs, Don Lafferty, Jonathan Maberry, Lucas Mangum, Marc Maurino, Jon McGoran, Kelly Simmons, Wallace Stroby, August Tarrier, and Laurie Webb.

I also have to single out my agents and indispensable friends, Alex Glass of Trident Media and Brooke Ehrlich of Brooke Ehrlich Artist Management. Thanks for this amazing and unexpected career.

Thanks also to Kelley Ragland, Elizabeth Lacks, Hector DeJean, Justine Gardner, and everyone at St. Martin's for endless patience and infectious enthusiasm.

Thanks, most of all, to my wife, Karen, who put up with all of this personal growth going on in the next room, and my kids, Elena, Rachel, and Dave. Please never do anything I write about.

*I'm a fighter. That's all I know how to do, is fight.*

—Christy Martin

# THE
# POOR BOY'S
# GAME

# 1

Frannie Mullen stood behind the counter at a sports memorabilia store on Arch Street, waiting for a felon. The felon's name was Otto Berman, and he had embezzled three hundred thousand dollars from a mobbed-up linen supply company in Atlantic City. When he got caught, he tried to turn state's evidence, offering up his bosses, and when he decided he was more frightened of his employers than he was of the feds, he jumped bail and ran.

Berman's office in a Point Pleasant strip mall had featured a water-stained ceiling, leaning stacks of dusty files, and a pressboard desk, but there had also been baseball cards neatly framed on the walls, some of which looked to Frannie like they were worth money. When they peeled open his cheap safe he had two more, including a signed Hank Aaron card in his Braves uniform. So she and Sleeper, her partner from the task force, dug through his credit card receipts (stuffed in a box from Discount Shoe Warehouse) and turned up the place he dealt with, so that three weeks later she was standing behind a low glass counter and waiting for Otto to pick up a Babe Ruth card from 1933 worth eighteen hundred dollars.

Now it was almost five and Otto hadn't shown, so they were beginning to think he wasn't coming. There were three on her team: Joe Carson in a UPS truck on the street; Eric "Sleeper" Hansen standing in the doorway to the back wearing a blue shirt with the name CHUCK in script over the pocket, pretending to look at a clipboard; Frank Russo out of sight with an automatic rifle, the barrel down along his left leg, and a black ballistic vest that read U.S. MARSHALS across the chest. He was paging through a catalog of sports memorabilia. He lifted his head to wink at her and mouthed, *Where you at?*

It was something he did: When he was one of her instructors at Glynco he had stopped her in the middle of a talk about search and seizure and asked her where she was at. She had looked around the room at all the other 1811s, the Treasury agents and ICE agents and the other Marshals, but they all sensed a trap and looked away. She had stammered something about the training, how it was going, and Russo smiled and said, *No, where are you at? Your location, right now, physically. If you need help, if somebody gets hurt, if you need backup, you have to know where you are all the time. Not how you're* doing, *Mullen. No one gives a shit how you're* doing. *Just where the hell you are.*

Now Frannie was lead on the team, and he smiled and tapped his watch, telling her time was almost up.

On the wall above the cash register a photo caught Frannie's eye; two men, brown skin slick with sweat and oil, one of them with blood spread bright and vivid across his nose and cheeks. Frannie knew it immediately and forgot everything, standing with her back to the open room: Hagler versus Hearns, a fight from 1985 that people still talked about. They called it "The War." She had the fight card signed by Hagler in a closet somewhere and looking around at all the framed cards and signed bats and balls she wondered what it was worth. Maybe she'd sell it. She had a walk-in closet full of junk from the house she'd grown up in, and she hadn't gotten around to throwing it away after her aunt Rodi died. Maybe she'd dump it all on eBay, find out what she could get.

In her earpiece she heard Joe Carson say, "You got a guy coming in." Carson was in the UPS truck, in front of the parking lot two doors up, with a newspaper on the dash and a Benelli M90 shotgun behind the seat. This part of Arch Street ran through Chinatown, and on the street Frannie could see bright signs decorated with ideograms that shimmered in the rain.

She cleared her throat. "Description?"

"Six-one, six-two, two hundred pounds. Black raincoat, gray hair, came from the parking lot on Race."

Sleeper looked at her, his eyebrows raised, but she shook her head. Into her mic she said, "Thanks for the heads-up." To Sleeper she said, "No, he's too tall and he's got hair." She had a photograph on the counter in front of her, the same one Sleeper had clipped to the clipboard he carried as a prop. Otto Berman from his license, a wide face, thin lips, a fringe of brown hair that seemed to recede while she watched it. Worried eyes that looked down and away, set in dark smudges. As if he had already been on the run when the picture was taken, as if he'd been born guilty of something he could never make right.

There was a muted chime and the door moved, the guy in the black raincoat coming in and going immediately to a framed Raúl Ibañez jersey by the door. He had neatly trimmed white hair, a suit and tie under the raincoat, looked like an executive, a lawyer maybe, from one of the white-shoe firms sprinkled around City Hall. She'd have to get rid of him, in case Berman was still coming. There was a flash from the street and she flinched, then a low, echoing boom that rattled the windows. Her earpiece hissed and snapped and the man with the raincoat smiled at her. "Here it comes," he said, nodding his head toward the street, and the rain came down in wide sheets that flexed and broke as the wind picked up.

Frannie looked at her watch and stepped from behind the counter. There was a hiss in her ear and she heard

Carson say something, his voice raised, but there was another blue flash of lightning in the street and whatever he said was lost in static. She turned discreetly and tapped the earpiece while it clicked and hummed, and then the bell chimed and Berman walked in. Frannie stopped, looked back at the desk and the open doorway to the storage area, but Sleeper and Russo were out of sight and she was too close to the customer and Berman to say anything over the radio to Carson.

Berman looked nervous, his head jerking from side to side, taking in the businessman, who stood, head cocked, in front of a jersey that Pete Rose had worn during his Philly years and then Frannie, who tried on a bland and distant smile. The accountant's clothes were rumpled, like he'd been sleeping in his car, and his sparse hair was lank and looked unwashed. He closed an umbrella clumsily with his left hand and dropped it on the carpet by the door. His right hand was in his raincoat pocket, and his eyes jumped in his head.

"May I help you?"

Berman looked toward the back. "Where's Emile?" Emile Frankel was the owner, and he had turned over the store for the day to the Marshals and made himself scarce. Frannie had the impression he was only too happy to help the feds because he didn't want anyone asking a lot of hard questions about his business, his tax status, and the provenance of some of the stuff on the walls, the signed jerseys and autographed footballs that sold for thousands of dollars because of the unrecognizable scrawl of some ballplayer who had been dead for twenty years.

"Mr. Frankel's just stepped out. Were you looking for something special?"

Berman didn't say anything, but turned for a long moment to look at the customer by the Pete Rose jersey, then out at the street, and then swung his head to look hard at Frannie. She saw the bulge in his pocket where his hand was in his coat and wondered if he had a weapon and if she could grab the arm before he could get it clear of his pocket. She took a small step back toward the counter, and she heard him shift and move with her. She was wearing a Tahari suit cut loose under the arms to cover a concealable ForceOne bulletproof vest and hemmed a little long in the legs to hide the Galco rig holding a small-frame Glock at her ankle. There were ten rounds in the pistol and a twenty-one-inch spring-loaded Peacekeeper baton under her coat. The vest would stop a magnum round, but if he had a knife, or if he pointed a gun at her head, or the customer, things could still go wrong.

"I'm here to pick something up?"

"Of course, sir. Just let me . . ." She pointed toward the counter, hoping that Sleeper would figure out what was going on without popping out and spooking Berman, or that Carson had noticed him come in and was getting a position on the guy to grab him when he walked out if she made the decision to let him walk rather than risk the arrest with a civilian standing three paces away. She hated this calculus, the figuring of lines and angles. She wanted to grab the accountant and throw him to the floor.

She crossed to the counter and turned to see Carson crossing the street in his UPS uniform, a long box under one arm. He was moving his lips, probably trying to reach her or Sleeper or Russo. The radio was dead, but she was still hearing a voice in her head, the voice that told her when things were slipping beyond her control. Now a van was pulling to the curb, cutting just behind Carson as he stepped from the street to the wide side-walk. The van had the words SCOLARI AND SONS PLUMB-ING on the door.

Frannie had just reached the counter when Carson got to the door, left arm around the box. He pushed at the heavy glass door and Berman was suddenly beside her, grabbing her arm with his free hand. She turned to see him staring out the window, the tension in his arm communicated to her directly, physically, as if in touch-ing they now shared the same nervous system. The van was idling at the curb, the side door slowly sliding open to reveal only a dark hole. Joe Carson shouldered aside the heavy glass front door, his hand slipping inside the box. There was a moment when everything slowed down and seemed to get very close, as if she could extend her arms and touch every single thing in front of her—the white van at the curb, Carson coming through the door with his eyes on her, the oblivious customer turned away, Berman's yellow, clawlike hand on her wrist. She saw that his nails were ragged and bitten down, and she could smell the rain in his coat and beneath that his unwashed hair and the curdled wine on his breath. She saw in his darting eyes and jerky movement that he was drunk and scared out of his mind.

She pulled the Peacekeeper out of her pocket and swung it down to snap it open, then reared back, pulling Berman off balance and bringing the baton down hard on his elbow as he tried to get the pistol clear of his coat. He screamed, slamming his arm back and catching Frannie across the bridge of her nose, a jolt that rattled her skull, and she tasted metal on her tongue as Sleeper came over the counter, cuffs out. She dropped to one knee and felt for the ankle rig.

Carson was through the door and closing the distance, the black shotgun coming up, when the man by the door in the raincoat, the man Frannie made for a lawyer, pulled a heavy dull-metal revolver and put it against Carson's head in one smooth motion, like it was a trick they'd worked out in advance. Outside there was a silent blue flash and the room went dark, so that for one long moment Carson and the man who held a gun to his head appeared in black silhouette against the windows. The lights clicked and buzzed and came back on and no one had moved that Frannie could tell. Sleeper had one of the cuffs locked on Berman's right hand, and Frannie herself was crouched at Berman's feet, her right hand on the butt of the small Glock 27 in her ankle holster. The man with the pistol whispered something and fanned back the hammer and the Benelli dropped slowly to the carpeted floor at Carson's feet. Sleeper opened his hand, releasing the handcuffs, and Berman took a step back. Frannie felt blood on her face and tasted it on her tongue.

Behind her Frank Russo said, "Nobody needs to get hurt, partner." Russo was dark and had razor-cut black hair, an Italian boy from Oregon Avenue, but he talked the way all the male Marshals talked, with the rhythms and tones of the Southern plains, a drawl that seemed to come with the badge, like it was issued at the federal training center at Glynco. Like they were all the sons of Wyatt Earp.

Berman took a step back, and then another. Frannie could feel Russo beside her and shifted her head to see him with the M4 up at his shoulder, the barrel trained on the face of the man wearing the black raincoat with the pistol at Carson's head. She touched her lips and her hand came away smeared with red.

Berman ducked behind Carson to reach the door, one handcuff dangling. "Let's go," he said, his voice thin with tension. The white-haired man looked at each of them in turn and grabbed Carson by the collar, pivoting him awkwardly to use him as a shield and backing toward the door, the barrel of his pistol tight against Carson's skull. Joe Carson's arms were up in front of him, showing them all his empty palms.

The man with the gun shook his head. "You said there'd be money here, Otto."

"Shut up, Arthur."

"I mean, what the hell, Otto? Who are these people?"

"Arthur!" Then he said something fast in what sounded like German. She couldn't catch it.

Berman grabbed Carson's shoulder and ducked behind him to claw at the door. Frannie heard Frank Russo say, "Otto. Don't do this."

He stopped, but didn't turn. "You think I want to do any of this?"

Frank Russo said, "Listen to me, Otto. You're in trouble, I know. You're scared, you feel trapped, but this is just a mistake and nobody's hurt. You go out that door with our guy and you throw away any chance you have to get clear of this."

"Man, I got no chance now." He crouched awkwardly behind Carson, who stood rigid, his eyes pinned to the right side of his head, trying to see the barrel of the gun jammed against his temple.

Arthur turned his head slightly to Otto and spoke again, fiercely, two quick words in the same language, a harsh clicking of the tongue that might be German.

"No, you do have a chance, Otto. The prosecutor will still help you—"

"The prosecutor? Who gives a shit about the prosecutor? You know who I owe money to? You know who those people are?"

"Otto, you got to think about what you're doing."

"Everybody wants me dead!" Berman looked back and forth between Frank and Sleeper and then down at

Frannie where she stood in her half crouch, one hand on the Glock. He said, "Jesus, look at her, look at her face. She wants to kill me so bad she can taste it." He found the door handle and was tugging on it with his thin arms, the heavy glass door swinging in. Arthur crowded in as Berman pulled and Frannie saw what was coming and tensed, narrowing her eyes and gritting her teeth as the door swung in and hit the tall man's gun hand.

The gun swung wide and Joe Carson moved fast, smacking at the man's wrist and trying to wrench free of his grasp. Frannie pulled her Glock as Berman yanked harder at the door, his face set, and the gun in Arthur's hand went off with a hard pop. Frannie saw a flash, a white star imprinted on her vision as she extended her arms toward the struggling men, her pistol locked in both hands. Carson yanked himself free and Frannie fired one shot and the man's head bounced off the door and he went down, his eyes rolled back and his muscles loose in death. Berman screamed, a sort of high-pitched wheeze, and launched himself through the door and took off down the street. Frannie could hear him screaming as he ran, his arms up as if to ward off the rain and the noise he made changing, becoming a throaty sob as he disappeared from view. The van at the curb pulled out, following Berman down the street.

There was a moment's silence, Frannie still standing with her pistol pointed at the dead man, Carson standing with his hands drawn up under his chin like an actor about to deliver a line. Frannie could hear something, a hiss or a rasp, and took a moment to realize it was coming from Frank Russo, who stood with his hands on his throat while bright blood jetted through his fingers.

Frannie threw the Glock down and grabbed at him, putting her long white hands over Frank's thick fingers and looking into his eyes. He was trying to talk, making terrible noises, and Carson stammered into the radio while Sleeper put away his pistol and helped her get Frank into a sitting position. In seconds she was covered in his blood while they both squeezed at the ragged hole. She heard Carson saying, "What? What? The corner, at the corner, come on." His voice caught in his throat, and Sleeper stood up and grabbed the radio from him and started walking whoever it was through the situation, repeating the address, saying there were plainclothes officers at the scene so nobody would come in shooting. He pointed at the door with one red hand, and Carson nodded, his eyes wild, and took off after Berman.

She tried to keep her face open so that Frank would see her and be calm. She remembered him telling her she had to know all the time where she was. The street, the directions, the flow of traffic. She said, almost to herself, "1013 Arch Street, tell them." Frank was too caught up in what was going on inside him to notice them, too lost in his own dimming mind, thinking maybe of his wife, his two girls. She said, "I'm here, Frank. I'm right here."

# 2

It was dark, had been dark for hours and Frannie had the sense that it was cold, saw the EMTs in their heavy jackets and sharing steaming white cups, but she herself could not tell. She tried to remember the date, but couldn't come up with anything except that it was October, and too early in the winter to be so cold. The rain had stopped, the rainwater on the sidewalks had become a kind of thick slurry, some state between ice and water, and Frannie thought that if it started up again it would be snow.

She wondered idly how she looked. She had one of those chemical ice packs that a tech had given her for what must be a bruise or mark between her eyes where Berman had clocked her with his elbow and she had held it to her face for a couple of minutes, but now she just passed it from hand to hand and felt it going warm.

The EMT had given her a sympathetic frown as she handed her the cold pack and touched her own face in the hollow between her eyes. Frannie thought at first that her nose might be broken again, and remembered the first time it had happened, when she was a teenager. She could feel blood crusted under her nose and around her lips. She could close her eyes and still see a faint green star, the flash of the gun fired by the man she had killed.

The situation was bad. The supervisory deputy had come down and stood by Joe Carson, the two of them leaning their heads together and talking. The SD was named Bill Scanlon and Frannie knew he didn't think much of her, had a way of scowling when she talked that let her know he thought she was too young, had come up too fast, and had too much responsibility for her years in. And there was more; a complaint against him that he had blamed on Frannie, an incident that had ended with a letter of reprimand in his file. And now here was Frank Russo down, maybe dead, and a high-profile fugitive in the wind. Scanlon would look for someone to blame. He raised his eyes over Carson's bowed head and looked hard at her.

She knew a story was forming about what had happened, strands of reality and impression and wish coming together into a narrative that would be the way everything that had happened would be judged. There were two ambulances and several cars from the Philadelphia PD, guys with different uniforms, evidence techs; down the block TV reporters doing stand-ups in showers of brilliant light. There would be segments on the news based on rumors from people who hadn't been there, witnesses that hadn't seen anything but only heard gunshots and breaking glass and screams. At 601 Market there would be an internal review, hard attention on everyone involved. An official version would be arrived at, rendered in the flat and toneless poetry of legal transcript, and as the team leader she'd take the weight.

She had positioned herself on the curb facing the big arch covered with Chinese characters, so she couldn't see through the starred glass into the dark cave of the store. She could hear people talking on cellphones; the strange accents and unfamiliar languages reduced to assonant song. On the wet sidewalk at her feet was a compress, lost from a gurney or dropped by an EMT. She had been stealing glances at it and now stared down, seeing a bright red dot and a couple of smears that might have been left by gloved fingers. She thought she smelled blood, but that might be just in her head. She felt she might see things that weren't there, hear sounds and voices. In her mind's eye she saw the photograph of the boxers that had caught her eye in the store, their shoulders slick with sweat, their eyes wild with pain and sunken beneath their swollen brows.

A Philly detective came and stood by her, flipping open a notebook. Carson drifted over from his conference with

Scanlon and Sleeper materialized at her elbow from somewhere, and the cop looked down at his notes and up at each of them and drew a breath. He said, "Tell me about your day?"

She said, "We knew our guy was coming in, to the memorabilia dealer. We thought he was picking up a baseball card he had ordered, but it looks like he had cooked up a scheme to rob the place. Probably he needed money to run with. If I was to guess." EMTs moved by with Arthur's body in a black bag, one wheel on the gurney spinning crazily. Frannie pointed at the body. "He brought this guy as muscle, and I guess they were going to get what they could off of Frankel, the owner. Berman and his accomplice pulled guns and one of my team was shot." She cleared her throat. "I shot the accomplice and Berman took off."

The cop blinked, keeping his face neutral. "Was he facing serious time, your guy Berman?"

"It wasn't the time so much. He stole money from the Catrambones. He was the accountant for one of their linen operations in Jersey."

"Okay, then. That might make you do something stupid."

Sleeper said, "If stealing from the Catrambones wasn't stupid enough."

The detective looked at his notebook again. "We think your guy Berman was found about a half hour ago in Camden. We're expecting a call from the watch commander over there, but word is that a body was found by kids under the Ben Franklin near Campbell's Field." The guy looked tired and depressed, the detective, and there were dark smudges under his narrowed eyes. Frannie thought his face was familiar but he wasn't one of the guys she knew by name. "You know what it's like across the river now. They're running half manpower with the budget cuts, got fucking park rangers riding patrol. So we'll hear when we hear. The patrolman who called it in said the body had multiple stab wounds and an apparent gunshot wound to the head. The ME is on scene and Camden will pass along the report as soon as they get it." He flipped some more pages. "A guy at the Asian grocery up the street said he saw Berman being pulled into a van with the name of a plumbing company. The guy said there was a struggle."

Sleeper looked at her. "The van."

Frannie said, "Yeah. On the side, it was . . . Scolari, something like that? I thought the van was Berman and his friends. A getaway car."

"Guess not. It was stolen yesterday up in Bensalem. We got pictures off the cameras at the bank and the parking lot. I guess Mr. Berman's previous employers had the same idea you did and camped on the store, too. He ran out of here and they grabbed him and . . ." He lifted a hand, a gesture that meant *There you go,* or *That's that,* or something. "We have the description and plates out here and in Jersey. We're looking at the photos from the cameras now." He pointed down the street without looking. "See if we can make the driver."

Frannie thought the cop looked as sad as she'd ever seen anyone look. She thought about being a city cop, about how much bad news they had to deliver in a day. How could you bear up under that? Her friend Mari was in uniform with Philly PD, and she teased Frannie all the time that as a Marshal she was a guest-star cop, a gunslinger who scooped up a bad guy or two and called it a day, while Mari and her friends got to clean up after. Looking at the sad-eyed detective, she had the impulse to grab his arm and tell him she understood how you could be run down by a river of other people's trouble. She pictured herself touching those dark grooves under his eyes and found herself on the verge of tears, had to look away and blink or risk losing it. She started to say something and found her mouth dry, her lips stuck together. "The, uh, accomplice, the guy in the raincoat? Do we know anything about him, what puts him with Berman?"

The detective reached into his pocket and pulled out a folded sheet of paper and handed it to her. "Berman's cousin, looks like. Arthur Felig, did two years for assault in New York, worked protection, some kind of half-assed bodyguard."

The paper was a printout, the white-haired guy with a placard with ID numbers and the words NY DOCS and CAPE VINCENT CORRECTIONAL FACILITY. She said, "They were talking to each other in German or something?"

"Yiddish," Sleeper said. "Berman told the white-haired guy to shut up. *Shtimm zic,* I think he said. And the guy told him to hurry up. *Nu, shoyn.* Like, 'Let's get moving.'" Frannie looked at him out of the corner of her eye. This was a surprise, that he spoke Yiddish, with his white-blond hair and pale blue eyes. His last name was Hansen. She didn't know a lot more about him except what he brought to the job, and he rarely said anything about his personal life. That was one of the reasons she liked having him on her team.

The supervising deputy, Scanlon, came over, closing a phone. "Frank Russo's dead. His heart stopped beating in the ambulance and they couldn't revive him."

She sagged and let a long breath go, then had to turn and look at nothing. The SD was talking again. "I got a lot of questions about what happened here."

Sleeper said, "Not now."

He kept going. "I see violations of procedure here. I see lack of definition."

Sleeper stepped in front of him and looked him in the face. The SD looked down, then stepped away and opened his phone again. Sleeper stood looking into the space where Scanlon had been, his blue eyes almost white. Then he looked at her, his expression impossible to read, his eyes bright, fixed, as they always were. He nodded, and she dropped her gaze. When she looked up again the EMTs were loading the ambulances, and at the corner of her vision she saw the blue-white flashes of cameras from inside the dark store, illuminating brass casings and splashes of dark blood.

She had been in the Marshals service for seven years and worked hundreds of apprehensions. It hadn't always worked out, there had been mistakes and screwups. People she'd wanted who slipped away. Terrible moments: A boy, maybe six, his face bent to a bowl of cereal and sobbing with shame and fear while she handcuffed his father. All the wives and children with pain and dread plain in their eyes so that sometimes she felt wrong even doing what she knew was right. Once she had once grabbed the wrong man and put him in cuffs. But she had never gotten one of her guys hurt before. Had never fired her gun except at the range. And now here were three men dead, one of them a friend, a mentor, and there was Scanlon staring at her, his face twisted.

She was good at her job, but she knew people who had been forced out for less. She'd answer the questions the SD put to her, she'd follow up with the Philly PD and talk to the prosecutors who had been trying to put Berman away or get him to give up his bosses. She'd go to the hospital and hug Claire Russo and tell her she was sorry, and Claire would wave off her apologies. She would never blame Frannie. But even if she stayed, it would be with this new identity; the one who screwed up a simple arrest. The one who got Frank Russo killed.

A guy she used to work with, Chris Bueckers, had been after her for a year to come work for him, doing risk assessment for insurance companies and multinationals. It would mean travel, more money. It would clear her head. No more meeting at Dunkin' Donuts at five in the morning to plan a day of knocking on doors, no more falling asleep in court. What was risk assessment? She thought of watching, listening. Keeping an ear to the ground. She'd talk to men in the comic opera uniforms that foreign cops all seemed to wear, shake hands, write reports. She pictured night-lit cities, signs with pictograms instead of words. A café on a quiet street, a young waiter with soulful eyes and unkempt hair bringing her a sweet roll and coffee. Unfamiliar languages and smiling strangers. Meetings in boardrooms. Onion-shaped domes, leaning spires, and the sound of bells at twilight.

Frannie stepped off the sidewalk into the street and looked down to see a white square framed in blue and glazed by ice and water, a kind of mosaic of tiles pressed into the street with crudely cut letters of red and blue that spelled out the words, TOYNBEE IDEA IN KUBRICK'S 2001, and RESURRECT DEAD ON PLANET JUPITER. She had seen these things before. They were pressed into the asphalt at intersections all over the city, and she'd heard, in cities all over the world. She'd read about these tiles, placed in the middle of the night by somebody no one had ever seen who maybe believed that someday the souls of the dead would be collected on Jupiter. It didn't seem any crazier than the things the nuns at Mother Grace had told her. She couldn't form an idea of heaven in her mind, but she could at least picture

Jupiter, a ball of yellow mist in the endless black of space where everyone might gather, waiting to come home.

That night a song came on at the bar and she had to call Wyatt. She wanted to sing it to him, and she thought he would know what she meant. She was leaning over, standing in the bathroom of a bar on Frankford Avenue and swaying slightly, opening and closing her fingers the way you had to do sometimes when you were drunk. She bent farther to let her face touch the wall, hoping it would cool her skin. The bar outside the door was loud and she said something to Wyatt that she forgot the moment it came out of her mouth.

He said, "Baby, what's going on?"

"Do you know this song? It's on now, can you hear?"

"Frannie? Are you okay, baby?"

"You ain't listening, are you listening?" She sang a few words, about raising your glass and praising and laughing and praising some more. Wyatt had been one of her fugitives, a biker who ran with Pagan and Breed clubs but who had straightened out and had a good business, a shop that customized bikes. He had a wall of photographs of celebrities with his bikes and had been on TV. She said, "Can you come get me, Wyatt?"

"What's wrong, Frannie? Tell me."

"I just wanted a drink. Everybody can't drink, but I can drink. Is it wrong?"

"No, baby, but you should stop now and let me come get you."

"It's a bar, you know it. You brought me here, maybe. Somebody brought me here."

"The place on Frankford? The Lost Bar? Is there pool tables?"

"I don't know where I am, baby. I'm supposed to know and I don't. I don't."

"Don't cry, Frannie. I'll be there. Don't get in your car."

Another song came on, one of those ones that sounded like people praying in the Middle East, maybe. It was too beautiful and she had to shake her head. She had to stand up straight. Wyatt was asking, "Where are you?" but somebody was knocking on the door and she hung up.


She woke up at five and was sick. Wyatt, who never slept when he was at her apartment, was watching TV with the sound off. He was still in his clothes but had taken off his boots. When she came out of the bathroom she pulled on her panties and sat at the edge of the bed, grimacing.

"I can't remember where my car is."

"It's in Kensington." He pointed at the TV. "Did you see this? Somebody got shot near the convention center. It's on every channel. Was it a cop?"

She looked over at the TV with one eye, her face

screwed up. "Jesus, turn that off. Yeah, I saw it." She patted the bridge of her nose, the skin over her cheekbones, now swollen and speckled yellow and black.

He turned to her, reached out a hand. "Jesus, Frannie. What happened to your face?"

She pulled back, turning away. "Ah, just . . . nothing. Looks worse than it is. Takes a while for the bruise to come up. You know how it goes. We wanted to take a guy to jail and he didn't want to go."

"I know all about it, don't I?" He watched the TV in silence, the legend LAST NIGHT appeared on screen and figures could be seen milling around, one of them wearing a vest bearing the words U.S. MARSHALS. "Frannie, do you know these guys? There are Marshals at this thing, this shooting. Is this friends of yours?"

"Yeah, it's all right." She waved a hand. "Turn it off."

"The phone rang a couple times. What's USP Pollock?"

"A prison. Did you answer it?"

"No, don't worry. I know better. The display on the phone said it." He watched the TV for a minute in silence, holding the remote. "They saying a Marshal got shot?"

"Yeah, but, it's over. I can't do anything now." She lunged across the bed to get the control from him, but had to stop herself and show her teeth to keep from being sick again.

"It was somebody you knew."

"Can you please?" She looked at him, her eyes narrowed. "Wyatt."

He turned off the TV and put the remote on the table.

Sleet ticked against the window. After a minute he said, "That's why you got drunk, isn't it? Because one of your friends got hurt. That's why you called me." He bent to pull on his boots.

"I just wanted to forget my life for a little while."

"I guess."

"You going to sulk now?" She covered her face with both hands, her fingers riding lightly on her swollen cheeks. "You know there's nobody more annoying than somebody who used to get high, right?"

"Okay," he said. He got up, nodded his head. He began pulling on his jacket. "I'll see you."

"Oh, Christ, Wyatt. I'm sick. It's not even, what time is it?" She squinted at her phone. "What do you want from me?"

"I don't know, Frannie. I guess I thought you keep calling me, it means something. How many times we done this now?"

She got back into bed and pulled the covers up to her chin. "Isn't it enough I call you?"

"You got beat up, your friend got shot. Were you just going to keep all that to yourself?" He sat back down on the edge of the bed, his jacket pulled around him. "And if you got hurt? Hurt bad, or killed? What would I do then?"

"What would you *do*?" She shook her head. What was he talking about?

"I tell you what I think. I think 'cause we met when you busted me I'm not real. I'm not a real person to you.

I'm like a wild story you can tell yourself about how you fucked an outlaw."

"Man, you're a lot more fun when you're drunk."

"I want to ask what you think of me. Who you think I am. But I don't think I want to know."

"You're a good guy, Wyatt," she said, forcing her breath out to stop the waves of nausea. Her face felt like a mask, like someone else's skin laid over hers. She kept lightly tapping her swollen cheeks, her nose.

"You know I don't know one thing about your life? Your mom, your dad. You got sisters? Brothers? Is there somebody gonna kick my ass I treat you bad? I been coming around here for almost a year, Frannie." He got up and went into the kitchen. She could hear him opening and closing drawers, the refrigerator. When he came back in he handed her a bag filled with ice. "You got those paintings, those pictures all stacked up in your office, I wonder who those people are. I tell you all kind of stories about my life, you never say shit about yours. I wonder sometimes if you're married or got a regular boyfriend or something."

"Have you been snooping around?"

"Okay, fuck this." He threw up his hands and turned his head. "I'll see you."

"Okay, wait a minute, can you?" She sat up slowly, put the bag across her eyes for a minute. From behind the bag she said quietly, "Okay, okay." There was a rattling of ice, a long sigh. Finally, she said, "The part of me, of my brain . . ." She lifted the bag again and he took it from her and wrapped it in a towel and gave it back to her. She patted the bed next to her, thinking this would be easier if he sat down next to her, but he didn't move.

She started again. "The part of my brain that holds all that? It's too full right now. It's not that I have anybody else. I don't. I'm not dating anybody. The calls from prisons. I get them. We all do. Guys I locked up. Guys in prison, they get bored, they get angry. You just ignore them. My father . . ." She lifted a hand to touch her bruises, talked through the screen of her fingers. "He's one of them. In federal prison in Atlanta. He used to call, but I think he stopped trying. I have a sister, she's in and out of rehab. Her ex-husband has custody of her daughter. She carries a picture around all the time of her little girl, like she's a murder victim or something. And what happened tonight. Things got out of control. I let them get out of control. I let my friends, the people I work with, I let them down and somebody got killed. I just don't have room, you know? I don't have enough room in my head right now. For someone."

He leaned against the wall, looked at his feet. The room was almost dark and he was a looming shape, his pale eyes standing out. He said, "Don't call me anymore." He took a step toward the door.

She lifted the bag from her face. "Thank you. For coming to get me. I mean it. And thanks for the ice."

He rattled his keys in his pocket and pulled out his

gloves. At the door he said, "That part of you, Frannie? That part of you where you keep all this stuff? The people you care about, your friends, your family. That ain't your brain. Anyway, it ain't supposed to be."

# 3

Frannie stopped sleeping. She had always been a night owl, liked to stay up late and watch TV, read through the mail stacked up under the slot: circulars for clothes from Peter Kate and shoes from Bus Stop, catalogs from Title Nine and Galls law enforcement supply. She had a little money saved and some more that came from her late aunt Rodi's life insurance and she lived frugally by long habit. She figured she could go three more months before things got dire and she'd have to make a decision about work. About what to do next. Chris Bueckers heard she'd left the Marshals and he wanted to fly her over to London to interview with his company. The firm was called Centurion and they did risk assessment and threat management for large corporations that paid millions for their expertise. She needed to line up work but she couldn't bring herself to say yes.

She wasn't drifting, exactly, but felt it was more that

she was in training for something that hadn't been re-vealed to her yet. She worked the heavy bag she had hung in the extra bedroom she used as an office and went for long, punishing runs. She still had friends at the Mar-shals and they would call to check up on her. Everybody wanting to know how she was coping with what hap-pened to Frank Russo. To tell her it wasn't her fault. Or hint that maybe it was. She thought about changing her number.

It got colder, the days got shorter but she'd find herself wired at two, at three in the morning, watching old mov-ies and cop shows. Wine didn't help and she didn't want to start pouring herself a shot to relax at the end of the day. Pills made her groggy and slow to wake. She'd go the gym and push herself, sometimes wander the clubs on Second, stunning herself with expensive vodka. Flirting that felt like argument and dancing that was like fighting, all sharp elbows and hard stares. She didn't call Wyatt, didn't want to be alone and didn't want company. She'd walk home through the October night, hearing the distorted screams of the dead from the haunted house they ran at the old prison down the street, the sound mixed up with the mock hysteria of stoned teenagers.

After a couple weeks of that she went into the spare room that she used as an office and pulled the tape from the boxes she'd brought home from the office at 601 Mar-ket on her last day with the Marshals and hadn't opened since. One of the other Marshals, Cathy Nava, a stylish woman in her late forties who'd led a regional fugitive task force, caught her by the elevator and passed her the card when they shook hands on her way out of the building with a box under her arm. Now she dug through the boxes and come up with the card where she'd thrown it. Amy Blanchard, the woman's name was. A psychologist. The card said, COUNSELING AND CONSULTING FOR LAW ENFORCEMENT.

The office was off Lancaster Avenue, behind a shopping center in one of those prosperous, indistinguishable Main Line towns with Welsh names, Bala Cynwyd or Bryn Mawr, and the Welsh, if that was who named them, long gone. She parked near a Whole Foods, watched twenty-somethings in their Lululemon sweats and carrying yoga mats and young mothers wearing J. Crew. The streets seemed wider, sunnier, not like the crowded warren of ancient breweries and stables in Fairmount. No wailing ghosts here. Inside, the low medical building was bland, quiet, and the woman who opened the door quiet herself, smiling and pointing to a comfortable chair, giving an impression less of healer than of efficient office administrator, maybe. White hair, neatly trimmed in a kind of page boy, a gray suit. There was a couch, Frannie noticed, but it was against a far wall and didn't seem to be the center of the action.

The woman sat in the other chair, nothing in her hands, no notebook or pen. There were no questions about insurance. Frannie adjusted herself, touching the buttons of her suit, tugging at her suit. *What to call her?* she thought. *Dr. Blanchard, Amy?*

"Cathy said you were good. You worked with her on a couple of cases, she said."

Dr. Blanchard smiled, nodded. "You work with Cathy? In the Marshals?"

"Yes. Well, no, not now. I did. I left."

"Recently?"

"Yes. No. A few weeks, I guess it is? Almost a month."

"Are you still in law enforcement?"

"I'm between jobs. A friend wants me to come work with him. A risk assessment firm based in London. They work with insurance companies, mostly, international investment companies. Oil companies. Tell them what the likely risks are for workers in insecure countries, places with local insurgencies or heavy OC activity. Organized crime. People likely to kidnap or terrorize their employees. Extort money."

"But you haven't taken the job yet?"

"No. He wants to fly me to London, do the interview. I just haven't pulled the trigger."

"I see. Then, how can I help you, Frances?"

"Frannie. Nobody's called me Frances since the nuns at Mother of Divine Grace." She waved her hand like she was waving away smoke. "Frannie. Please." She smoothed her skirt and started again. "I'm having some trouble. Sleeping." She lifted a shoulder, smiled. It was no big thing.

"Can I ask, why did you leave the Marshals?"

Frannie paused. "I don't . . ." She looked at the wall, a picture of a man in a boat. "I'm not here to get into a lot of, you know." She smiled. "I just can't sleep. I'm having trouble sleeping." She couldn't take her eyes off the print. A black man in a sailboat with its mast gone, gape-mouthed sharks, and blood in the water.

The doctor followed her gaze to the wall and smiled. "Winslow Homer."

"Right, that's right. I remember it." She had been to the Met, in New York, a day with Mae a couple of years before. They'd stayed at a boutique hotel overlooking the library at Forty-first, Mae's treat after she'd sold some big property in University City. She'd been making good money then, before the drinking had gotten out of control. Their mother had painted, had pushed the girls to notice art, design. Mae had taken it in but it made Frannie edgy, mostly. Thinking there was something to get that she wasn't getting.

Frannie nodded at the picture. "It's a little bleak or something, isn't it? For a doctor's office?"

"People who first saw it worried about the sailor so much, I read that Homer had to add the little ship in the distance, to give people hope. Had to tell a woman who saw it that the man got home all right and lived happily ever after."

Frannie got up and walked over to it. She could see, closer now, the twister, a waterspout, over the sailor's left shoulder, the eye of the shark as it looked to the man. The ship, or schooner or whatever it was called, so far away as to be not much more than a smudge on the horizon. "It's funny. Or, you know, odd. He doesn't look like he cares that much. The man. The sailor."

She crossed the room, self-conscious again, arranged herself in the chair. "Is it some kind of test? Having that there?" She smiled, trying to be in on the joke. "Something for the regular patients? To see what they make of it?" A little edge in her voice, like maybe she'd fallen for a trick.

"No, no. I just like it. I know it's a little melodramatic, but it fits, somehow, I think, in the room. When I bought it, I was having that kind of moment. You know, the sharks circling, and it just made me smile, really. It was just like a reality check. I was struggling a bit, but you know, there were no actual sharks. Most people don't notice the picture. The, uh, *regular* patients. They don't see it, not right away. They're too wrapped up in what brought them here."

"Too busy watching the sharks."

"Right, something like that." There was a long pause, and the woman watched Frannie's eyes. "I've noticed that my law enforcement patients do notice, though. The detectives and policemen. They always comment on it."

"We're trained to notice, I guess you'd say. Look at people, their surroundings."

"I'm sure that's it."

"Situational awareness, it's something they teach us."

"And it's also a kind of deflection, isn't it?"

"Ma'am?"

"I mean, if we're talking about Winslow Homer, we're not talking about whatever brought you here."

"Right." Frannie nodded and passed a hand across her eyes.

"How long since you've slept?"

"I get catnaps." Frannie smiled and made another motion with her hand, trying to make it all less dramatic. "Zone out on the couch for a few minutes."

"How long has it been going on?"

"A few weeks. Maybe a little longer."

"You're not looking forward to the new opportunity?"

"Oh, sure it looks great. I'd get to travel. All over the world. My friend is talking about twice what I made with the government. And I just got bumped a GS grade." Dr. Blanchard's eyes went up. "A four-thousand-dollar raise. Right before I left."

"And now you can't sleep."

"Right."

"You know I'm a psychologist. I don't write prescriptions."

"Definitely. I mean, I don't want to get dependent on anything, anyway."

The doctor let a moment pass. The sharks rolled, showing white bellies to the sun. The man in the boat looked away. "So, then. What do you see us doing here?"

"I don't, uh. I don't know, specifically. Cathy said you were good."

"Frances." She held up a hand to stop herself. "Frannie. If we're not sending you to a doctor to get Ambien, we're talking."

"I get that. I thought maybe there were, I don't know. Relaxation techniques? A friend of mine quit smoking, she had a rubber band on her wrist and she'd snap it when she wanted a cigarette. To distract her? I know we have to talk, I know that. But I mean, there are just things it's not worth going into. There are, you know, these *areas*. Everybody has areas, don't they?" She felt herself rambling. She touched the gray Dyna bag in her lap that held the short-barreled Colt she carried now. "Ma'am, I just don't want this going on and on."

"Call me Amy, please. I'll call you Frannie, you call me Amy. Did you enjoy being in the Marshals?"

"Enjoy? I don't know about enjoy." Frannie curled her lip. "I liked the people I worked with. Most of them. I liked doing a job, you know. Being good at it."

"Do you keep in touch with the people you worked with?"

"No. Not after the way things went. I didn't feel, you know . . ." She shook her head. "People call, but I don't know what they want to hear. It's easier to just . . ." She trailed off again, made a chopping motion with her hand; a connection broken, or maybe a limb cleanly severed.

" 'The way things went,' " she repeated. "If you were good at it, why did you feel you couldn't do it anymore?"

She opened her mouth and closed it again, thinking of the quiet, tense minutes on Arch Street before everything went wrong. She saw the photo again as she had seen it behind glass at the store. The men, the boxers, hunched and bleeding in the ring under the harsh lights. She remembered her father watching the fight over and over in their dark basement. He had tapes of the fights he liked and kept them labeled in neat rows in a dark bookshelf near his lounger. Six years old, seven, she'd sit on the leather couch while he narrated. "There's your man Hearns breaking his hand on Hagler's skull. Think of it! To hit somebody that hard." He'd stop the tape, rewind it, the boxers' arms windmilling fast, blurred like smears of wet ink. "And still he goes, look at him." She knew the whole fight by heart, every stagger and punch, and the picture had brought it back. The two men slamming away at each other, nothing like any other fight she'd ever seen, not boxing but *warring*, truly, as if their lives depended on it, and her father watching, moving his arms, twisting his hands sympathetically with the slight, shining figures in the square of light that were men giving and taking pain.

Is that where her mind was that night on Arch Street? Did she lose her focus, thinking of her vicious father and her dead mother and lost sister? The night before she'd visited Mae at Sunrise House, watched her twist a tissue to ribbons while she talked about hitting bottom in a motel at the end of the Black Horse Pike, waking up with a knot over her eye and a man she didn't know going through her purse. Frannie had known it was wrong to be distracted in that moment, to have had all that going through her head while they waited for Berman at the store, pulling her out of the work. Something had happened that day, though, some door opened in her head and all these memories, these terrible pictures of her ruined family drifted across her vision like blue clouds. She remembered that day in the store, turning from the picture and Sleeper looking hard at her from the open doorway, like he knew what she was thinking. But what could he know? She had never talked about any of it to anyone at work. To anyone, really. Believed instead that working hard, keeping her head down, keeping her distance from her family's mess would immunize her. That not being like them, she was no longer *of* them.

Frannie stood up and smoothed her skirt. "See, this is why this is a bad idea." She spoke quietly, talking to herself, maybe. She walked over to the painting again. "*That's* someone in trouble. That guy in the boat. Me, I just . . ." She shrugged. "I just quit my job and it's an adjustment."

"Are you married?" Frannie shook her head. "A boyfriend? A girlfriend?"

Frannie put a hand out and almost touched the print. Held the fingers of one hand out as if there was energy or something coming off the scene that could be felt at a distance. She thought of a day years before, sitting on a pier in Ocean City with her mother, watching a storm come across the bay. Her mother had grabbed her and Mae from in front of the house on Almond Street and piled them in the car and they'd driven aimlessly around, circling farther into Jersey, windows open in the heat, her mother saying they'd just keep going till they felt a breeze. How old was Frannie then? Seven? And Mae maybe eight, then, or nine.

Late in the day they'd ended up eating ice cream and French fries sitting on some splintered gray boards at the end of a dock. The salt on the fries burned Frannie's mouth and she'd moved the cold, sweet ice cream over her lips like balm. Her mother smoked and looked out over the water, finally pointing with her cigarette hand at a dark line, a blue shadow that raced toward them, and in the last moment before the rain swept over them the temperature suddenly dropped ten degrees. She and Mae ran back to the car, squealing at each other as the cold rain ran down their necks. Their mother sat at the edge of the bay until she was soaked through, raising her cold cigarette to look at the damp circle of ash. It was years later she realized they'd been hiding from her father. It couldn't have been much later that her mother took them out of school and ran away, the three of them holing up in a motel in the Pine Barrens. One last, doomed attempt to get away.

To Dr. Blanchard she said, "Do you think he made it, really? The sailor in the boat. How could he?" Her voice trailed off. "Look at that water. The shape of it." Thinking of her mother and father, and their voices raised as she and Mae sat holding each other on the floor of the bathroom.

"Tell me about your family." The woman knew something, could read something in Frannie's distraction.

"I have a sister."

"Are you close?"

"We talk. Close? I don't know. What does 'close' mean, exactly? Talk every day? Every week?"

"What about your mother and father, are they living?"

"I come to you with a simple problem, ma'am. I need eight hours a night. I don't want to start talking about dreams."

"Amy, Frannie. Call me Amy." She smiled. "Okay, no dreams. Tell me one thing, okay? Can we talk about one . . . area?"

"If you think that's the way to go." Frannie was aware of herself talking, her clipped cop voice. Trying to keep the woman at arm's length. And what would happen if she stopped?

"Tell me . . ." Amy tucked her chin down against her chest, maybe thinking she had one chance to get it right or Frannie would pack up and go home. "Tell me about your last day with the Marshals. Just that one day." Frannie looked trapped, the look of someone who'd answered the door to a kid with glassy eyes and pamphlets about Jesus. "You were sleeping then, right? Getting a good night's rest?"

Frannie nodded. What to say about that? She felt the woman was trying to trick her somehow, get her to admit some weakness. To talk about Frank's blood on her hands and the man found dead in the weeds under the bridge in Camden.

"You got up, got dressed?"

Frannie waved her hand, she wasn't going step by step. She knew what the doctor wanted, the payoff. It wasn't where she ate breakfast, or what she wore. It was: Why did she quit her job? She said, "It was a long day."

# 4

The two kids touched gloves and then backed off, looking hard at each other. A tall black kid and a shorter, wider Latino, his back inked with Aztec symbols and grinning skulls under sombreros. Patrick Mullen watched from the back of the gym, his hands in his pockets as the boys circled. The Latino kid made the first move, a fast jab at the stomach that his opponent easily blocked, and then it was on. The black kid used his height, kept his hands up and his head down like he'd been taught, moved his feet to keep himself right. The Mexican kid planted his feet and swung hard, his eyes burning, trying to land that one that would have an effect he could see. Stagger the black kid and make him forget his moves.

In the black kid's corner, Rudy Wurtz bobbed and threw his right fist in sympathetic motion with his fighter, calling out warnings and instructions, and making a round "oh" sound every time the kid's gloved hand found the Mexican's head. Rudy looked around the gym and Patrick stepped backward, flattening himself against the wall in the shadow of a metal storage closet under a fifteen-year-old poster for a recently paroled Mike Tyson fighting Buster Mathis at the Spectrum. Under the picture of Tyson looking like a mountain of dark muscle were the words PRESUMED INNOCENT.

Mullen was taking a chance following Rudy into this place, but he enjoyed being in a gym again and watching the two young men squaring off. He thought he knew what was in their heads. Another gym had been his hangout: Cas Brodzinski's place on Richmond, the place Rudy's father Adolph had first seen Patrick Mullen. Mullen had been like the Latino kid, a tough fighter but a lousy boxer, in the ring to take and give punishment so that he forgot what he'd been taught and kept swinging through the bell and old Polish Cas would come off the corner and smack him on the forehead to get him to break off, like throwing a bucket of water on a snapping dog. The old gym on Richmond was gone, he'd seen, but this place was the same, he thought. They were all the same; the sour smell of sweat and the tang of ointment and salts, the fading posters of hopeful local boys and the hard-eyed visitors who laid them out.

When Mullen left, backing out through the doorway, the Latino boy's shoulders were heaving, his breath whistling around the mouthpiece, spit and blood shining on his chin while he flailed with his gloved hands. It was over, that fast, and the Latino kid was finished. The tall black kid standing him off with hard snaps to the head while the short kid slumped and the light went out of his eyes, and Rudy Wurtz nodded his head and said, "yes" to himself. It was like Mullen was watching his own life, and he wanted the tough little Mexican with the tattoos to come back, find some last reserve of power, step inside the other boy's arms and knock him down. The kid with the concentration, the moves, the system that meant he was counting in his head—he was the one who any second now would raise his arms, and Mullen wanted to be away before it happened. And, anyway, Mullen was pushing his luck, wanting to stay close to Rudy, and it wasn't smart to stay any one place long enough to be remembered.

He came down the stairs from the gym onto Clearfield just as a police car went by, the cop looking right at him. Mullen hunched into himself and kept his eyes front. He had been known in the neighborhood once upon a time, and there were cops looking for him, and probably FBI and federal Marshals. His right hand closed around a linoleum knife in his pocket, a short blade with a hook. He'd shoplifted it in a hardware store in Charleston, West Virginia, and at night he'd sit on the edge of the bed and work the knife on a ceramic whetstone until it was so sharp he'd had to make an improvised sheath out of a leather glove to keep from cutting his hands. While he moved the blade on the stone he thought of his father in his stained apron using a long steel on his knives in the butcher shop on Christian Street, the old man's hands a blur. He could picture the old shop, and smell the sawdust and the blood. He stepped into the doorway of a liquor store to wait for Rudy to come out of the gym.

The cop car kept going down the block toward Aramingo. What would the cop see, if he even noticed Patrick Mullen? *An old man,* Patrick thought, *an old neighborhood guy with gray hair, a little paunch, maybe.* Thrift store jacket, flannel shirt, and watch cap. Stooped shoulders and hard eyes, if he looked that close. What his cellmate Tommy Reynosa used to call his Manson lamps, something Tommy got from TV. *Crazy eye,* he'd say, and shake his head, but it wasn't something Patrick did consciously. He'd just spent his life around dangerous people and got in the habit. It was just better for you if you turned away from Patrick Mullen, and his way of staring was like a warning, a reminder.

The old gym was where Adolph Wurtz had seen in Patrick what he wanted. Not a boxer, this kid, but a street fighter, a brawler. Put him to work at Roofers Local 225, going out with Wurtz and his son Rudy to check for cards in the crews working roofing jobs. If a contractor was using guys who didn't have the card, or had one of the phony cards guys would trade in the bars on Frankford Avenue, Patrick's job was to hit the boss on the knee with the blunt end of a hatchet or drag him to the edge of the pitch and force his head and shoulders out into the empty air. Throw a seam roller down and let the guy watch it fall and think about what it would be like to fol-low it over, spinning down to shatter in the street. Pat-rick did what he was told, and he liked the money and he liked the feeling of being somebody nobody would fuck with.

Rudy came out of the gym and walked by Patrick, talk-ing on a cell phone, doing a recap of the fight to whoever was on the line. Mullen watched him walk a few steps up Clearfield and hook left down Coral, and he counted to ten in his head before following, stopping at the cor-ner to peer around at Rudy's back. He found the street blocked off to cars. It was something the neighborhood people had done, an improvised barrier of lawn chairs and old cones and silver duct tape, and beyond that the street was full of kids in Halloween costumes, parents on the stoops with flashlights or watching with cans of beer and soda in their hands. Night was coming on and it was getting colder, the kids running around and screaming. Boys in wrestling masks and girls as angels, tinfoil halos and cotton wings. Screaming to each other, to their parents and, Patrick thought, just screaming to make the noise, to hear themselves. The way you did when you were a little kid, your head thrown back and your mouth wide. Patrick saw the house where Rudy's girl lived toward the far end of the block, and he saw Rudy talking to two men standing in front of it and passing a can of Tecate back and forth. Mullen took it all in and then turned away, crossing Coral to circle around from Frankford Avenue.

Patrick knew the short blocks and narrow streets. He knew there was an alley between Frankford and Coral, really a vacant space made when two houses had been knocked down back to back, and it was better than going right down the street past the neighbors. It got darker, Patrick walking between the circles of light as he made his way around the block, everything familiar and strange at the same time. The same houses but different people since he went away. More Spanish on the storefront signs, more families from Mexico and Guatemala and the markets with racks of the same Mexican junk food that Tommy Reynosa's family used to bring to him in Pollock, the federal prison where he and Patrick were cellmates. Little snack cakes with strawberry filling and coconut-covered cookies that Patrick thought were pretty good, though he couldn't pronounce the names.

Patrick found the vacant lot near the far end of the block. It was planted with squash and a few rows of spindly white cornstalks like ragged, upright bones, and while he was standing there, trying to get a glimpse of Coral Street through the junk and waist-high weeds beyond the garden the cop came back. He saw the car move down Frankford, slow, and took a few steps among the plants and dropped to his knees and began to pull weeds from between rows of winter squash. Behind him he could feel the space filled by the slowing car, feel the eyes of the cop on the back of his neck, and he waited a good long while. It felt good to be doing something with his hands, and to smell the bitter, dusty smell of the plants. He had cleared a short row before slowly coming off his knees and looking up and down the darkening street to make sure the cop was gone.

He made his way slowly through the lot. Halfway across, where the foundation of the missing house was still plain as a gray line of dust under the twisted grass, an old man sat on a rotten log and drank something from a bottle hidden in a bag. When he noticed Mullen he pulled into himself and said something under his breath. Ahead of him on Coral Street a man wearing a hockey mask dumped out a cooler and water on the street moved like a river under the green lights. Patrick could hear doors slamming and people calling and children complaining and he understood though some of it wasn't in English. He came to the edge of the first house at the edge of the lot and stood quietly. Two doors down, a man was smoking a cigar, his back turned and saying something through a screen door to a woman with dark hair. Patrick waited for an older woman carrying one of the angels to go inside a redbrick house at the end of Coral, then stood motionless until they were out of sight. He took a few steps into the street, watching.

The woman with dark hair who had been talking to Rudy turned away from the screen door and Patrick crossed the tiny street in two steps and put his arm around Rudy's neck and pulled him backward toward the lot, whispering for him to be quiet. Rudy began to struggle, but Patrick set the hook at the end of the lino-leum knife tight under the knot of cartilage at his Adam's apple and walked him around the corner into the weeds and trash. Rudy still held his cigar and stood facing away from Patrick. They touched at the knees and the hips and Rudy held his head stiff above Patrick's hand cupped around the knife and said, "All right, all right," a few times under his breath.

They stopped moving and Rudy swallowed, Patrick feeling the movement in his hands. Rudy's voice was tight. "I heard you walked out. Where was it, Atlanta?"

"Pollock. In Louisiana. Atlanta's not maximum secu-rity anymore." Mullen spoke quietly, his mouth a few inches from Rudy's ear. He reached slowly, took the cigar and put it in his own mouth. "You're getting gray there."

"My kid is three steps away inside that house, Pat."

"With any luck it will be somebody else who finds you, then." Mullen felt the younger man tense in his arms. He thought about what he wanted, and what he would have to do. Rudy's hair smelled of cigar smoke and sweat.

"I didn't—" Rudy said, and stopped. "It wasn't my call, what happened to you."

"You're going to say what, now? That it was all Adolph, all your father and what he had to do for his wee Italian friend? And you, poor Rudy, you just did what you were told and cried yourself to sleep?" Patrick saw an easy chair a few paces ahead, caught in the oblong of pallid light from the streetlights and looking out of place in the long grass of the lot. It was an old sprung lounger gone green from sitting out in the rain and dust, and he walked Rudy over to it. The two of them moving together, Rudy's legs gone weak and his hands hanging useless or plucking weakly at the tail of Patrick's shirt.

"Jesus, Pat. We grew up together. My father took care of you."

"I remember. I went to see you at the fights today, and I was thinking about all that."

"You were there?" Rudy's breaths came ragged and wet, and Patrick wondered if he was crying. Would he cry, he wondered, when it was his turn? Rudy was talking again. "You need money? On the run, you have to need money. I can get you something. Jesus, talk to me."

Patrick kicked Rudy's legs from behind, pushing him closer to the chair. Rudy said, "Jesus, Patrick, Jesus. My father taught you how to fight. He taught us both."

"That's nearly true, Rudy. He taught you to *box*. He taught you the moves and the style and how to breathe and all that. But not me, Rudy. Me, he took one look and he knew I'd never be able to hold it in. I'd never be able to count in my head and move my feet, 'cause I'm not patient and I'm not smart." He forced Rudy down over the arm of the chair, their touch intimate, Patrick feeling Rudy's breath on his fingers. "Like that poor Mexican kid your man beat down at the gym." Rudy made a move, pushing back on his heels so that Patrick had to hold him tighter. "Right, so, it was you he taught to box, and you parading in the lights, and you he gave the prize." Mullen covered Rudy's mouth and felt his scream as a vibration in the bones of his hand. "And me, I was the one got took out into the dark, out into the alley and got taught how to beat all those poor fucks trying to put food on the table." Patrick moved his right hand and the other man bucked and thrashed like something caught in a net. Patrick held him until he stopped moving. He whispered, "So it was you he taught to box, Rudy, and me he taught to fight."

But he was talking to himself.

Mullen walked back the way he'd come, past the old man hunched in his coat and making strange signs with his hands, to bless Patrick or to ward him off. When he came to himself, he was standing in front of the old house on Almond Street, someone else's house now, and ghosts and green paper skeletons on the window, limbs splayed, and didn't that mean something? Even all these years later, here's the dead in every window.

Tina pulled the car up and he got in and sat in himself, staring as she drove. After a minute she asked, "Right, so, how did it go, then?"

"What? How did what go?"

"The man, you said, the man you came to see? Will he help you, then?"

"Shut up." He looked at her a long while, and she stole glances at him.

"Where am I going, Patrick?" Her voice rising. She

wasn't used to the car and would get panicky driving the city at night.

"Pull over."

"Where?"

"Just here." He yanked at the wheel and she gave a small cry, dropping her hands protectively over the swell of her stomach. When they bumped the curb lightly she dropped her eyes, hugged herself, and trembled.

She stole glances at him, her eyes pained. "Is that blood, Patrick? Are you hurt?"

The heater was whistling, putting out waves of heat and he swiped off his cap and snapped off the fan. He said, "Get out."

"What? Out? Where do I go, then?"

"What do I care, you muck savage?" It was what he called her when he was angry. That, or *culchie*, because she was from a small town tucked into the hills west of Kenmare. When she went to visit him at the prison and he was feeling tender he called her bog sprite and sang old songs, but that was rare now he was back here in Philadelphia, his mood black, just black, all the time. He came across the seat and reached over her to throw open the door and she retreated, squeezed her eyes shut and turned awkwardly to shelter her belly from his fists as if from a cold rain.

The blows didn't come, and she opened her eyes to see him hunched on the seat, his hands held clasped at his chin as if in prayer. He opened them and looked down at his fingers, his scarred, bunched knuckles.

"Don't be afraid," he said. "Please don't. It's just I'm lost now. They'll kill me out here and I don't know how to do these things anymore. These terrible things. When I was young I could just call it up and go. My head was full of that red fire and I'd do anything. Any awful thing. For any reason, or no reason. Now, I have to, you see? It's what I have to do." She reached out a hand then, to touch him but he shook his head and opened his hands to her. He didn't look up. "No, no, you can't," he said. He opened his hands to her and she saw them, then, the whorls of red on his palm, edged in rust and black. The blood. She edged out of the car and closed the door.

When he was alone he drove west across the city to sit on Aspen Street and wait. He pulled the knife out of his jacket and yanked his shirt tail free and rubbed at the blade, never taking his eyes off the street. After a few minutes he watched his daughter Frannie pull up in a sporty car, an Audi in midnight blue and herself visible from a block away with her mother's red hair, though he saw it was cut short as if slashed away. He saw her turn off the motor and sit, watching the street for a minute, or just lost in her thoughts, and then get out and walk across the street to her door. He'd forgotten how tall she was, and the pictures he'd seen in the last years hadn't shown much. Glimpses of her in news stories on the Internet, working in her dark clothes and Kevlar vest, escorting men in handcuffs, standing hard-eyed outside a courthouse with a pistol at her hip. What would she do if she saw him? Scream, or run, or call for help? Pull a gun and point it at him? Patrick lowered his head and watched, flexing his hands on the wheel. She opened her door, closed it, and was gone.

He watched to see lights come on inside, thinking about Rudy Wurtz and the street full of angels. After a minute he fumbled at the switches in the unfamiliar car until he got a pale blue light on over his head. He pulled his wallet out of his pants, unfolded the picture again of his daughters, Frannie and Mae on a beach. The girls were small, then, six and eight, maybe. Frannie's open smile and Mae's shy, anxious look, Frannie's brilliant copper hair and Mae's dark mop. And of his poor, dead Nora just her hands, her long and slender fingers, touching each girl's head. Where were they, then, when the picture was taken, and where was he? Working, or fighting. Drinking. Locked up, as he was now and then.

He held the linoleum knife up to see the blade, clean now and shining blue, saw the blood crusted around his blunt nails as he laid it on the dash. Lifted the photo again with his bloody fingers, holding it loosely, by the edge, where his wife's pale hands were just visible, reaching in from that torn fringe toward his girls, as if to take them with her to the land of the dead.

# 5

Frannie got up at dawn and dressed in flannels, her sweats, the Blackhawk fanny pack with her keys, ID, and the little Glock she'd been wearing her last day on the Marshals. She stood in her doorway awhile, watching the street, then jogged up Aspen toward the park and the river, moving slow. At Twenty-fourth Street she put on a burst of speed and cut left, then made a quick right down Meredith, running flat out. The street was narrow, not much more than an alley, and the noise of her running shoes on the street came back at her hard from the house fronts just a few feet away. In the middle of the block she stopped, breathing hard, and turned, standing behind a parked car. A white van moved down Twenty-fourth and crossed Meredith, too far away now to see anyone inside. Had it slowed? Was there a stutter as the driver lifted his foot from the accelerator to look down the tiny street?

She'd had a feeling. In the last week she'd had a feeling there was someone near all the time, someone watching. It had been getting worse, along with the sleeplessness; her edginess and irritability and the paranoia of a watchful life coming together so that she felt exposed, thinking of eyes on her from cars and windows, binoculars or rifle scopes. Red leaves tumbled out of the wet trees and lay in streaming clots in the gutter. She stood for a full minute watching the street, then slowly began to walk west again, stopping twice to look back.

At the end of the block she picked up the pace and ran hard down the hill toward the river drive. Most days she liked to run along the river, past the boathouses, the statue of the tall Viking, and farther on, pushing herself around the bend of the Schuylkill to the figure of John B. Kelly bent to his oars. She let her earbuds dangle, not wanting to be isolated behind the wall of sound, and even running flat out she was strangely conscious of the cars going by, letting herself sort through the traffic for a white panel van. There had been something written on the door, she remembered, but it had been too far away and moving too fast for her to pick out intelligible words.

She slowed when she came back around the bend of the river, and stopped at one of the terraces to open a bottle of water. There were statues all around her, some recognizable as people from the city's past, in tricornes and frock coats, some distorted and broken as if, struggling against some titanic force, they had been pulled inside out. On the river a woman pulled at the oars of a racing shell, pushing hard upstream against the current.

By the art museum was a billboard, a photo of a kid somersaulting over a stack of old mattresses. She'd seen these things around the neighborhoods, billboards that weren't ads but some kind of art for the city. People's faces, scenes that must be from Katrina of sunken cars and messages scrawled on buildings. There was something about the pictures that unsettled her when she saw one. The faces showing anguish, or doubt, or even the unguarded moments of happiness. Wordless, without captions or explanations. They demanded something of her, they were clues about something. Down on Grays Ferry there were a couple she couldn't stop thinking about: In one an anxious woman holding a man's shirt up to the camera; in another a woman sitting on the edge of the bed, looking like maybe she was getting dressed for work.

Those two pictures looming over the streets, they both felt aimed at her somehow. She wanted to find whoever took the pictures and ask them, but she knew it said something about *her*, not the artist. If these pictures of women alone got under her skin it was something she carried with her, some guilt or anger or fear that she'd never let go. Something about somebody she'd locked up? Somebody not around to take care of their family? Somebody who got away from her to hurt somebody else? And her own family, all the things she didn't want to think about. All those shadows and ghosts. All the business of her life felt unfinished.

Frannie had begun to jog south again, slowly, breathing hard and sweat in the hollows under her eyes despite the chill, when she saw the van again. It stood out, moving slowly, coming north out of the city, and next to the driver a man with gray hair pointing across Kelly Drive. Pointing at *her*. She sped up, her heart moving in her chest, suddenly racing, and her hand going to the pack at the hollow of her back with her cell phone and the pistol. She watched the van slow, the brake lights bright in the mist, and she could see the driver's elbows as he spun the wheel and cut across the drive, almost clipping a Suburban as the van executed a wide, clumsy circle to follow her.

She thought about stopping, taking the few seconds to stop and open the pack and get her hands on the Glock and then see if whoever it was would keep coming. She'd locked up a lot of people, usually not knowing much about them other than there were federal warrants out on them and they were hiding in the city. Most days it had been a kind of culling, sweeping through the neighborhoods for people who knew they had only so much time to say good-bye to family or score one last time, or hide like children in closets or under beds, but there were people who would do anything to stay out, dangerous people who cursed and spit at them or pulled knives or guns and swore they'd remember Frannie and her friends and come back and do something. The ones who called in the middle of the night, the display reading USP Victorville, or Atlanta, or Marion.

So who was this, then? She decided to run a little harder, get away from the Drive and either get them to get out of the van and show themselves or to fade away back up the parkway into Philly. She cut between cars as she ran, crossing the four broad lanes and angling toward a bench on the other side. Something, maybe, to give her cover in the flat space, and beyond the bench she saw a statue, a man cradling an infant, and vaulted the bench and made for that, hearing the screech of tires behind her and a hard pop.

She turned when she reached the statue, going for the pack, rolling the zipper out of the way and putting her hand on the pebbled butt of the pistol. She looked up then, as the gun came free of the straps, her finger along the barrel as she'd been trained and the gun barrel pointed down. There was honking and the distorted sounds of screams from moving cars and someone shouting through an open window, calling someone else an asshole, but the van was past, moving back into the city, toward the museum and the Circle, getting smaller. Across Kelly Drive a Volvo station wagon was pulled over and a woman was getting out, a cell phone in her hands and pointing after the van. Frannie moved closer to the road, her hands shaking and her pulse banging in her ears, and she saw black tire marks and a red puddle of shattered plastic.

She looked after the van and saw its right side taillight was punched out, the light flashing bright white as the van braked hard to make the turn around the museum. And then it was gone.

A second later a police car pulled up in front of her, and she was instantly conscious of the gun in her hand. The white Philly PD Impala fishtailed, the dome lights coming on as the car slid onto the grass and two cops jumped out, going for their guns. Frannie hesitated for a full second, the dropped the Glock and lifted her hands, palms out. One of the cops advanced on her, shouting, and she got to her knees and put her hands behind her head. She was conscious of the people in the cars going by, watching her. The woman from the Volvo held her hand over her mouth, transfixed. A big Mercedes slowed, the driver pivoting his head to see what was going on and a white Mini Cooper plowed into its rear fender, bouncing and spinning. There was more screaming, and horns going, and the cop, now just a few feet away, looked like he wanted to pull the trigger.

Frannie heard another car pull onto the grass behind her and stop, but she couldn't take her eyes off the startled, angry young cop with the pistol pointed at her chest. She winced, feeling the heat from the engine of the car as it stopped just inches from her exposed back, and she flashed back to the white van and the man pointing at her, feeling herself vulnerable to whatever was coming from behind.

She heard a voice say, "Jesus, Mullen," and turned her

head just enough to see Sleeper stepping out of a government Crown Vic, slamming the door and walking slowly forward, his credentials held out for the cops and his free hand patting the air, making a gesture of calm. Drivers were swarming out of the knot of traffic on Kelly Drive, people pointing to crushed fenders and broken taillights or watching the cops with their guns out. Sleeper identified himself, and the cops gradually came down. Frannie didn't get up, but slowly let her hands drop down to the cold grass as Sleeper talked to the cops. She shivered, aware again of the chill, the wind off the river.

The cops talked to Sleeper for a minute, then they shook hands and he waved Frannie over. She didn't move but thought about what she'd say, about what she knew for sure. The van turning, her fast impression of the driver—young, pale, long black hair—and the man who'd pointed, a man with a bullet head and gray hair cut close. Were they after her, really? Could they have just been looking for a place to turn around on Kelly Drive and been impatient and stupid enough to cause an accident?

And if she'd been right and they were coming, what did it mean? Who was looking for her? She stooped to pick up the pistol and found it heavy and rattling in her shaking hands. She ejected the clip and worked the slide, dropping the bright shell into her palm. She held the breech open and blew into it. It gave her something to do, someplace to look while the cops took her measure and compared it to whatever Sleeper had told them.

When she looked over again, he was pointing toward the Crown Vic and nodding, and she stowed the pistol again and went over and got in the passenger seat. She watched the men shaking hands again and felt the lack of credentials, the federal ID she used to carry that separated her from the bystanders and victims milling and muttering at the side of the road like frightened birds. She wasn't one of those people, she wanted to tell the cops; she moved through the world the way they did, observant, controlled, conscious, aware, making choices. An actor in the world, not one of these hapless, acted-upon civilians. It couldn't matter, but she wanted it known. When she'd been a Marshal the badge had made that clear. What would it say for her now?

In the car she told Sleeper about the van and the guys, about them chasing her, or seeming to. How it all happened so fast she couldn't be sure. They were there, then they were gone, and what had really happened?

Sleeper looked at her out of the corner of his eye while they drove. "Where you been?"

"I was out running." She pointed toward the river. "I was just out running and those guys came after me. Anyway, they turned and followed me."

"No, where have you been? The last, I don't know, two days?"

"Around, I don't know."

"We tried to call you."

"Who's 'we'?"

"The office."

"I needed a break. It was a couple days, Jesus."

He nodded. "I get it."

"All those fucking calls about how was I doing? How was I feeling? What am I doing next? I don't fucking know. I just needed a couple days to let myself think." He looked over at her and she let a breath go. She said, "Sorry. What's it all about anyway?"

"It's about your father."

She sat up straighter, looked out the window. "What about him?" She saw they were heading down Vine Street. Heading downtown, she figured to the courthouse. "What the hell is going on?"

"Your father's out. He escaped from Pollock." He watched her face. She closed her eyes, shook her head. "You okay?"

"Pull over." She reached for the door.

"Wait a minute, there's no place to—" She grabbed at the wheel and he stopped her hand. "Frannie. Wait."

"Pull over now. Now!"

"Wait a minute, for Christ's sake." She was already yanking the door open as he swerved to the curb. She got out and stood by the curb for a minute, feeling the rush of air on her exposed back, hearing the distorted notes of the car horns moving past on the street. There was a low wall with Chinese characters inscribed on it, and she ducked around it away from the road, bent at the waist and breathing through her mouth, trying not to be sick. She heard Sleeper behind her, yelling at the drivers on Vine to go around him. She looked up and saw that they were at the Sixth District station house, the street full of white Philly cop cars. Her stomach moved, unmoored inside her. The panic and adrenaline of the morning, and now this. She tried to sort it out—her feeling of being watched, men in a van who might be after her, and her father out of prison and running. She finally looked over at Sleeper, who looked into her wild eyes, said, "Wait here," and got back in the Crown Vic and pulled away.

When he pulled the car up among the white city RMPs and got out, she was sitting with her back to the brick wall and looking up at the buildings downtown. He sat next to her and waited. A cop went by, a woman who looked down at them, her eyebrows up. She saw the badge at Sleeper's waist, or the gun at his hip, or just made a judgment that satisfied her curiosity and walked on, nodding. The wall muted the sounds of the traffic from Vine Street and the expressway below, and they sat for minute.

He said, "Christ, look at you. You look like maybe you're in shock. Your color."

"I'm all right, I just needed . . ." She shook her head, lifted one shoulder. "I'm okay. Really."

"That thing this morning? Do you think it had something to do with him? With your father?"

She stared straight ahead. The sound of the cars on Vine Street was like surf, rising and falling behind the brick wall. She couldn't think. Finally, she said, "How did you get that name? Sleeper? I never got that story."

He looked at her hard. She wanted to hear about this *now*? After a minute he nodded at the cars and the building, the station house. "I came out of the cops, you knew that, right?"

"I heard it. Somewhere. From Frank, maybe."

"I was partnered with a cop, Terry Randolph, he was a tough old guy. Had been on the job since the cop cars in Philly were red." He watched her, followed the movement of her hands, her eyes. "Terry taught me the choke hold. We weren't supposed to use it, but Terry didn't much give a shit what anyone thought. About anything. He told me, man, they come at you, you better know every way there is to slow 'em down. So he taught it to me."

"I saw a report from the DOJ said it was a better tool than it got credit for. Not as dangerous."

"Well, you know how to do it, it works just fine."

"So?"

"So, I was new in the Marshals, and there was a guy, Ken Miller."

"I remember him."

"Yeah, he had come out of Secret Service, and didn't think much of street cops. We were down on a boat seizure, down in Cape May, me and him and Frank. I heard later Miller was going through a divorce, I don't know, so maybe he was a little messed up about all that. Anyway, we were standing on the dock, he was talking a lot of shit. Somebody had died in L.A. and they said it was cops using the sleeper hold, so I had to hear about that for an hour. I made the mistake of saying, you know, it worked if you did it right. Then he said a guy at his dojo had taught him how to break a hold, and he kept on me about it, about trying him out. Saying it was one thing to throw a choke hold on some doped-up kid with a heart condition, I should try that shit on a grown man. I guess he thought I was going to talk back to him or something."

"He didn't know you."

Sleeper moved his lips. He might have been smiling.

Frannie said, "So . . ."

"So I put him to sleep. When he went down, Frank was singing that lullaby, you know. You know how Frank is. How he was. Every time he'd see Miller, he'd do it. *Lullaby and good night.* I think he transferred to Miami, Miller. He liked boats."

She shivered, and he took off his windbreaker and handed it to her. She held up a hand.

"I was running. I'm still all sweaty."

He looked at her, the way he did, and she shrugged and put it on. They sat for another minute, waiting. Finally she said, "I thought he'd die in there. In prison. Patrick. I thought he'd get old or sick, or somebody would, you know. Cut him." She wrapped the jacket tighter and drew her legs up. "I thought, man, he had a lot of enemies. He hurt a lot of people." She thought of a time when she was small, and him coming into the house on Almond Street one night, going to the laundry room, his knuckles covered in fresh, seeping cuts and old scars. He'd put his head under the faucet and blood had run out of his hair. He was drunk, blinking and shuddering with the effort to stay upright, and singing to himself. Elvis, "Can't Help Falling in Love With You." Singing, whistling through the parts when he couldn't remember the words. *Wise men say*, he sang. *Only fools rush in*. Then more of the memories came, the things she didn't let herself think about. Her mother running through the house. Her sister screaming and the house on fire.

"I should have known, right? Tough old fucker. Somehow maybe I did know that he'd come back."

She smiled, and Sleeper said, "What?"

She said, "Just thinking of something my mother used to say. When I was little he'd come home all busted up, his hands, you know, from fighting." She held up her own hands, seeing a few scars there, from her own fights. "Anyway Mae and I, we used to get upset when he'd come home like that, all covered in blood, not knowing it wasn't his blood. Mostly, it wasn't. But my mother, she'd just shake her head. She'd shake her head and say, *He'll bury us all*."

# 6

Sleeper took her to the courthouse and they got in an elevator to go up to the Marshals office on twelve. She hadn't been back since the day she walked out, boxes in her arms. There was a picture of Frank by the reception area, an official-looking one of Frank in a suit and tie, a flag behind his right shoulder. She knew he'd hated that picture, the one where his big shoulders were squeezed into a blue sport coat, but she had told him no, he looked like a high school football coach who took his team to state for the finals.

Sleeper left her in the conference room nearest the elevator, and she could hear people moving and the phones going. She wondered who was sitting at her desk, what had replaced the drawings her niece had done for her. She felt displaced, lost. She was about to get up and pace when Scanlon came in, the door held open for him by a younger man she didn't know.

"Come with me."

Scanlon went back out again and the other man stood at the door, so after a minute Frannie got up and followed. Scanlon was already halfway down the hall and Frannie followed him into a large open area divided by cubicles, and there was a white board, a new one, with a picture of her father and under it written, "Patrick Mullen." Frannie felt a pulse start at her throat, a hard clenching that grew in her chest as if the blood were working its way around a stone just over her heart. *He got old,* she said to herself, the hair in the photograph longer and much grayer than in her memories, almost white. The placard under his name read USP POLLOCK, and had his inmate number and the date. There were other pictures and names, lines drawn. Grainy surveillance photos of men on street corners, men in prison uniforms moving down hallways. A car at night, a young girl biting her thumbnail and looking nervously at something beyond the edge of the photo. She was blond and fair and seemed very frail.

Sleeper was looking at her from his desk, the space around him still clean, as it had always been. No photos, nothing personal, just files and flyers. She thought he was trying to communicate something with his look, but she couldn't guess what it might be. Scanlon walked into his office and she followed.

"Your father is Patrick Mullen?" He held up a photo and let it drop.

"You know he is."

"Do you know where he is now?"

"Last I knew, he was locked up in federal prison in Atlanta."

"So you haven't spoken to him?"

"Not in years."

"Bullshit." He held up a hand and turned in his chair. She looked away from him, trying to suppress the urge to grab his throat. "We know he called you." He lifted a printout that she could see was a list of phone numbers. "He called you twice from Pollock. How many more times has he called you since he's been on the run?"

"You pulled my phone records?"

"We've been trying to reach you for the last two days. If you had cooperated with us . . ."

"I ignored a few calls."

"Why?"

"You know why. I needed a break."

"So you told Hansen. We'll see."

She breathed through her nose, trying to control herself. "You'll see shit. Stay out of my life."

"That's not how it works. You used to work here, you ought to know that."

And she did know. She had asked a thousand husbands and wives and sons and daughters about fugitives on the run and knew the frustrations of getting the trust and cooperation that so much of the time made the difference in bringing someone in safely. It made her crazy to be here, on the wrong side of the table, expected to tell her story, to cooperate, and that fast she knew something nobody else in the room did, could never learn in a life-time of asking questions and expecting lies.

"You want to help him, you'll help us. He's running around out there hurting people."

"Yeah, well, that's what he does. It's all he ever does."

"Why don't you help us?"

"Why don't you stop working me?"

Another man came to the door, a man about Scanlon's age, silver hair and a neat goatee. Scanlon waved him in and he took out his identification and held it out to her. FBI. Scanlon pointed.

"This is Agent Ahearn."

"Call me Red." He shook her hand and smiled. "I'm sorry for your trouble, Frances." The guy was trying to be nice, but she couldn't catch up with the new reality where she was the family of a wanted felon, and she looked away into a corner of the room (like she had seen the guilty do a thousand times). Ahearn came in and put a thick file on the table in front of him. "I understand you were with the Marshals, so you know what we're trying to do here. We just want to get him off the street as quickly as possible before anybody else gets hurt."

She looked from the FBI agent to Scanlon, and Ahearn raised his eyebrows. "Does she know what's been going on?"

Scanlon gave a tight shake of his head. "We've been trying to reach her for two days. She's been ignoring our calls."

"You pulled my phone records, you know I never spoke to him."

Scanlon said, "He calls you, you call him back on a burner cell."

"Oh, bullshit." She was half out of her chair.

"Wait a minute, wait a minute." Ahearn smiled, pivoted his hands up to keep her in her seat. "Bill, give us a minute?" Scanlon sat back, a gesture saying he was going to do whatever he wanted, he could leave or stay and it was his call. After a minute he gave a slight nod, got up stiffly and walked out. Ahearn waited for the room to change, for something to dissipate in the air.

He said, "You haven't been briefed."

"Agent . . ."

"Ahearn. Red."

"Agent Ahearn, I don't know any more than what they just told me two minutes ago, that my . . ." She waved one hand toward the other room, the picture of her father. "That Patrick Mullen escaped from Pollock. I didn't even know he was there. Last I heard he was in Atlanta."

There was a pause while he looked at her, idly tapping the file with one hand. He said, "Your father wasn't doing easy time. He got into some kind of gang scrape in Atlanta, got transferred to Pollock two years ago." He opened the file and leafed through it. She wanted to reach over and take it from him, but now that she was a civilian—worse, the family of the wanted man—that access was denied her. Ahearn slid some photos out of the file across the table. Men in a line, men in prison jumpsuits, caught by an overhead camera. The first shot showed them in some kind of rough order, the next couple featuring a knot of men forming, at the center her father, elbows up. Fighting. "Two months ago something went wrong at Pollock. There were at least two incidents, inmates connected with the Royals. They went for him in a lineup and in the yard. You know the Royals?"

"A white prison gang. I've read the intelligence, and I've seen a few of their guys on wants and warrants. Why would the Royals want to hurt him?"

Ahearn shrugged. "Your father makes friends wherever he goes." Smiled, and she nodded.

"Yeah, he was like that on the outside, too."

"So, for whatever reason, business, or personality problems, whatever, I guess he knew he was in trouble. And your father's not exactly the kind of guy who's going to come to the authorities, is he?"

"No." She sifted through the photos, finding one showing his face contorted in rage and his hands a blur of motion as he fought. "So he escaped. How did he get out?"

"He had help." Ahearn fished around in the file again and came out with another series of photos. A truck at a dock, the rear doors standing open. Shots inside the truck, a stack of pallets. "He made himself a box, got inside it, and somebody—another prisoner, maybe a guard—put him on a truck out of the facility. A couple miles away he broke out of the box and jumped off the back of the truck." More photos. A highway through green bottomland taken from the air, close-ups of tire tracks, a white nest of discarded cigarettes printed with waxy red stains. Ahearn tapped the photo. "He had help on the outside, too."

"Lipstick." Frannie looked at him. "A woman."

Another photograph. "This woman, maybe." A shot of a young woman, not much more than a girl. The same woman in the photograph out on the white board. Bright frizz of hair and wide eyes. "Tina O'Bannon." The picture is head-on, an ID photo, her eyes startled and worried.

"Jesus, what is she, seventeen?"

"Twenty-six. She came over on a tourist visa from Dublin and stayed. We think your father brought her over. We think he met her when he was hiding in Ireland. You know what your father did for a living."

"He was an enforcer for the roofers union. He . . . beat people up for Adolph Wurtz, the guy who ran Local 225."

"He didn't just beat them up, Frannie."

"I know."

"He's suspected in at least two—"

She held up a hand to cut him off. "I know. I know what he's suspected of."

"I'm sorry."

"There's nothing you can tell me about what he's capable of, Agent Ahearn. I know what he is and I know what he did."

She got up from the table and went to a corner, surveying the room. "You know how many times I sat at this table?" She pointed at him. "Sat right where you're sitting, trying to get the mothers and wives and sons and daughters of some dealer or smuggler or thief to give up somebody they love? And they tell us we're wrong, and they love him, and if we only knew him the way they did, knew he was generous, or kind to animals, or gave his grandmother a new car." She shook her head. "Or they go the other way, you know. They know he's a bad guy, they want him out of their lives, they want him locked up, they'd love to help. And the funny thing? The funny thing is whatever they say, they're usually lying." She smiled, but there was nothing in it.

"The ones who say they want to help, half the time you know that's a lie. The mother's telling you she's done with him, she hates what he's become, a thief, a killer, and you find him hiding under her bed. You cuff him and she cries and curses you out, calls you all kind of filthy names and says leave her baby alone." She lifted the sleeve of her pullover and showed him a puckered scar running along her forearm. "Two years ago. The woman, the mother, she's broke, all her money gone when her son, the drug dealer, the rapist, jumped and the bond forfeited. Lost her job as a teacher, living in a rat-hole motel in Hunting Park, trying to take care of her granddaughter and watching the kids of the prostitutes who worked out of the rooms on either side of her. We picked the son up when he came to her trying to borrow more money from this poor, broke, just defeated woman. And what does she do? When we put the cuffs on him, she pulls a knife. Comes right at me. I was standing there flatfooted, I couldn't believe it. Takes two guys to hold her down and I get eight stitches and a tetanus shot. "

Ahearn smiled and nodded, he knew these stories and probably had some of his own. Frannie said, "But the other ones, the ones who say he's a good boy, a good husband, a loyal son. They're full of shit, too, right? Mostly? Mostly I think they're terrified. More afraid of him than they are of you, that's all."

"So, then," Ahearn finally said. "Which one are you?"

"You're missing the point, Agent Ahearn."

"Red."

"Red." She nodded. "I'm saying I know it doesn't matter what I say, you'll think I'm lying."

"I don't know it's lying exactly," he said. "I think it's people don't know, half the time. They don't know *what* they feel. They can't sort it out themselves, the families, the wives, the girlfriends." He looked at her. "The children. We tell them, your son, your husband. Your father. He's a drug dealer, a rapist, a killer, and they don't know what to think. What to feel. What do you know about anyone? Even the ones closest to us?"

"You don't have to give me an out."

"Whatever he is, your father? You made your own way. You made good decisions. You joined the Marshals."

Her face tightened. "I don't need anybody's permission to be who I am."

"I'm sorry. I didn't mean to presume anything."

She moved her head, a gesture. "I'm sorry. Days like

this I find out I'm holding on to a lot from when I was a kid."

He smiled. It was okay. He said, "But you'd help us? You'd give him up without looking back? Worrying about what it means?"

"If I could draw you a map to whatever hole he's hiding in."

Ahearn nodded. He looked down at the files on the table, then back at her as if trying to decide something. After a long second he nodded to himself as if making up his mind. "That's not all, though, Frannie."

"What?"

He sorted through the file, came up with digital photos of what looked like a notebook filled with a tight, furious scrawl of blue ink. He laid his hand on the photos and paused, touching his tongue to his teeth as if silently running the words he needed to say.

"What?"

"These were in his cell. Pages and pages of this . . . I don't know what to call it."

"What does it say?" She picked up one of the pictures and tried to read the handwriting but couldn't make much out. She saw the words "never forgive" underlined. She saw the word "murder."

"A lot of it, I don't think anyone could figure out. It's not particularly clear, but the parts we can read and understand?" He lowered his voice. "It's full of death, Frannie, and rage. He talks about working up to killing his family. Your mother, your sister, and you."

She reached out for another page but he stopped her hand, gently, and took the photos up. "It's probably not a good idea for you to go through the files. All of this?" He waved a hand at the stack of documents, the photos, the prison intake forms, the A0205s, incident reports. "This is evidence. We pick him up, this will help get him locked up again forever. And we don't want a defense lawyer having an in here, right? Asking what you saw? What you touched?" He finished stacking everything and sat on the edge of the table. He looked at her, and then away. His voice quiet. "I wanted you to see. In case, I don't know. He comes near you or Mae. But you don't want these things in your head." On the top of the stack a picture of a section of text, blown up, circled in red pen. She could read the words "all of them dead."

She nodded, a barely perceptible ducking of the head. "Like I said, there's nothing you can tell me about him that I don't already know." But she could feel the blood draining out of her face, felt she must have gone white and colorless. She felt heat on her face, plain as if the papers on the table had burst into flame.

Red Ahearn spoke quietly. "So you know, then. That he may be coming. To hurt you and your sister, if he can."

"I know."

"How? Did he threaten you? From prison?"

"No, already tried. To kill us, me and my sister. He came close."

"He tried to kill you? When?"

"The night he murdered my mother."

They were sitting there, the words hanging in the air, and Sleeper opened the door. They looked at him and he said, "The cops found Rudy Wurtz."

# 7

Sleeper drove her to her place first and waited in the car while she showered and changed into jeans, steel-toed CAT boots, and a turtleneck. She stood for a minute at the front window, watching Hansen talking on the phone in the car, then into the room she used as an office. There were the cartons she had carried home the day she left the Marshals, still mostly unopened, the drawings Tansy had done that had hung over her desk. Stacked against the wall were two paintings by her mother, the only two that survived the fire the night she died. One was of a woman suspended in blue that might have been water. She remembered her mother working on the painting, her hands daubed with paint, and Mae asking about it. Her mother had said, *It's a woman in the river*, and Mae had asked if she was drowning or swimming. There were figures watching from the shore, small figures that might have been children. Frannie didn't remember what her mother had said, but she remembered saying she'd never let her mother drown. She'd jump in and save her.

She went to the gun safe and got the short-barreled Colt and stuck a Yaqui slide holster into her belt. She lifted a wool blazer off the rack that she'd picked up at Joan Shepp when she'd gotten her last raise, then threw it on a chair and rooted in the back of the closet for a black leather coat she'd taken off a guy named Levi Tucker, a former member of the Vagos biker gang who had killed a young student in a bar fight in Nevada, then dropped out of sight for twenty years. When Frannie found him, he'd been living quietly in Jersey and had grandchildren who thought of him as a sweet old man, which by then he probably was. He was sitting in his old colors at his breakfast table and when they came in he'd stripped off the jacket and handed it to Frannie. The back of the jacket had the word VAGOS over what looked like a red demon riding a single wheel and a rocker that read, RENO, NEVADA. Levi Tucker brushed the back of the jacket with his cuffed hands and told her it wasn't a demon on the jacket, it was Loki, the Norse trickster god, the shape-shifter, the troublemaker. Levi Tucker said, *The god of stirring shit up*.

Now she walked out as Sleeper was hanging up his phone. He watched her come across the street.

"What?"

"Nothing."

"Come on." She stood at the passenger door.

"Nothing. You just, you know." He lifted a corner of his mouth. "Got your hunting clothes on."

Sleeper drove her northeast up Frankford Avenue, and when they crossed Lehigh she felt herself tighten up. They were getting closer to the place she'd grown up, to the bars she first drank in, to the houses of the kids she grew up with, to the house where her mother died.

They reached a knot of police cars and vans at Elkhart and slowed down. Sleeper made the turn, Frannie watching the neighborhood people, kids pointing at the lights and talking to each other out of the corner of their mouths and keeping their distance from the uniforms. A block down at Coral, a young cop with a high-and-tight haircut waved them to the curb near a vacant lot and guys in uniforms and plainclothes stood in clumps on the sidewalk while evidence techs poked in the high grass. They got out, Sleeper on a cell phone while she looked at him impatiently. She followed him around a corner while somebody talked him in, and he showed his ID to another cop manning the yellow tape. Scanlon sat in the open door of a Suburban, his face contorted by rage as he whispered into his phone. Red Ahearn and a young Hispanic detective from Philly PD walked toward them and they shook hands.

The cops formed a rough circle, and in the center of the circle was a dead man. He was sitting in a blue easy chair, his eyes barely open, his shirt black with blood.

His mouth hung open, too, as if he was just about to say something but the words wouldn't come. Most of the death Frannie had seen was in photographs of crime scenes, and the day she had shot the man in the raincoat was a blur, but here the dead man sat like the guest of honor at a party. Surrounded by action, movement, the flash of cameras. *Wait a minute,* she wanted to say, *wait a minute and be still. He's going to speak. He's about to tell you what happened.*

Sleeper and Red Ahearn came back to where she stood at the tape. Ahearn said, "Do you recognize him?"

She nodded her head. "I think so. I think he used to come over to the house when we were kids."

"Rudy Wurtz. He and his father ran the local for years. The father is Adolph. Philly PD says he's on his way down here."

"To see this?" She shook her head. "To see his son like this?"

A detective tapped Sleeper on the arm, his shield hanging on a chain around his neck, and showed him an image on a phone. He and Ahearn looked at it for a minute, then at her, then Sleeper held it out to her and she took a slow step forward. Sleeper pointed up toward Frankford Avenue. "This is from the camera at the beer distributor up the street." It was a still from a digital camera, washed out and grainy, but she recognized her father, hunched and furtive on the street.

She looked back at the dead man, the milling cops. "Why would he kill Rudy Wurtz?"

Ahearn said, "It's a good question. Patrick worked for Adolph and Rudy. Like you said, he was an enforcer. He kept the contractors in line, kept nonunion jobs from getting done. The Wurtz family ran the local, and there was a lot more going on than just strong-arming for the union. They had a second-story crew, burglars who worked all over the East Coast, did work for the Philly mob. Worked protection schemes, extorted money for the Catrambones and their friends. I worked those cases." He nodded toward the open door of the SUV where Scanlon sat scowling and muttering. "Bill Scanlon, too. In those days he was an investigator for the U.S. Attorney, before he went to the Marshals. It was a big case and it went on for years. Even after we started locking them up, Wurtz and his people, they kept coming. Bribing judges, trying to muscle the guys who ran against Adolph for president of the local."

They all watched as a crew from the medical examiner's office positioned a gurney on the sidewalk and began to open a body bag. Ahearn said, "This thing goes back a lot of years. People don't talk about it anymore, but this all goes back twenty, thirty years. There was a time the roofers owned a lot of people in this town. Cops, judges. They used to hand out envelopes, give people free roofing jobs." He smiled. "We were doing the racketeering prosecutions, trying to put Adolph and his pals in jail. Me and Bill used to ride by the judges' houses, see what kind of shape the roofs were in. If a judge had a new roof, we'd open a file, start a wiretap. We indicted three judges and a handful of cops, but there were a lot more that were dirty."

Somebody screamed. They all turned, watched a young woman with black hair and tattoos on her arms trying to rush the tape to get at the body. A policewoman was holding the woman but it was a close thing, and Frannie stepped across the street and helped hold the woman back. She was wiry, large-breasted, wore feathery false eyelashes and smelled to Frannie like Pall Malls and Playboy body mist. She had *"Rudy and Rosie"* in script on her arm. The policewoman cocked her head toward an open door where a stocky older woman held a toddler with his fingers in his mouth, so Frannie helped guide the young woman through the door and onto a couch with plastic slipcovers. On the walls were pictures of the couple together, the baby between them, and an animated picture of a waterfall that issued a rushing sound from a speaker on the frame. The older woman was speaking Spanish under her breath and shaking her head, probably at the spectacle of it all and the shame it brought on the house. The young woman collapsed, sobbing and scream-ing into her fists, and Frannie nodded to the policewoman and retreated to the cold street.

The Hispanic detective thanked Frannie for the help, guided her away from the door so they could talk. He said his name was Camacho, like the fighter, and handed her his card. "Call me Lino," he said, and pointed back at the house. "That's Rosie Porrera, she was Wurtz's girl-friend, and the neighbors say that's his kid."

"He live here, Lino?"

He shook his head, a quick, furtive movement, like *Are you kidding?* "No, he's got a family up in the Northeast, off Roosevelt Boulevard. A nice blond wife and three grown kids. Rudy and his father train fighters at the gyms around here. Rosie's a neighborhood girl."

"So he's got the wife uptown and the girlfriend down here. What about the grown kids? They in the life, too?"

"One of them is in L.A., trying to become a movie star, one of them is in business school at Wharton, so I guess the jury's still out on him. The youngest one, Marty? That one's a straight-up thug."

"He in the family business?"

"He's twenty-two, that kid, but he's got a motor on him. Burglary, assault. We liked him pretty good for the murder of an informant, but we couldn't make it stick." He watched her, trying to read her face. "Why, you know something about these birds?"

She shook her head, but was thinking about the white van on Kelly Drive. She had only the quickest impression of them, but she remembered an old man and young man. Who knew who they were? And if her father was out of prison and killing his old friends, was it coming back on her? She said, "I don't know. I don't know how much help I can be, but give me your card."

A car honked, and they all turned to watch an Escalade nose up onto Coral Street and three men get out, an older man in a tracksuit on the passenger side and two young men, each a head taller than the older man and bulked up in the chest and shoulders.

Camacho said, "Shit." He drew a breath and walked toward the man, holding up his shield.

Ahearn talked into his shoulder, quietly. "Adolph Wurtz. The old man. He did five years, did a deal to keep Rudy from going up for racketeering. He built the local, put guys like your father to work keeping everybody in line. Pulled them out of the gyms, guys who knew how to fight. I bet he knows everything that's happening here and why."

Frannie said, "I remember him."

"From when?"

"When I was young. He used to come by the house once or twice a year. Always a crowd with him, always a big show. My father would get tense when he was in the house, drink and shout at my mother. Even more than usual."

The old man walked by them without acknowledging their presence, pushing through the yellow tape and going to where the body had been. He stood motionless looking at the sprung, rotted chair, the spattered blood. Frannie noticed the sides of the chair had been tagged, scrawled with numbers and signs. The cops looked at each other but nobody made a move to stop him.

Frannie said quietly, "When Wurtz would leave, my

old man would go nuts and my mother would have to try to talk him down. Me and my sister would hide in the bathroom and listen to him tear the place apart."

Ahearn said, "What I know about your old man, it must have been a hell of a way to grow up. Is she in law enforcement, too, your sister?"

Frannie shook her head.

"What's she do, then?"

"She drinks."

They watched Camacho talk quietly to Wurtz until he nodded and stepped back behind the tape. He wasn't as tall as the two men he was with, but he looked hard, the veins in his neck standing out. Whatever he was feeling, he was holding it inside. Lino Camacho walked back to Frannie and Ahearn, shaking his head.

To Ahearn, she said, "What's he, seventy?"

"Seventy-three, I think." They watched him walk back to the car. "He did three of his five at Marion. Back when it was a supermax, in permanent lockdown. They wore handcuffs to the showers in that place. Kept some guys in Plexiglas cages in the basement." Adolph stopped at the open door, looked around at the place. The lot and its scattered trash, the neighborhood guys with shaved heads, speaking Spanish to each other. Frannie couldn't guess what was in his head. Whatever he was feeling didn't show in his face. Ahearn looked at her. "They could never pin it on him, but I heard he killed a guy in there. An Aryan Brotherhood guy from Chino."

Lino Camacho said, "Jesus, you don't got enough trouble doing federal time, you stick some Brotherhood guy in the lunch line?"

"Nah, he didn't use a knife. The way I heard it, the guy took a run at him in the shower, and even with cuffs on him, Adolph took him on." Ahearn held up his own hands, joining them together at the wrists as if cuffed there. "Beat the guy to death with his hands." She looked at the old man, his head bent, arms rigid. She could believe the violence. He gave off an electricity, some motion that was there even when he stood still. After a long minute he got back in the SUV.

Lino said, "All that shit they got up to, he only did five years?"

Ahearn shrugged. "We were lucky to get that. A guy that smart it's tough to make anything stick. We had a couple witnesses disappear."

"He still run the union?"

"No, the Justice Department pulled the plug on the local, put a trustee in charge, a retired federal judge. It's all over now."

The Escalade backed up and the driver straightened out on Elkhart to drive away. Before he did, the old man reached one hand out and put it on the wheel and said something to the driver and the car stopped. All three men turned together and looked straight at her. They paused there, staring, and Frannie squared herself to the car. A delivery van came up to their bumper and blew its horn, but the Escalade didn't move. She saw the old man's lips moving, talking, and the two men looked at him, then back out at her. Finally, she made a motion with her right hand, sweeping back the jacket slightly, letting it fall away to show the gun at her hip. The old man's face got rigid, then he nodded and the big SUV moved slowly down the street and was gone.

Ahearn and Camacho looked at each other. Camacho said, "Damn, girl. You call out Adolph Wurtz in his own neighborhood? At the place where his son just got his ticket punched?"

Watching the Escalade move slowly away, she said, "They saw me. They know who I am." She turned and looked at their faces, Ahearn squinting, Camacho looking pained. "What am I supposed to do? Run away?"

Ahearn said, "You know, I didn't see it before. But yeah, you're Patrick Mullen's kid."

Ahearn and Camacho went off to talk to the evidence techs and Sleeper was deep in a phone conversation, the phone propped on his shoulder while he wrote in a notepad. For a minute she was alone. She looked back at the empty lot and the bloodstained chair. She noticed something she hadn't seen before, graffiti on the wall of the house on the far side of the lot. It took her a minute to recognize the numbers "225" and a picture of an eye. It was everywhere, she saw now, the pattern emerging on the walls and sidewalks and the chair itself, the bloody chair that had held Rudy Wurtz's lifeless body. Two-twenty-five was the Roofers local that Adolph and Rudy had run, that her father had beaten and killed people for. Some of the tags were old, she could see, weathered and barely there. A hieroglyphic now, from a lost empire. From a time when the local had just about run the city, when the eye told people they knew everything, were hooked in everywhere.

But some of the tags were fresh, bright, like if you touched them they'd still be wet. She crossed the street and ducked under the tape and went to the wall and was reaching out to touch one of the scrawled numbers when she felt a hand on her arm and looked to see Camacho shaking his head at her.

"Don't touch."

She stopped and pointed. "This is fresh," she said. "And I don't think it's paint."

He cocked his head, sidestepped to get an angle on the graffiti. "No," he said. "No, I think you're right." He looked around and caught the eye of one of the evidence techs, a slender Asian woman wearing thick blue gloves and carrying a digital camera. She lifted the camera and Frannie had to turn her head from the bright flash. Camacho squinted at her. "Bet you ten dollars," he said.

Ahearn came over, his eyebrows raised. "What are we betting on?"

Camacho pointed at the wall. "That this? These tags? That's Rudy's blood."

They all came over the wall to look, the other techs and Sleeper and Ahearn. Frannie stepped back and crossed the street, lifting the tape and heading to the opposite curb. She turned to see them absorbed in the messages scrawled on the wall, then she ducked around the corner onto Elkhart and headed down, toward the river.

She came out from under the overpass at Martha Street to a deserted stretch of Clearfield Street bordered by empty lots full of weeds that had been beaten down by the early snow, and farther south she could see cars and people on the road. She walked slowly, trying to sort out the day. How long had Patrick been out, three days? Four? Had he been here all that time? And did he kill Rudy Wurtz? Patrick had stood with Adolph and Rudy for years, she knew, had beaten and threatened people for them and gone to jail for them. He could have gotten a deal, she was sure, could have ratted on the Wurtz family and drawn easy time. She hadn't talked to her father in years, but she had gotten updates from her aunt Rodi when she was alive, and of course from Mae, who had followed the news compulsively for years, trying to make sense of it.

So why, if he'd done time for them, taken their secrets away with him, why would he break out now and kill one of them?

At Collins she saw a flyer on a telephone pole for a haunted tour of Philadelphia that started at St. Peter's Cemetery on Almond. There were blurry, much-copied photos of a pale girl in a top hat in front of the Poe House down on Spring Garden Street and perched on a headstone in Laurel Hill Cemetery. Frannie had an impulse to go, hijack the bus full of vacationers, and drive them on her own haunted tour of the city. Here the Chinatown street where she got one of her best friends killed, here the motel on Westmoreland where a sixty-year-old former teacher stabbed Frannie in the arm, trying to keep her drug-dealing son out of jail. Or they could just walk half a block from St. Peter's and see the house where she'd grown up. Not the original house, of course, not as it was. That was gone in a twister of black smoke and a shower of red embers the night her mother died. She remembered the drifting, burning sparks coming down everywhere while she and Mae stood on the street, a Polish woman from across the block holding them both in her wide arms and trying to keep them from watching their house burn. Sometimes she'd wake up from a dream expecting to see the room filled with glowing red specks. She'd make the pale tourists from Montreal and Wheeling and Dayton stand on Almond Street and close their eyes and imagine the narrow road at night, the fire engines and police cars and neighbors drunk and sober and two small girls with ash in their hair watching sparks drifting to heaven and one of those sparks maybe the soul of her mother, if you believed in that.

That's where the ghosts ought to be in this town. Not in the cemeteries, the tidy forests of marble and granite in Holy Cross and Laurel Hill, but on the street corners in Strawberry Mansion and Frankford and in front of the social clubs on North Broad and the Kensington bars with no names where the young men got heads full of Hennessy and cocaine and retired to the street to have their showdowns. Ben Franklin might be buried down on Arch Street somewhere, but the restless dead, the young dead, the murdered ones whose rage and thwarted ambition would make for wrathful spirits, they were out in the empty prairies of Mutter Street and Westmoreland and Somerset. There was no tour for that.

The phone in her pocket vibrated, and she looked at the display before she answered.

She said, "Mae. How're you holding up?"

"Okay," Mae said. "I'm cooking." Her sister had gotten home from rehab the day before. Frannie could picture her slamming around her kitchen, a contained frenzy of restless energy and nerves.

"Cooking? For who?"

"Me, I guess. I've been away a month. I emptied the fridge and everything that wasn't spoiled I cooked. You want to come over and eat?"

"What's on the menu?"

"Pasta with corn and . . . hotdogs. I think they're hotdogs. They were pretty covered with frost."

"Thanks, but . . ."

"Yeah, I don't know that I'm really going to eat it. Remember when we used to make breakfast in bed for Mom?"

"Who could forget? Eggs with chocolate jimmies. She thought they were ants."

"A few of them might have been. She wasn't the greatest housekeeper."

"No." They laughed, Frannie thinking her sister sounded manic, a little shrill, her mind jumping from one thing to the next. Still, that was better than the other, the deep silences and crying jags. "So you're . . . okay, then?"

"Sure. Keeping busy. That's the main thing. Not sitting around, thinking too much."

"Right."

"You working tomorrow? Want to do lunch?"

That brought Frannie up short, thinking, *Are you nuts? Our father's out killing people,* but she realized Mae knew nothing about any of that and she needed to. Even if it upset her, even if it erased whatever progress she'd made at Sunrise House. She shook her head, damning her father again in her mind.

"No? You're busy. I'm sorry, I just thought since you were in town."

"Oh, no, that would be great. We should . . ." Was going to say, *We should talk,* but didn't want to leave her sister with anything that would upset her, nag at her. "I'll pick you up, how about that?"

"Sure," Mae said brightly, "that would be great."

"Eleven?"

"You bet. I'll be here. Still cooking, or defrosting the fridge, or dusting the fruit at the bottom of the bowl."

"You should take it easy, Mae."

"Oh, I will. It's this first day out, you know. It's always just . . ."

"Right." Because this wasn't the first time she'd come out of rehab. "Mae, I'll talk to you tomorrow, okay?"

"Sure. Love you, sis."

"See you at eleven."

# 8

When Frannie was thirteen, a girl named Mariposa Rivera broke her nose. She had gone a few times to the old gym on Richmond Street and thought she knew something. Old Cas, the trainer, would shake his head when he saw her coming, try to get her to keep her hands up, protect her head. He'd step on her toes to remind her to stop planting her feet before she punched. Old Cas would say, *Jesus, here comes another Mullen ready to take on the world*, or, the last few times just, *Here comes trouble*.

Mariposa was Puerto Rican, from the other side of Kensington Avenue in Juniata. She was an inch shorter than Frannie but easily stood her off, slipping off her jabs and rolling when she hooked her arm, getting ready to throw the haymaker (the one that had gotten Frannie thrown out of Mother of Divine Grace on the day she overheard one of the janitors saying that Frannie was going to *for sure kill somebody*). So she danced and threw punches at Mariposa but she couldn't land anything and just bruised her arms on the smaller girl's hard biceps. The trainer's voice was an insect buzzing in her ear, teaching her nothing, and after the fight Frannie couldn't let it go. She threw down the gloves, stalked her to the lockers talking shit, and the girl had turned and popped her hard and she felt the bridge of her nose give way and the blood come. Cas packed her nose with an iced tampon and told her to stop coming around. She remembered the long walk up to the Ready Care across Aramingo, her nose swelling so that she had to breathe through her mouth, and she remembered that when she came out, Mariposa Rivera was waiting on the steps and walked her home.

Now as Frannie drifted south down Clearfield Avenue she heard the liquid warble of a siren and turned quick to see Mariposa in uniform at the wheel of a white Philadelphia police car, lifting her hands off the wheel in a *What the fuck?* gesture while her partner leaned back against the passenger window and looked at the two of them through heavy-lidded eyes. Mari, twenty years older than the day she broke Mullen's nose but still a tough girl from Juniata, still wiry though she had two boys of her own.

"Jesus, I thought there was a cop following me for a minute."

"What I hear you need a cop following you." Mariposa put the car in park and opened the door, the radio coughing and sighing quietly. "I hear right your old man is on the street?"

Frannie lifted a shoulder. "And back at it. I just walked down from Frankford Avenue."

Mariposa's face changed, her eyes going big. "Christ, the dead guy in the lot? That was Patrick, did that? It was on the radio."

"Looks like it."

"Jesus, does your sister know?"

Frannie shook her head. "No. I haven't said anything." She dropped her voice and leaned in close. "Mari, she just got out of Sunrise yesterday. She's got twenty-eight days sober and she's running on nerves as it is."

"Jesus, that's right. But Frannie, at some point you got to tell her."

Her partner leaned forward, the front of his blues dusted white. "Rivera, we need to get back."

She rolled her eyes. "*Mira, puñeta*. Eat another *paczki* and let me talk to my friend." She shook her head. "He makes me drive him all the way down to Richmond Street to the Polish bakery lady, then he wants me to run code with the goddamn lights to get back in time for roll call."

"You go on ahead. I'll be okay."

"You got your phone?"

She touched her pocket and nodded. Mari looked unsure. "Why don't you ride up with us? I can take you home when we're done."

"I'm okay, really. I got my phone."

"You carrying?"

Frannie lifted the leather coat to show the Colt on her hip, nearly the same gesture she had used on Adolph Wurtz.

"Why does that make me more worried?"

"Go, Mari. I'll call you later and check in."

Mariposa's partner made a noise inside the car. She shook her head. "Okay, I see you. I want updates."

She watched them go and thought she maybe should have gone with them. Wondered if she really needed to be alone to think or if she was trying to make something happen. The day felt unreal, the chain of normal life snapped.

Frannie moved south and the dead and empty lots gave way to houses and convenience stores and bars. At Weikel was a little bar that used to be the Corner Spot but was something else now, and she walked inside. There were a couple of older neighborhood guys looking into their beers and a young woman with bright green eyeliner and tattoos on her arms throwing darts at the board in the back and singing quietly to the Coldplay song "Paradise." The place had been cleaned up since the old days, fresh paint and better lighting. On the wall near the door was a sign that said ZERO TOLERANCE DRUG POLICY! and IF YOU SMOKED WET TODAY, DON'T ASK FOR SHIT! For all the new lights and paint, she thought, it was still Port Richmond.

The bartender raised his eyebrows and she ordered a Coke and stood by the bar. The last time she'd been in here it had been the Corner Spot, and she'd been twenty-one and had a drink with a sweet boy from Belgrade Street named Richie Barnett who left for Fort Benning a few weeks later and was killed in a helicopter crash in Iraq. She took a few sips of the Coke and walked back out and stood on the sidewalk and the girl who had been playing darts came out after her. She pointed a cigarette at Frannie, but Frannie shook her head. "No, thanks."

The thin woman squinted at her while she fired up her Lucky Strike. "I know you."

Frannie looked at her. She was pretty in her way, bony and hard-eyed and with tattoos of crosses and roses on her arms. Her eyes had a metallic glint and darted in her head, like the eyes of a bird. Meth, Frannie thought, or crack, maybe. Or maybe that's just how she was. The woman said, "You're a Mullen, right?"

Frannie nodded, "Yeah. I'm sorry, I don't . . ."

The woman lifted a thumb on the hand that held the cigarette. "Bertie. McCullough. From down Cedar Street."

"Oh, Jesus, Bertie, sure." She nodded, remembering her as a skinny kid throwing rocks and tennis balls at the wires for the trolley on Richmond Street. The kids called it "wireball."

"I was going to say, you know, you don't remember? You were ahead of me at Carroll. You went out with my cousin Danny."

"I don't know that we went out, exactly. Hung out, more like."

"Yeah, he didn't tell it that way." She smiled. "He thought it was the big romance."

"He was a handful."

"That's what the nuns used to say. A handful."

"He still live around here?"

She squinted and leaned in, and Frannie could see she was more than a little drunk. "Locked up," she stage-whispered. "Him and Donald. My idiot husband. Tried to rob a jewelry store up on Frankford. So, that's that."

Frannie couldn't get a fix on how old the woman was, trying to do the math in her head. "You were married?"

"I divorced him when he got sent to Graterford. Stupid bastard. And me with his kids to take care of."

So, maybe in her late twenties, then. Married, divorced, kids, the husband in prison upstate. She wanted to ask who was watching the kids when she was drunk on Clearfield Street at noon, but just nodded and thought, here was the life she had left when she went away to Glynco and the Marshals. Bertie asked, "But you got away. You still with the cops? Somebody said you was with the cops."

"The Marshals. I was, but now I'm out."

"Better, huh? All that cop bullshit. Busting kids for joints when the big crooks steal everything that isn't nailed down." She smoked her cigarette, pulling hard at it, the end glowing and the ash stacking up at the tip.

Frannie didn't know what to say to that, so she asked about the kids. That fast, the woman switched gears, her voice getting hoarse with emotion. "Little Phil and Donald junior are at Divine Grace. I lost one, Brianna." She lifted her sleeve to show a cross and roses, dates of birth and death a year apart. Her hands shook, Frannie saw. "She never could breathe right." Her eyes filled with tears. "They said down at Children's Hospital it was all the crap in the air down here from the refineries on the river."

Or meth fumes from the basement, Frannie thought, but she just nodded. The phone in her pocket rang, and she smiled apologetically and stepped away to pull it from her pocket. Sleeper's number on the display. Behind her she heard Bertie say, "I seen your dad."

Frannie stopped, the phone vibrating in her hand, and turned back to Bertie, who was fishing in her purse and came out with a broken cigarette. "Crap. I need more smokes."

"What did you say? About my father?"

"I seen him. I just seen him yesterday. Walked right by here." She pointed with the ruined cigarette, the end dangling. "I said it to John, the bartender?" She pointed back in toward the bar. "That's how I knew it was you right away. 'Cause I just seen Patrick and you was all in my head. The Mullens. I said to him, *What are you, lost?* I thought he was still locked up. And here you are, like old home week for the Mullens in Port Richmond. So, is he out?"

"He escaped from a federal prison, Bertie."

"Aww. No shit?"

"You don't want to go near him now. Did he say anything to you?"

"Nah, he just kept moving down the street, so I left him be. He looked like he was in a dream, you know?

Or high, but I don't remember him using, Patrick." *Pay-atrick*, the way she said it. And *schtreet* for "street." The consonants tumbling into each other, the vowels tortured into two and three syllables. Frannie wondered how much she herself still sounded like Bertie. In her own head she thought she'd lost her accent, but some of the guys from the Midwest or the South would make fun of the way she talked. *Crown*, for "crayon." One of the Marshals from Kansas City would point to street signs to hear her pronounce "Passyunk" and "Sigel" and "Schuylkill."

Bertie smiled. "He could drink, though. Jesus, could he drink."

Frannie went into her pocket and got out a card, then found a pen and crossed out everything but the number for the Marshals office downtown. After a second she flipped the car and wrote her own number. "You see him again, you call me?" She could say call the police, but Bertie wasn't going to do that. She took the card and looked at it, and on her forearm just above the wrist was a tattoo of a razor and the words *"Snitches Get Stitches."*

"You sure you ain't still a cop?" But laughed to show she was still being friendly.

"When was it you saw him?"

"Oh, like dinnertime? Like six?" Bertie snapped off the ruined end of the cigarette and lit it. "The Mullens. Back in Port Richmond. He in trouble again, Patrick?"

Frannie shook her head. "Always."

---

She stepped away into the narrow side street to use the phone away from the bar and Bertie and anyone who might be listening or watching. There was a gap between two cars; cones and lawn chairs and a plastic paint bucket marking off a parking spot that somebody was trying to claim in front of one of the two-story row homes on Weikel. They were a fixture on the narrow Philly streets, these constructions, somewhere between street barriers and art installations.

The phone barely rang at the other end. "Mullen," Sleeper said, managing to convey in the single quiet word concern, disappointment, and exasperation.

She could picture him shaking his head and felt herself getting defensive. "I needed to get out of there."

"Where are you now?"

"I'm on Clearfield. But—"

"I'm sending a black-and-white."

"Oh, get over yourself. Listen to me."

"I'm listening. I'm not hanging up until I hear a cop get out of an RMP."

This was a lot of talk from Sleeper. It made her smile to think of him worked up. "I talked to a woman who says she saw Patrick here last night."

There was a pause, then she heard him conferring with somebody else and voices telling somebody else to shut up. "Where?"

"On the street in front of a bar on Clearfield." She gave him the intersection and heard him repeat it to somebody else.

"Don't leave." The phone went dead.

On the corner in front of the bar Bertie was talking on her own cell phone. Catching Frannie's eye she held the phone away from her ear and made a flapping motion with her free hand, mouthing *blah, blah, blah* silently. Disinterested in whatever her mother or friend or boyfriend was telling her, probably about doing something other than drinking and hanging out in the middle of the day. Frannie thought again that if she'd stayed in Port Richmond another couple of years she'd have been Bertie, or some harder, angrier version of her. The darkness of her father's life and her mother's death ready to eat her alive all the time, the way it had Mae.

Bertie smiled at her, and then her face changed, her head cocked like a bird's and her eyes lifted to look over Frannie's shoulder and down the street. Frannie turned to follow her gaze and saw the white van coming up the street. It was the van from Kelly Drive, the engine racing. It was about four car lengths away, coming fast, the tall kid from earlier at the wheel. Her right hand swept her coat back and she felt for the butt of the Colt. She heard Bertie scream. Maybe it was Frannie's name, or just a sound, the kind of jumbled syllables that come out of somebody's mouth when they're terrified, but Frannie's attention was fixed on the van.

Bertie screamed again and Frannie stepped back and swung right to look toward the corner, pulling the small, heavy pistol out of the holster at her hip and catching a blur of motion as a man materialized a few steps away with a baseball bat cocked over his right shoulder. A second later she'd know it was the older man she'd seen in the white van when it was down on the river, but for now what caught her eye was the bat, its bright metallic blue, the color of a beer can, with the name DeMarini in bold letters. The man wound up and hesitated, making a small feint and moving back a half step. Maybe he'd seen the pistol, maybe he'd been distracted by Bertie's scream, but then he committed and swung the bat hard against her right forearm just as she began to raise the gun. The aluminum bat made a small, sharp ping as it connected with her arm, and Frannie screamed.

She wanted to make sense, to form words, to tell Bertie to get help, call the cops, somebody, but it came out as something like the cry of a bird. There was a deep pain, a vibrating burn that rattled through the bones in her arm, and she tried to point the gun at the man as he wound up again with the bat but the gun hung useless in her dead hand.

She lifted her good arm to try to fend off the next blow as the van stopped hard next to her, the brakes shrieking. She had one moment of clarity, the realization that if the bat came down on her upraised left hand the man would break her fingers with the bat and she'd be left with no way to respond. With both of her hands useless and empty, he'd raise the bat again and again until she was dead or unconscious and then throw her in the van and take her away to dump her body somewhere, and no one but the incoherent Bertie to tell the police what had happened.

The van was stopped right behind her. She registered its position as much from the rattle and rasp of the old engine and another sound, the shriek of metal as the side door opened even as the van was still moving toward them. She felt herself going blank from panic, struggled to tear her attention from her lifeless hand and useless gun and concentrate on the man with the bat. She heard his breath coming hard. He was big, not tall but wide across the shoulders. The sleeves of his tracksuit pushed back to show thick forearms, and his shoes were polished to a bright shine. *Not a working man,* she thought. His nose was wide, flat across the bridge where it had been broken a long time ago. The aluminum bat was a blur of silver and blue as the man raised it again, pivoting, feinting, trying to figure the best way to bring it down on her before she could get a shot off.

And then she lost the gun.

The heavy Colt dropped from her frozen hand and hit the top of her boot, skittering away under a parked car. The gray-haired man swiveled his head to watch it go and then turned to her and she heard him draw a sharp breath through his ruined nose as he wound up to deliver one last hard shot and end it.

# 9

Frannie had first learned to fight in the street, the way these men had. In the quiet second before the man came at her again with the bat, before the driver and whoever else was in the van got out and joined in, she could see from his body language, the way he stood tall, canted back to swing the bat, and worried more about not getting hit than about landing a shot that would count, from all these things that the man with the broken nose was a brawler who fought in bars and parking lots and relied on his size and the willingness to hurt. The difference between them wasn't just size and weight and age, but that Frannie had left the streets and gone to the boxing gyms and the Police Athletic League and then Glynco, and she'd learned how to defend herself against men like this. For a second she let her face go slack, let the tension go out of her for one silent moment and felt the power in her arms and legs, flexed her hands against the wasp sting as her right arm came back to life. She drew a breath, felt the way her heavy boots anchored her to the street, and then she moved.

The man swung the bat, and Frannie stepped inside his swing and grabbed his head. He was moving forward with the effort, following the motion of the bat, and she pulled him easily off his feet, using his own momentum so that his head smacked against the side mirror of the van and she felt a physical rush of relief to hear the gasp of air from the man's lungs and the mirror mount crack as his head connected. The effort of lifting her right arm, of grabbing and pulling, made her grit her teeth against the pain that was like a knot in her arm, but she could use her own fear and adrenaline to keep moving, the way she had used the momentum of the man with the bat to put him on the ground. The man groaned and fell and Frannie lifted her steel-toed CAT boot and brought it down hard, missing his head by an inch and stomping the fingers of his left hand.

She could hear the door slamming on the driver's side of the van as the younger man got out but could only see the gray-haired man as he rolled, moaning and trying to protect his head. She saw something bright and green at the curb and she glanced down to see a Sprite can that had been run over so many times it was crushed flat. She had the crazy thought that she could grab the flattened can with her good left hand, but as she pivoted to grab the can the man at her feet kicked out and she fell back hard onto the curb, the air rushing out of her lungs so that she gasped and couldn't catch her breath.

She lost a second to the pain and surprise and lifted her head to see the driver, a taller, youngish man with a spiky mop of black hair crossing the street toward her. She heard herself trying to talk, to ask for help or for more time to think or prepare, but she couldn't draw a breath and the words were trapped in her throat. The older guy in the tracksuit was moving on the ground, moaning and trying to sit upright.

The kid registered the older man down and stopped, scrabbling for something at his waistband. He pulled at some kind of tool or weapon, something with a long wooden handle that he had trouble getting free. Frannie rolled, tried to get to her feet, her right hand and arm flaring with pain. She staggered up as the driver stood flatfooted, working to get the long-handled weapon out of his coat. He jerked at it once, then again and then he raised it high and she had just enough time to register that it was a small ax before she dropped and pivoted and kicked his left leg out from under him, and he went down, the ax head striking a spark off the asphalt as it fell.

She heard a sound; a scuffling noise and a squeak of springs that might have been someone else getting out of the van, and she looked over her shoulder to see a figure looming, a man, younger than the others, wearing a faded red Phillies jacket and swinging something, bringing it forward from way back over his shoulder. Somebody screamed. Maybe it was her.

She woke up in the ambulance, fists clenched. She tried to sit up, ready to fight, her head a ball of flame and her eyes clouded. She found her hands tied to a stretcher and she screamed and a woman in a uniform jacket, an EMT said, "She's awake again." To Frannie she said, "You're okay, it's okay," but Frannie couldn't follow what was going on and it was only when Mari Rivera leaned past the woman into Frannie's field of view that she began to calm down, though her heart raced and her breath came in uneven gasps that burned her throat. She looked wildly around her, registered where she was and that Mariposa sat next to her and Sleeper crouched in the back of the ambulance, gripping the frame of the stretcher as the ambulance rocked.

Mari looked into her eyes. "Calm down, Frannie. It's okay now." She touched Frannie's tethered hands. "You were still fighting when they picked you off the ground."

Sleeper reached over and began to untie the soft restraints, but the EMT put her hand on Sleeper's arm. "Wait a minute, cowboy. This one's been in and out and every time she wakes up she starts swinging."

"It's okay." He looked into Frannie's eyes. "You're okay, Mullen? You're not going to go off again, right?"

Frannie nodded, but was aware of herself staring, her eyes unfocused. "I'm . . ." She cleared her throat, which was raw and dry. "I'm okay. It's okay." Sleeper moved in again and freed her hands. She raised her now weight-less arms and touched her face, feeling scrapes on her cheeks and then gingerly touching a hard knot at her temple. The EMT reached toward her and Frannie flinched, but the woman took her hand gently and said, "Don't touch your head, okay, Frannie? We need to clean out that cut and get a doctor to look at everything. That make sense?"

Frannie nodded and began to relax a little. She re-membered fighting but couldn't sort it all out. There was the third man coming out of nowhere and she remem-bered trying to hit him, but those were the last things she remembered. The ambulance was loud and that made it harder to concentrate.

"Where's my gun?" She tried to sit up again. "Did you get my gun?"

Mari held up a hand. "It's okay, the cops have it. It's okay." Frannie could hear the radio from the cab, the en-gine straining, the liquid drone of the siren cutting through everything. There were wires and tubes swing-ing, arcane tools and bits of plastic hanging from every surface. The EMT was a woman with strawberry blond hair and freckles on the bridge of her nose, and she moved with assurance as the ambulance bucked and swayed on the rutted street. Frannie thought that must be something you mastered working in a rig like this, the way a blue-water sailor would keep her footing in a rough sea.

"Mae," she said, struggling to sit up again. "My sister."

She grabbed at Sleeper's sleeve. "If they tried to get to me they might go after her."

He put his cell phone to his ear. "Give me her address. I'll get Philly PD over there right now."

"I want to talk to her, can I talk to her? She's already . . . She's got a lot going on right now. " She shook her head, unsure what to say, hating to put her sister's problems in front of people she didn't know.

Mari put a hand on Frannie's leg. "I got it." Sleeper looked from Frannie to Mari and then handed her his cell. Mari made a call, talked to the watch commander at the fifth district out in Roxborough near where Mae lived, giving him the address, then handed the phone back to Sleeper who told him Marshals would be on the way to meet the cops at Mae's house. Frannie heard him make more calls, to Scanlon and Camacho, the detective from Philly PD. Mari told Frannie that cars were on the way to her sister's and she nodded.

"How long was I out?"

Sleeper said, "Not long. The first RMP was on-site in a couple of minutes, a couple of guys from the twenty-fourth district, and Mari was there a minute later. The guys from the twenty-fourth said you were still conscious when they rolled up."

Frannie closed her eyes, felt the pain in her head, a rhythmic banging timed to her heartbeat. She couldn't think straight. "Jesus, I can't remember. Did you pick up the guys I was fighting? Did they get away?"

Sleeper looked at Mari for a second, then opened and closed his mouth like he couldn't think of what to say. Mari finally said, "Don't worry about anything. We'll be at the ER in two minutes and get some X-rays and get you seen by the doctor." She looked at Sleeper, but spoke to Frannie. "Everything else can wait." Sleeper nodded.

There was confusion at the hospital, cops and reporters and more Marshals. She saw the Philly detective Camacho and Red Ahearn from the FBI, and it was like the same cast from the earlier crime scene had reconvened in the halls at Temple Hospital. Frannie said to herself, *Didn't I just leave this party?* Mari came back and touched her arm to say she had to go pick up her kids and Frannie grabbed her hand and was reluctant to let her go. She felt an odd panic watching Mari leave, knew that having a familiar face had given her some slim purchase on what was going on and she didn't trust anyone else to keep her grounded.

There was some kind of argument outside the cubicle where they had left her on a gurney. She could hear Scanlon's low, insistent rumble and Sleeper's terse rejoinders but she couldn't make sense of it. A nurse came in with a gown and held it up to her, but Frannie waved her off. "I'm not staying." The woman was young and had a neat, squared-away look and a tiny Purple Heart pin at her collar. She raised an eyebrow.

"You got insurance?"

"Yes." She had to think but it was hard to concentrate. The throb in her head seemed to scatter her thoughts.

"You get hit on the head?"

"Yeah, but—"

"Get the X-rays." She dropped the gown in Frannie's lap. She walked back through the curtain. Frannie slowly raised her arms to pull off her top. She had a knot in her arm where the gray-haired man had used the bat on her, and it seemed to grow larger and hotter as she moved. She was aware of her bones grating as if her joints were full of dust. She breathed through clenched teeth against the pain of lifting her arms overhead, but satisfied herself that at least her arms were not broken. When she put her arms through the gown she let herself sink back to the gurney, exhausted.

The nurse came back in and took her blood pressure and temperature. Her name plate said DEVERAUX, and Frannie nodded toward the Purple Heart pin and asked her if she'd been a nurse in the army, her swelling lips clumsy around the thermometer. In the halls there were running footsteps, birdlike yips of pain, a muffled roaring that was like the sound of a crowd in a theater before the curtain rises.

"Combat medic. Two tours." She smiled. "Did you serve? You got the look."

"No, I was with the Marshals."

"Not anymore?"

Frannie smiled, feeling a cut on her lip part. "I'm retired."

The woman laughed. "Yeah, you look retired."

There was more shouting outside the cubicle, and Frannie asked the nurse, "Where did the other guys go?"

The nurse shook her head, "Other guys?"

"The ones who did this to me. I know they were messed up."

"Got your licks in?"

"At least one of them I know was unconscious."

"I'll find out, okay?" She reached a gloved hand out to Frannie's face. "And I'll get some water and a washcloth, get you cleaned up before they take you down to X-ray."

"Thanks."

The woman paused at the curtain. "How's your head?"

Frannie shrugged. "It hurts."

"I'll keep checking in with you. A head injury is nothing to fool with."

"Thanks."

"I'm Khandi," she said, "With a 'K-H-I,' not a 'C-A-Y.' "

"Got it."

The nurse went out and the doctor came in, a quiet, sad-eyed man who looked like hadn't slept in weeks. He shone a light into her eyes and had her grip each of his hands in turn and gently touched the base of her neck. He told her to try not to move around much until they could do the X-rays.

Sleeper and Ahearn came in and stood looking significantly at each other, Ahearn rolling on the balls of his feet, like he was getting ready to run somewhere. Sleeper, as always, stood rock still but watched her face.

"Okay," she said when the doctor went back out, "somebody better tell me something."

Sleeper said, "What do you remember?"

"I remember getting jumped by two guys. I lost my gun under a car, so I fought them, got them off their feet. Then, I don't know."

"You passed out."

She looked puzzled, trying to remember. Her head throbbed. "There was a third guy. There was Broken Nose," and here she touched her own nose, with its faint crease where Mari Rivera had broken it twenty years before, "and the one with the ax."

Ahearn cocked his head. "An ax?"

"A hatchet, I guess you'd say. Short, stuck in his belt."

He looked at Sleeper. "A roofer's ax. I'd bet money."

"Well, there was those two and then another one came out of the van, or somewhere, and that was it." She shrugged. "He hit me with something, I don't know. Next thing I remember was the ambulance."

Sleeper said, "They came out of a van?"

"The van, the white van." She looked at each of the men in turn. "The one in the middle of the street."

Ahearn cleared his throat. "There was no van when the police got there."

"Okay, so number three drove it away. Did you get the other two? Were they down when the cops got there?"

Ahearn looked at Sleeper and Frannie snapped her fingers, annoyed. "Don't look at him, look at me. What happened to the two guys?"

Sleeper stepped toward her and lowered his voice. "Frannie, they're dead."

# 10

Outside in the hall somewhere there was a low hum and a light went on, a bright white glare that filled the gap between the curtain and the bed and threw shadows edged in red and blue. There was a hard ball in Frannie's throat that stopped air and sound and she felt pressure in her head as if the blood from her heart had rushed to her brain and was trapped there. The lights moved as if searching, and while some part of her knew the lights were from news cameras and photographers it was impossible not to feel they were searchlights that would find her, pin her in place so that she could be held and punished. She struggled to keep herself under control. She forced air out through her nose and cleared her throat before she trusted herself to speak.

"How?"

Sleeper said, "Frannie," but she gave him a look that stopped him.

"How are they dead? What happened to them?"

Ahearn cleared his throat again. "The bodies are on the way to the morgue. We'll know more when the ME's had a chance to look at them."

"Come on, come on!" She felt as if someone had fired a white flare into her head, the pain now coming with bright sparks across her vision. She clenched her hands, could feel herself losing control. She swiped at tears at the corner of her eyes. "Christ, can't anybody give me a straight answer about anything?"

Ahearn looked unhappy. "You carry a Colt, right?"

"I never fired the gun. I told you."

"Philly PD has it. There's blood and hair on the butt and the grip, Frannie. If had to guess, and it's just a guess . . . I'd say they were beaten to death with the Colt."

"Jesus. I hit them, but I don't remember anything like that."

Sleeper put a hand up. "Mullen. Stop talking about this, and I mean right now."

She knew he was trying to protect her, but she couldn't stop her hot, racing brain and the words spilling out of her. "What was I supposed to do? I thought they were going to kill me."

Ahearn said, "He's right, Frannie. Philly PD will be talking to you about this. You want to think carefully about what you say. Whatever happened to those guys I'm sure they had coming, but the wrong thing gets into the record and you got the prosecutor asking questions, and maybe families of the dead guys coming after you with lawyers."

She shook her head, opened and closed her mouth. "But I don't remember . . ." What *did* she remember? Fighting, and the men on the ground. Being frightened, but focused on putting them down.

The curtain moved and Wyatt stepped in. She almost broke down when she saw him, and he stepped across the room and grabbed her hand. Ahearn and Sleeper looked at each other and slipped out again. She bit her lip and held his hands to her face, smelling his familiar tang of motor oil and cigarette smoke and cut metal from his shop up in Northeast Philly.

He said, "I didn't have time to wash my hands."

She had trouble getting words out over rucked and trembling lips. "I don't know what's going on. I just want a straight answer."

"They taking care of you here?"

She nodded, getting control of herself. She started to tell him what happened, but it came out as a disjointed collection of violent episodes and disconnected family history. She thought she must sound like a beat-up drunk trying to tell her life story to a sympathetic bartender. Finally he put his arms around her, gently, felt her flinch. He stood awkwardly back, held a hand under her chin and looked at her face, wincing. She said, "Every time you see me I'm a mess." She tried to smile.

"You look fine."

"Yeah?"

"Well, you're breathing and sitting up and you still got your teeth and all."

"You're easy to please."

"I'm an Oklahoma boy. We tend to be realistic."

"Doc says I have a concussion."

"My daddy used to say wouldn't be a party without someone gets concussed."

"Maybe I'll have to meet him sometime."

He curled his lip in a tough-guy smile. "I think visiting days up at McAlester is Friday, Saturday, and Sunday."

Her voice was quiet. "So we've got that in common, then. Our fathers are both locked up. Or were locked up, anyway."

She moved over and he sat next to her, holding her hand.

"My uncles, too," he said. "My brother Dalton was, but he's out of prison now. He's a one-percenter, rides with the Bandidos."

"I've heard that, 'one-percenter,' but I don't know what it means."

"The hardcore guys, the outlaws, they call themselves that. Somebody said one time that ninety-nine percent of motorcycle riders was okay. So Dalton, guys like him, they use that one percent as a way to tell you who they are. Serious fellers." She noticed, as she had before, that when he talked about home his accent got thicker.

"That's another thing, then. We both came from that life, but we went another way."

"Yeah, some of us figured it out faster than others, though." Meaning himself, the things he'd done to get himself in trouble with the law. The way they'd met, when she'd arrested him on a failure-to-appear warrant for missing a court date.

"Well, you could say if you got straightened out any sooner we'd have never met."

He smiled at her. "There you go. The silver lining."

They sat in companionable silence for a minute. The curtain was opened by two Philadelphia cops and a tech, and they got her onto another gurney to take her to X-ray. He touched her hand before she went. She said, "Be here when I get back?"

"I'll run up and close the shop, check those motor-heads that work for me don't steal me blind. Be back in an hour." He tapped his watch.


When they brought her back from X-ray the uniformed cops were still there. She felt embarrassed that they were there to look after her and had to remind herself to thank them. Even after the fight on Clearfield Street it seemed more dramatic than necessary, though there was a TV playing soundlessly in the corner of the room and she recognized shots of Port Richmond and remembered that she'd been at two crime scenes in the last eight hours.

Alone for a moment, she thought about Wyatt and how she felt seeing him again, afraid she was just feel-ing overwhelmed and alone and turning to him out of need. And what would happen tomorrow, or next week, when her father was back behind bars and all this was gone, and it was just the two of them? He'd expect things from her, and she didn't know if she could give them.

The nurse came back in, Khandi with a "K-H-I," and Frannie asked her where her cell phone was. She handed Frannie a plastic bag that held her coat, her car keys and wallet, but there was no phone. She wanted to call her sister, check her messages. She'd ask Wyatt for his phone when he came back.

The doctor came back in and told her she could go home if there was someone who could stay with her. The X-rays were good, he said, no fractures in her arms or skull, but he'd feel better if there was someone who'd keep tabs on her for the next twenty-four hours. Make sure she slept, check her for slurred speech or vision. She said she'd work it out.

While she was getting dressed the curtains opened again and a small blond woman came in carrying a clipboard. Frannie held up a hand and asked to give her a minute and the woman nodded, backing out, smiling apologetically, though in the second before the curtain closed again Frannie thought the woman looked familiar. Frannie clumsily pulled her turtleneck over her head, drawing sharp breaths as she flexed her arm, which already had turned to a mottled purple around a yellow center in a way that reminded her of the lowering sky and storm clouds. She was sitting on the edge of the gurney, her jeans unsnapped, her body canted so that she could see the dappled blue welts on her back and arms when Mae came in trailing an exasperated-looking patrolman who stopped short at the curtain and backed out, holding his hands up in apology.

Mae's face was white. "When did you know?"

She pulled her shirt down, avoiding her sister's wide, red-rimmed eyes.

"Answer me: When did you know he'd escaped from prison?"

"This morning. I lost my cell phone or I would have called you."

"Jesus, look at you, Frannie. Are you all right? What happened?"

"I'm fine, really." She found herself speaking slowly and calmly, as if to someone with one foot on a high ledge. She forced herself to smile. "They just checked me out, the X-rays are all fine. I'm clear to leave."

Mae put a hand on her face and hissed through her fingers. "Did he do that?"

"No, no, it was . . ." She threw up her hands. "No. It was just these guys. I don't even know if it has anything to do with Patrick."

"You don't know."

"Well, no, I don't know. But we're okay, the police are with us and we're okay. The Marshals will have people keeping an eye on us, too." She crossed her arms, aware that she should be doing something, hugging her sister, but couldn't bring herself to cross the small space. She picked up her jacket and absently touched the void at her hip where her holster should be.

Mae let herself lean, then sagged onto a small stool. "I can't do this now. Not now. You know I can't."

"I know, Mae. But listen, you can hold it together." She clenched one fist. "Look, he's nothing to us. I know this eats at you, but you got to build a wall between you and all of this. All this history. You got to just get through it."

"Don't lose patience with me."

"Mae."

"God, look at you, you're all beat up. And you still want, what? To deny it has anything to do with you?"

Frannie lowered her voice, aware of the room full of cops and Marshals on the other side of the thin curtain. "No, but it doesn't tell me who I am. I can't do anything about who he is, but being his daughter doesn't make me his victim."

"Wow, okay. Is that how you see me? As a victim?"

Frannie shook her head, defeated by the conversation. "Let's go home, Mae. Let's just get you home and safe and we'll figure out what to do next." She put her hand out and Mae leaned away from her.

"I'm sorry I'm a burden to you, Frannie." Mae sat folded on the stool, her eyes red, her pale skin papery and translucent.

"Oh, God, Mae. I didn't say that."

Frannie stepped through the curtains to find the cops

talking to Wyatt, looking skeptically at his long hair and boots. They turned to her and she nodded. "He's with me." Mae came out and Frannie looked from Wyatt to Mae, not sure what to say next. Wyatt looked at her and smiled, shaking his head. He put his hand out to Mae, who took it, looking back and forth between her sister and Wyatt. Frannie tried to control her expression, tried not to look like she wanted to run from the explanations of who was who.

"I'm Wyatt."

"I've seen you on TV."

"Was it *America's Most Wanted*? 'Cause you're supposed to keep in mind that we're all presumed innocent on there."

"I'm Mae." And then, realizing that didn't mean anything to Wyatt, "Frannie's sister."

"Oh, sure. Frannie's told me all about you."

While they talked, Frannie noticed the slight blond woman she'd seen before, sitting in a wheelchair. She had a clipboard in her hands, but she looked out of place and her gaze was fixed down at her lap, as if she knew she was being watched. Frannie could see now that she was pregnant, and she wondered again how she knew her. It was not unusual for her to see the families of fugitives she'd chased before, and put it down to the woman being somebody's girlfriend or sister, embarrassed to be seen by a Marshal. It would come to her.

———

She drove Mae home as the lights along the parkway came on and the city faded to black and white. Behind them was Wyatt on a bike she'd seen before, a restored Triumph with blacked-out chrome, and behind him were two police cars and Sleeper in a black Suburban. Frannie said, "Look at this. We're a parade."

"I'm sorry, Frannie."

"Don't be sorry. There's nothing to be sorry for. I just want you to be safe. That's what these people do for a living, they keep people safe." They drove west through the city and along the bluffs on the eastern shore of the Schuylkill, night collecting in the hollows like black water.

"Jesus, though, it's humiliating, isn't it?" The sisters looked at each other. Mae said, "The fact that he's our father. That all of this comes from our being his . . ." She shook her head. "His *family*. Don't tell me you don't feel it. It's not just me being oversensitive. I can see in your face it's making you crazy that we're being singled out."

Frannie watched the road. They veered away from the river into Manayunk, turned east up into the tangle of narrow streets and houses clustered on leaning cliffs the color of blood and ash. After a minute she shook her head. "Yeah, maybe."

Mae shook her head. "Maybe?"

"Yeah, you're right." She took her hands off the wheel and made a hopeless gesture, looking over at her sister. "What? I said you're right."

"Jesus, Frannie. What does it cost you to admit you're just like everybody else?"

"Here we go. Tell me, Mae, what's everybody else like?"

"I don't know, Frannie. They get scared, or mad or whatever. They're human."

"So now, what? You don't think I'm human?"

"No, of course you are. I just mean it's okay to *act* human. To cry, or break down."

Frannie shifted in her seat, feeling the tortured muscles in her arms and legs. "I don't know, Mae. I just never saw the point in falling apart, I guess."

"Like I do?"

"Ah, no. I don't know, Mae, Jesus. Look, I'm sorry, I don't mean you always fall apart. I'm no good at this kind of conversation."

They drove in silence for a few minutes. Mae tilted her head to get the view through the mirror. "He seems nice."

"Who, Wyatt? He's a good guy."

"Pretty cool to be dating a guy with a TV show."

"Well, I don't know that we're dating, exactly. Officially."

"Officially? He came to the emergency room, Frannie. You know how many guys I've *officially* dated who wouldn't come see me in a hospital room?"

"Yeah, he's . . ." She shrugged.

"A good guy?"

Frannie screwed up her face in pain. "Can we not do this?"

"What? Talk to each other like we're sisters?"

"Ah, Mae. Am I not there for you? Whatever you need?"

Mae sighed. "You've always been there for me, Frannie. And I know you'd do anything for me, protect me if you could, if that was possible. Even take a bullet for me. I just think it's funny you'd rather take a bullet than talk about whether you're dating the guy you're dating. Officially." They reached the sloping driveway, Mae's small house that seemed carved from the gray schist of the hill. Her sister put her hand on Frannie's cheek and she flinched.

Mae said, "Poor Frannie."

"Poor Frannie? What's that mean?" Her sister just shrugged and got out of the car to wave at Wyatt as he pulled in. Frannie called, "What's that mean?" But Mae was gone up the driveway talking to Wyatt, and Frannie stood at the curb and watched them go into the house.

# 11

Frannie didn't go in right away but watched one of the police cars back into a spot on the narrow street and nodded to the guy behind the wheel. It was full dark now, fog rising from the Schuylkill so that while she watched the ends of the street disappeared into haze lit yellow by the streetlights and drops of water rose on the stones of the house as if it had rained. She felt she should go inside and apologize to her sister for rearing at her touch, but how was she supposed to explain that she was out of the habit of being touched? Telling her that would mean explaining everything that had happened with Wyatt and start a general review of Frannie's emotional life, with Mae weighing in, and there would be tears and hurt feelings.

And now Wyatt was inside talking to Mae. Though she could admit to herself that she was glad he was there, and there was something exciting in all of it, the crisis atmosphere, the sense of something dangerous out beyond the porch lights, something that woke her up, made her senses keen and her pulse run faster.

When Sleeper made his way up the walk she was sitting under a neighbor's spindly sourwood tree and watching the streets that tilted away toward the river. He said, "Scanlon is pushing the DA to indict you." She'd been away from Sleeper long enough to have forgotten his conversational style, the way he launched into dialogue like someone ripping off a Band-Aid. It was as if he thought all information was bad news and there was nothing to do but get it over with.

"Does he have a working theory? Or is he just being an asshole?"

"Well, my working theory is that he's an asshole."

"He's got a problem with women."

"He's got a problem with competence." Sleeper stepped off the walk and sat on a low stone wall. "He thinks you're in cahoots with Patrick."

"Of course he does. Did he use the word 'cahoots'?" A porch light snapped on next door, a weak glow that left Sleeper's face in blue shadow. She said, "Do we know who those guys were? The guys on Clearfield?"

"Camacho's coming by to fill us in." She tilted her head and he said, "I don't know everything. I'm not getting the briefings."

"What's that about?"

"He doesn't trust me."

She looked at him and pursed her lips, thinking.

"Because you trust me." There was a moment, silent but for water dripping. She said, "You can ask me. Anything you need to."

"I know that."

Headlights appeared out of the fog at the crest of the hill and they both stopped and watched the car pass. When it was quiet again Sleeper said, "What can I do?"

"Get my sister out of town, Eric."

He nodded. "What else?"

"I need my guns." She went into her coat pocket and gave him her keys. She thought about asking him to bring clothes but couldn't picture him picking through her closets trying to match pants and tops. She'd get something clean from Mae for tonight, then worry about next steps tomorrow when her sister was safely out of town.

Sleeper left and Frannie went inside, through the narrow rooms filled with pictures of Mae's daughter Tansy and the simple, tasteful furniture her sister had bought when she'd been making good money in real estate. She went to the back door and checked the police locks she'd given Mae as a housewarming gift and about which she'd received endless shit ever since. The backyard was a narrow strip running steeply uphill that ended in bare black rock. She flipped on the light and a startled gray cat vaulted the fence and disappeared. A plastic playhouse with matching table and chairs stood untouched in a carpet of red, wet leaves, as sad as anything Frannie had ever seen. She called to Mae that she needed a shower and Mae dropped a clean towel on the sink and said she'd scare up something for her sister to wear. Frannie let the water run until it was hot and the room filled with steam.

This was Frannie Mullen out of her clothes: pale rose skin, freckles across her cheeks and the tops of her breasts and the bridge of her nose that was parted by the faint silver line where it had been broken. She'd trained to box and that was how she kept in shape, though she hadn't been in a ring in years. So, hard muscle in her arms from dumbbell punches and the overhead press. Fading scars and lines: the pale runnel on her right arm where the woman in Hunting Park had hit her with the knife, a faint oval of raised flesh like a kiss on her left shoulder from a bit of white-hot ash the night the house burned and her mother died. A thin band across one knuckle from tearing a tendon in a fight, a red line bordered by dots running below her knee from surgery on a torn ACL. The new marks from the fight in the street; blue and lavender and waxy yellow on her forearms and back and at her hairline. A small tattoo in script on her bruise-darkened bicep. Muhammad Ali, *"Can't nobody stop me."*

She got out into the steam-whitened bathroom and moved her arms, cautiously flexed her neck. The pain in her head had receded to a dull ache. She'd need to keep moving so she wouldn't tighten up under the bruises. She should be exhausted but was strangely alert and awake. Was that a sign of head injury, brain trauma? What would bleeding in the brain feel like? She found a pair of Mae's old jeans and a sweater where her sister had left them on the top of the toilet and put them on. Mae was taller, a little wider in the hips than Frannie, but she rolled the cuffs on the jeans once and they were fine.

She used a corner of the towel to wipe the mirror and looked at herself. There was the red hair that the boys liked so much, that her mother used to say was like rope when she worked at the tangles with a stiff brush and a bottle of cider vinegar, a cigarette in the corner of her mouth, and her face balled as she set to the task. She could hear her mother's voice in her head, telling stories of Limerick, where she'd grown up, and meeting their father. Mae had asked if he was from the same place and she'd laughed and said, no, he was a *bog trotter*, a person from the country, but the girls should never say that to him because he might not like it.

She lifted her hair where it lay long across her forehead to see the dark bruise at her temple. Had she killed the men on Clearfield Street? She went over it in her mind as she had a hundred times since coming to in the ambulance. No, she remembered them moving, at least the gray-haired one, and making noises. She had violence in her, she knew, the will to fight that was always there coiled in the tight muscles of her arms, and when she was younger she would lose herself to a kind of red mist that came down over her eyes when she felt wronged and afraid, but on the street today she thought she'd been in control, fighting hard but not carried away by rage or fear.

Now she needed to get out and do something. She'd make sure Mae was safe, get Sleeper to stash her somewhere out of town and then get to work finding out what was going on. She'd never been an investigator, not officially, but she knew how to find people who didn't want to be found. If she got her hands on Patrick, or the third man in the van, she'd get answers, or at least put a stop to whatever was going on. Inaction was something she felt not as the absence of motion but as a physical sensation, like a hand pushing on her chest to keep her in place. She couldn't wait. It wasn't in her to wait.

Mae made dinner, a pasta dish everybody picked at without enthusiasm, though Wyatt told Mae it was the first home-cooked meal he'd had in a long while. He told them stories about growing up in Okemah, Oklahoma, where Woody Guthrie was from. When Detective Camacho knocked on the door Frannie looked at Wyatt, so he took Mae into the kitchen and helped wash the dishes. Sleeper followed Camacho into the house, carrying a black duffel bag that he held high for Frannie to see and then stashed behind the couch in the living room.

Wyatt asked Mae if there was a radio, and she put some CDs into a player and Wyatt closed the door to the kitchen, winking at Frannie. When they were alone,

Camacho got out his notebook and Frannie walked him through what happened on Clearfield while he listened and took notes. She kept her voice low, told them everything she could remember: The walk into Port Richmond. Meeting Bertie, the van coming up the street. The two men she saw clearly and the one she couldn't bring into focus. When she was done Lino Camacho went into a briefcase and brought out photographs. He pointed at each in turn.

"This is Tommy Fitzgerald, DOA number one. Twenty-seven years old, four arrests, one conviction for assault. Grew up in Frankford, definitely was on a crew run by Rudy Wurtz. He came out of one of the gyms they recruit out of, on Duncannon Street." She recognized him immediately as the one with the hatchet. Camacho tapped the other photo. "This one is more interesting. DOA number two. John Testa." Broken Nose. The picture was a few years old, his hair less gray and fewer broken capillaries in his face. "They called him Lead Pipe John, which the name isn't too tough to figure."

"Why is he more interesting?"

"He's not a union guy, and I wouldn't have put him with Adolph or Rudy Wurtz. He's with Tony Buck. You know Tony Buck?"

Frannie nodded. "The Catrambones." The Philly mob had imploded twenty years before, there had been a series of successions and low-grade turf wars and Anthony "Tony Buck" Catrambone had come out on top. She remembered how frightened Otto Berman had been of them, so frightened he'd reneged on the deal to testify against them, and how they'd gotten him anyway. She remembered the crime scene photos, the dead accountant on his back at the base of a concrete pylon painted with a sacred heart ringed in flame.

"So," she said, "you've got a Wurtz guy and one of the old Passyunk Avenue crew. What's it mean? What's it got to do with me?"

Camacho shrugged. "I don't know. I do know that when Adolph Wurtz ran the show, he did it with help from the mob."

"But he doesn't run the show anymore."

"Yeah, maybe."

"Maybe? Ahearn said the union was run by a federal trustee and the Wurtz family was all through."

"Yeah, that's what he said."

"But?"

Lino said, "I hope it's true. But I don't know."

Camacho told her there would be an investigation and that she'd have to answer more questions, but it didn't sound to him like there would be charges filed against her unless there was more to the case than he could see. Civil suits by the families of the dead men? He couldn't say about that. She and Sleeper looked at each other. Scanlon would do his best to see the DA's office make her life miserable.

She shook her head, frustrated. "I know I was knocked out and I don't remember everything, but I just don't think I hurt them that bad."

"We'll keep looking for the girl."

Frannie had told them about Bertie, that she had seen the start of the fight and maybe the whole thing, though she remembered her tattoos (*"Snitches get stitches"*) and didn't know that even if they could find her again she'd say anything to help Frannie. And she knew that keeping your mouth shut about what you saw on the street in Philly wasn't just tough-girl posing. The cops she knew complained constantly about not being able to make cases because witnesses had to put up with threats on the street and on the phone and online. A witness to a drug killing in Fairhill had been shot six times because she'd been seen getting out of an unmarked police car. Judges had started having people arrested in their courtrooms for pantomiming cocked guns and slit throats when witnesses were giving testimony. Kids learned it early, wore STOP SNITCHING T-shirts and tagged it on walls.

Lino said, "I know Bertie. I locked up her husband. Donald for a robbery he did with her cousin Danny."

"She told me about that."

"She tell you Donald used a BB gun? And his idiot cousin used a bug spray flamethrower."

"What, now?"

"Yeah, like pyromaniac kids use. A can of Raid and a Zippo. They went into Sheldon's, up on Frankford. Mrs. Sheldon threw a chair at Danny and knocked him down. Mr. Sheldon came out of the back with a .380 and chased the two of them out onto the street where Donald got himself hit by the Sixty-six bus. I think the video made it onto *World's Dumbest*."

"Do you think you can get her to talk to you? Tell you what she saw?"

"I can try. She did say that me arresting Donald was the best thing a man ever did for her."

After they left, Frannie sat with Mae while she lay in bed. There was a picture of Mae's daughter, Tansy, on the nightstand and another cluster of pictures on the dresser. Tansy was achingly beautiful, with her mother's high cheekbones and wide-set blue eyes and her father's flyaway African hair and toffee skin. Mae's ex-husband, Tobi, was a sculptor, a Nigerian who lived in Mount Airy and created unsettling figures in bright costumes with the heads of foxes and cattle. He loved Mae but since the divorce had kept his distance from her life, feared for what she would pass to their daughter by blood or bad example.

Mae lit a candle by the picture and touched it with the tips of her fingers and Frannie turned off the light. Mae said, "Twenty-nine days."

"That's something."

"Yeah." They could hear the faraway murmur of a radio in the police car at the curb. "Do you think he loved us? Patrick?"

"God, Mae. I don't know. I don't know if somebody like that is capable of love."

"I try to remember what he was like when he wasn't drunk, when he wasn't beating on Mom."

"I can't."

"You can't, or you don't want to?"

"I can't," she said, her voice too hard, maybe. "And I wouldn't want to if I could."

"I wish I could forget."

"You can. You just . . ." Frannie made a gesture, a hand sliding in front of her face. "You just push it all away."

"You mean you don't remember any of it? Mom, too?"

Frannie looked away into a corner of the room. "Bits and pieces."

"I wish I could do that. I wish I was like you."

"No, you don't."

"Maybe not. But maybe tougher, like you. I could use the strength."

Frannie smiled, and Mae lifted her eyebrows. "Well, there you go, something I do remember."

"What?"

"I remember her saying that. Mom. Whenever he came through the door. That slam, he'd always slammed the door and you knew it was him."

"I remember."

"I just remember her, when we'd hear that slam, she'd close her eyes and say, you know, like a prayer: *Give me strength.*"

Mae laughed, and they sat in the near black. "I do remember him bringing her flowers, or CDs. She had that vase, do you remember that? This little white thing, a horn. A cornucopia, you know, just balanced on a rock. I kept one of his cards to her, I had it for the longest time. His handwriting, that slanted scrawl, just about impossible to read. But she read it to me. It said, 'To chase away the blue clouds.' "

"So he brought her flowers."

"Don't get angry."

"I'm not angry." But she was, felt it like heat in her blood, and she had to clench her teeth. "I just don't know why you do this to yourself, Mae. Yeah, I'm sure he was good to her sometimes. I'm sure there were good days. Everybody I ever arrested, I'm sure they brought somebody flowers. They still hurt people."

Mae turned away from her. The turn changed the sound of her voice, coming now from the corner of the room. "I guess, to arrest people, that's all you have to know."

Frannie and Wyatt alone in the front room, on the narrow couch. They sat next to each other stiffly, a little shyly. There was a history of drunken coupling, late-night calls from Frannie and awkward mornings. Maybe they'd be different with each other now, Frannie thought, but what would that look like? She had a feeling of being on a first date and things going too far, of wanting and not wanting.

He took her hands in his and she let him. He said, "You heard me talking about Pell Carver, my father. Locked up at McAlester, back in Oklahoma. He was a hardcore biker, from back when they just called them riders. He used to beat on us, all of us, but my brother Dalton got it worst because he stood up for me and my sister when he came after us. Pell got locked up when I was fifteen. Best thing that could happen for us. He was running a meth lab in his Camaro, in that big trunk they have. That's what those boys do, make Nazi dope, or 'Nazi cold,' they call it, that you don't need a kitchen or anything. Anyway, Pell. My father. He shot a state trooper up in Comanche County. The state trooper pulled him over and Pell went for his gun. Shot the man in the back when he walked away from the car, then again while he was asking my father not to kill him, praying for Jesus to stay his hand."

Frannie watched his eyes and waited for him to tell the story. "My brother Dalton went to the trial every day, carrying a pistol. Drove all the way up to Perry, in Noble County. So one day the mother of this poor dead cop sees Dalton's carrying a gun and tells the bailiff, and they grab my brother and cuff him and haul him out. They ask him, *Son, you going to break out your old man? What were you thinking?* And Dalton says, *Break him out? No, sir. I was thinking that if you all turned him loose I was going to kill him.*"

Frannie said, "Know what I think of first, when I think of my father? He used to make us fight. Me and Mae. We were just little." She held her hand out, showing him how small they were, the gesture of patting a child on the head. "Three? Four? I don't even know. Patrick would lift us up on the dining room table, make us put up our fists. Try to get us to really connect. Mae would cry and ask to get down, but that just made him worse. I'd think, *Just do it. Just come on and hit me. Then he'll leave us alone.* I used to get so mad at her. You know, why couldn't she learn?"

Wyatt said, "All that stuff in your apartment, all those pictures of boxers. The heavy bag you train on."

"Yeah, I can't explain it."

"You became what he wanted, even still. You hate him, you never speak his name, but . . ."

"I don't know how else to be."

"I think maybe it's the same for everybody. Me and Dalton both took up with motorcycles, just like Pell. And Dalton went with the Bandidos. Riding with the same bunch, living the same life." Something to wonder at, and they sat in silence, their shoulders touching.

Frannie said, "My mother was an artist. Wanted to be. I used to think, why didn't I turn out like her?"

Wyatt said, "The paintings, I've seen them in your office."

"I have two. The rest burned up."

"A fire, you said."

"She tried to run, take us and run. We stayed away at a motel out in Jersey, in the Pine Barrens. She ran out of money, I guess, and we went back to get some things from the house. He found us there. I don't know it all. Mae and I fell asleep and when I woke up my mother was dead and the house was on fire. He was standing over her and there was blood on her hands and face. I guess she'd tried to fight him off. He looked at us, I think for a minute he didn't know who we were. I guess he thought he'd burn down the house, we'd all be dead and no one left to tell it."

Wyatt was silent but put his dark hand over her pale one. He had a Band-Aid on his ring finger and she touched it lightly, smoothing it where it had puckered. She said, "I'll always think he hoped we would just sleep through it, the smoke and fire would take us and leave no trace."

"But you got out."

"He picked us up and carried us out. It was one thing to leave and not see us again, I guess, but when we woke up and saw him he couldn't go through with it. He took us out to the street and handed us to a neighbor, a Polish lady who lived a few doors away, Mrs. Kosmati. Then he disappeared."

"The police, what did they say?"

"When they found her they couldn't tell what happened. How she died. He went to jail for ten years, but not for killing my mother. For the things he did for the union. Beating people, burning trucks. Time went by, everybody forgot about it but me and Mae. By the time he got out again the Feds were building RICO cases against the local and they eventually indicted my father. He ran away, but they caught him in Ireland and put him in federal prison. That was the last I knew of him.

Mae used to follow it all, used to try to read me the articles every time he got arrested, but I couldn't hear about it. I know everything I want to know about Patrick Mullen."

He kept his voice low. "Poor Mae."

"She got the worst of it, somehow. In and out of therapy, in and out of rehab. Always trying to process it, I guess, or make it come out different, but I think there's things you can't process. There's things you just have to leave behind."

"I guess. We sure keep moving, anyway."

"But?"

"But what did we ever leave behind?"


They fell asleep on the couch, Frannie's sleep disturbed by vivid dreams of chasing someone through narrow streets, climbing walls and squeezing through impossibly tight passages and she heard a voice say, "She's not dead."

She came awake fast and her movement woke Wyatt. She said, "Who called you?"

"What?" He pulled at his sleep-rucked hair and forced his eyes wide.

"You said somebody called you. When you came to the hospital."

"Oh. Oh." He nodded, blinked, tried to focus. "The police. A woman who said she was with the police. She had your phone."

"What?"

"It was your number. I knew it when it rang."

"Get your phone." She went into the kitchen and found Camacho's card and sat back down with Wyatt. He showed her the call, the number he'd stored in her name. She sat thinking for minute, then called Camacho and he answered on the first ring.

"Lino, it's Frannie Mullen."

"Everything okay?"

"Yes, but, tell me, do you have my phone?"

"No. I can check with the techs who worked the scene, but nobody mentioned it and I didn't see it on the list of things they collected."

"Somebody used it. They called Wyatt at a little after noon."

"Who called? Did he get a name?"

Wyatt shook his head at her. "It was a woman. Young, I think. I don't remember her giving a name but she said she was with the Philadelphia police and that you were at Temple Hospital."

Frannie asked Camacho if he'd heard. He said, "Let me make sure it wasn't anyone on my end, but I have to ask why anybody from the cops would call anyone listed on your phone. Did they call anyone else?"

"I'll ask my sister."

Next to her Wyatt closed his eyes, then opened them again. "She had an accent."

"Tell me."

"I don't know, something." He closed his eyes again as if listening. "There was a girl come to the shop for the show one time. She was an actress, wanted a bike done like the girl had in the *Dragon Tattoo* movie. An old Honda with blacked-out wheels. A friend of mine did all that work so I called him. She had the same accent, that girl. I told her I was just a hick and she said that where she came from they said *bogger*. For a hick or a hillbilly. A bogger."

Frannie stared hard at him for minute. "Oh, Jesus Christ." She told Camacho she'd call him and hung up. She got up and started rifling through Mae's purse and came out with her keys. "I know who it was."

"Where you going?"

"Back to the hospital." She reached behind the couch and grabbed the duffel. "Stay here, with Mae?"

"Why the hospital?"

"She was there. I saw her."

"Who? Who did you see?"

But she was gone.

# 12

Her mind was racing, and she got turned around somehow at Roosevelt Boulevard, so she pulled into an empty lot in Nicetown and sat for a minute, trying to slow her racing mind. She heaved the duffel bag that Sleeper had brought to Mae's onto the seat and opened it to find the small Glock she wore in the ankle rig and the big Glock 22 that had been her service pistol. She also found boxes of .40 caliber shells and beneath the handguns a Winchester pump shotgun broken down to two pieces that must have come from Sleeper's gun safe. She sat in the dark, the lights from passing cars touching each of the brass shells with gold as she loaded the pistol. She could see a billboard in the distance, a black oblong against a sky full of yellow mist and after a minute of staring she knew it was another of the art installations or whatever they were, another visual trick to pry at the edges of her brain. The sign was a picture of some kind of red-lit digital marquee with the words EXPECT EVERYTHING, and she looked from the sign to the bag full of guns and the heavy brass slugs and she had to smile. She would, she thought. *Expect everything.* There was nothing else to do.

It was after midnight and the emergency room was crowded with people from all over Philly and ambulances kept bringing more. Frannie moved slowly through the crowd, looking carefully at faces and keeping close to the wall, trying to stay aware of who was close enough to be a danger. She thought of that movie where Arnold Schwarzenegger is a robot and when the camera shows you what the robot sees all the threats are tagged and there are alarms and crosshairs. She wanted that now.

But the people she saw were all distracted or tired or in pain, and all of them looked back at her with a resigned misery in their eyes. A huge man had a T-shirt wrapped around his jaw like a cartoon of a man with a toothache. A woman was crying and telling someone on a cell phone, *He has to lie very still. Just very still,* and she heard a nurse ask *Is it like a squeezing or a pinching? Like a tearing or a stabbing?*

She walked through the rooms and hallways looking at each face, alert, searching and occasionally touching the wall nearest her as if she were orienting herself, as if she were navigating by feel. When she had come through the long room of cubicles and the waiting area she came to deserted hallways and she turned around and did it again, seeing the same anxious or broken or grieving faces and no one she recognized. When she came back out to the parking lot she kept going, walked out to Ontario and stood looking back at the hospital and out at North Broad Street. Mae's phone buzzed in her pocket and she answered it.

A voice said, "Mullen?"

"Sleeper. I'm back at the hospital."

"Are you staying in the building? Near people?"

"Yeah, I'm okay."

"I'm going to come down there. Your sister is unhappy."

"She's always unhappy." She stood looking into the little square between the entrance to the ER and the street. There were a few parking spaces, a line of trees. A few homeless people bundled in layers of jackets and coats.

"Tell me what's going on."

"I thought I saw . . ." There she was, a small figure sitting on the steps. A man in uniform, a Temple University cop in a yellow jacket bent over her, talking. "I'm going to call you back in two minutes," she said, and hung up. She jogged across the square, reaching the pair just as the cop stepped back and unclipped a radio from his belt.

"Tina," she said, smiling. The young woman turned, got clumsily to her feet. "I thought that was you."

The cop stopped, raised his eyebrows. "You know this young lady?"

"Sure, she's with me." The cop raised a hand, satisfied and started walking back toward the hospital, more for him to do than check on every midnight wanderer in the park.

When they were alone the girl said, "How'd you know it was me?"

"I saw your picture."

"Right, so," she said, "lucky you came back. I thought your man was going to take me off to jail," and Frannie heard in the girl's voice her mother talking, and her father, the brogue she'd grown up hearing in the house and that she sometimes came upon in her own speech, long vowels stretched into a kind of singing. She turned into the light and Frannie saw she was exhausted, her eyes red and her black eye makeup pressed into rings. She'd been crying, and she swayed a little as she stood. "Jesus, I'm that tired," and she sat back down again, losing her feet so that Frannie had to grab her arms as she fell to keep her from going over.

"We need to get you out of here."

"It doesn't matter. Is he really your dad?"

"Why doesn't it matter?"

"Sure he'll kill me. Just the same he'll find me and he'll kill me."

"Why, Tina? Didn't you help him?"

"I did, I did help him. I helped get him out of the jail down there in Louisiana. But I know all the rest," she said, and then she turned her head and was sick. Frannie went through her pockets and came up with a napkin from Dunkin' Donuts and did her best to clean the girl's face, so that she seemed even more a child, though her swollen belly pressed against her thin pink coat.

"What do you know? Do you know where he is?"

"I know he killed that man." She sobbed, holding the sleeve of Frannie's jacket. "The blood on his hands. He'll kill us all." Frannie cradled her head, watching the park around them, thinking what to do next, who to call. "Oh Christ Jesus, what did I do?"

Frannie walked Tina back toward the hospital just as a figure came out of the door, Khandi, with her bright scrubs and the Purple Heart pin. She looked from one to the other. Frannie's face red in the cold, and the girl with her smeared black eyes and her skin green and bloodless.

"Will you help us?"

The woman shook her head no, but said, "Come on, we'll get you seen."

As they put Tina into a wheelchair Frannie bent to Khandi and talked to her quietly. "She's a witness to a homicide."

"Oh, of course she is. And?"

"And she's illegal. No insurance, no ID."

"You know, I thought you were going to be trouble. I could see it in your face when I pulled back that curtain this afternoon."

"I never like to disappoint."

They wheeled her down a corridor to a room with a closed door. Khandi asked, "Is she hurt?"

"I don't think so. But she's sick."

"Look, I'll take a quick look, but if there's anything going on with her I'll have to admit her."

"I get it. We'll do what we have to do. I'm just trying to keep her out of the system if I can."

Khandi turned on the light and they helped Tina up onto an examining table. The girl's skin was white and slick as if she'd been pulled from boiling water. Frannie looked at Khandi and the woman said, "Give us a minute," so Frannie went back outside and stood by the closed door, her hand under her jacket. She walked back out the narrow corridor and watched the crowd, looking for Sleeper. A man about her father's age stood by the nurses' station looking out at the room, gray hair and a trim beard flecked with gray. He caught her eye and smiled, commiserating that here they were stuck in this place at midnight. Somebody was sick, somebody was hurt, but what could you do?

Sleeper came through a few minutes later and she inclined her head and stepped back down the corridor by the door. When he got close she leaned in and pointed. "I've got Tina O'Bannon."

"She cooperating?"

Frannie shrugged. "She's scared and pregnant and illegal."

"What do you want to do?"

"Do you trust this FBI guy? Ahearn?"

"I don't know him."

The door opened and Khandi stepped out. She looked from Frannie to Sleeper and Frannie said, "Khandi, this is Eric Hansen. He's with the Marshals. How's she?"

"I'm not a doctor, you know? She needs blood tests and a workup."

"I trust your judgment."

"She seems okay. She's dehydrated, she's exhausted, and I think she's scared shitless."

"What can we do for her?"

"She needs IV fluids and to be off her feet for a couple days." She looked back and forth between Frannie and Sleeper. "Not possible? Okay, if that's off the table, keep her drinking. Get her clean water and something to replace her electrolytes."

"Okay."

"Listen to me. If she throws up again, if her urine is dark, if she spikes a fever, you need to get her to an ER. No bullshit. She gets a urinary tract infection she could go into labor."


Sleeper took Tina out through a deserted part of the hospital, Frannie watching them disappear down a darkened corridor and then walking back out through the ER toward where her sister's Mazda was parked. As she came past the nurses' station the man she'd seen smiling was still there and he fell in behind her as if they had agreed to walk out together.

She stopped and turned to him, "Can I help you?"

"Maybe." He pointed at her, a comical, artificial little gesture that someone playing a salesman on a TV show might make. "Could we step outside and talk? Maybe we can help each other." He was still smiling.

"What's that mean?" She let her hand go under her jacket and he held up his hands.

"Let's not get excited, Frannie," he said, "I think we might both want the same thing."

"And what would that be?" He had working hands, rough and yellow palms, one finger that bent inward where it had probably been broken. He sounded like the city. *Egg-cide-it*, for "excited," he said, and *ou'side*, the words caught in his teeth.

He looked around them and lowered his voice, never losing the smile or the reasonable tone. "You know, I met you, and your sister when you were small. And your poor mother."

She put her hand on her gun now, her fingers curled around the grip and her body canted toward him. She felt a line of sweat materializing at her hairline, the salt stinging her battered skin.

"I was an associate of your father. We used to work together."

"Yeah? Making license plates at Pollock?"

"Before that. I've known him a long time."

"If you know my father, you need to tell him to turn himself in. He keeps out on the street he's going to end up shot."

"It's not his welfare I'm concerned with. It's you, and your sister. Struggling, isn't she?"

Frannie pulled the gun. She did it quickly, quietly, and held the Glock flat against the back of her thigh. She thought the man couldn't be here alone. There had to be more men with him, and she looked beyond him into the crowd and wondered if one of the men who attacked her was in the room. She wanted to point it at the man, make demands, but knew there would be a panic and the security guards would pull their guns and it would get bad.

He said, "I'm not threatening you. I'm trying to clear up a difficult situation so everybody gets what they want."

She heard the door open behind her and stepped to the side. She glanced out through the glass and could see Sleeper in his car parked by an ambulance from Children's Hospital. When she looked back the man had taken a step back. He was holding out a card, and he slowly laid it on the counter by the triage desk.

He said, "I know what he did to your family. I can guarantee nobody else gets hurt." He winked and pointed to the card, then walked back into the waiting room and disappeared around a corner. Frannie backed up slowly until her hip connected with the wall and stood that way for a long moment before she holstered the gun. She walked to the counter and picked up the card. A nurse turned to her and asked what brought her to the emergency room.

Frannie walked outside and stood for a minute in the cold air, her heart banging so that she could feel the blood pulsing in her neck, her eyes going to the shadows. An ambulance stood open, a woman with a ponytail dumping sterile water from a plastic bottle onto the floor. She was talking over her shoulder to another woman who worked with a spray bottle and a rag, saying "You got to keep them people from bleeding in my ambulance, you hear?" They were laughing, and one of them waved at Frannie and said, "People need to do their bleeding at home."

Frannie looked at the card, the cell number printed in block letters and the name JIMMY, and then put it away. She flexed her hands and then shook them, trying to stop the tremors. It wasn't fear, not exactly, but a feeling of physical frustration, like having her head held underwater. She walked to her car and waved to Sleeper and they pulled out. Frannie didn't know where they were headed and was happy to let someone else make the decision. Sleeper would take Tina someplace safe, and she'd follow. They stopped at the light at the corner of Broad and she went into her holster and pulled the gun and held it in her lap as she drove. The streets were empty, the city black and drowned as if at the bottom of the river. She wondered if she had seen the man before and forced herself to think of her family, of them all at home together. Patrick and Nora, Frances and Mae. Letting the doors open on all that memory. All she got was her father, his wild moods, his stare that was something she experienced physically, something that had weight and substance like a cold iron bar laid across her cheek.

# 13

Outside the hospital again, Jimmy Coonan shooed his nephew Cam out of the driver's seat and drove east and then north out of the city along Kensington Avenue. He was thoughtful, remembering his last days in the minimum-security camp at Canaan, the federal prison near Scranton, waiting for his paperwork to come through.

Cam asked, "He going to be pissed? Mr. Wurtz?"

Jimmy didn't answer, but asked Cam, "Ever see a documentary on sharks? What they look like in the water?"

"What, like Shark Week?"

"Shark Week?"

"A thing on TV, like a week of shows about sharks."

"Shark Week. I have to watch that."

"What about it?"

Jimmy fished in his pockets, looking for cigarettes. "So, they got these fish, the sharks. These little fish that swim alongside, ever see that?" Cam got nervous watching him take his eyes off the road and reached into the back to get his coat and fish out a Marlboro and hand it to his uncle. "I was up at Canaan, not the maximum-security part, the camp. I was waiting on my paperwork and I was so fucking nervous something was going to go wrong, I don't know. The fucking lawyers, they say this, that. You don't fucking know. So I was watching TV the whole time, which I never really done much of, I just didn't know what the hell and thought I'd at least take my mind off waiting." Cam nods, but he's twenty-two and doesn't know much about it. "So I'm watching this show about the ocean, whatever. And these little fish swim right up near the shark's mouth, right? I mean, right on it. And they clean up the shark, I don't know, like eat little parasites or whatever, so the shark gets that deal and the fish, they're called something." Cam leaned over and lit the cigarette and Jimmy felt around the door until he found the button and opened the window. He blew a stream of air out of the side of his mouth into the night. "Pilot fish, they're called." They turned onto Frankford and came out from under the El so that Cam could see the night sky. Clouds pulled close overhead, a sickle-shaped moon sharp and white low over the black skyline. "So the shark gets that, the parasites cleaned out, and the pilot fish, he gets to eat when the shark eats. The shark bites something, all that stuff goes in the water, and the pilot fish gets to eat, too."

He was quiet a minute, Jimmy, then asked Cam, "Where

did he say?" and Cam had to think, his uncle switching gears on him. "Adolph, what did he say about where we meet him?"

"Oh. The Walgreens at Bustleton," he said. Cam waited, but there didn't seem to be any more of the story about the sharks. They pulled into the Walgreens across from the cemetery at Bustleton Avenue. Adolph was standing at the edge of the lot by his car and looking out across Frankford Avenue.

"You got her?" Adolph's voice echoed. Everything was wet and night-slick. Cam got out and hung back, giving them space to talk.

"It was all security guards and cops, Adolph. It was never going to happen there."

"So, no, you mean."

"I'm telling you why."

"I didn't ask why, did I? I ask a yes or no."

"I'm telling you."

"You know what's going on, who's watching, right?"

"I know."

"I got Harry Buono in my office, I'm out here talking to you. I have to go in and put him and Tony off again. About is this situation resolved."

"I understand, Adolph."

"You understand. He killed my son. Do you understand that?"

"Rudy was my friend, Adolph."

"What do I tell his mother?"

"Did Edda say something? Does she know about

Patrick killed Rudy?" Jimmy pictured Edda, Adolph's wife, who stayed home and kept house and, as far as Jimmy knew, had never been anywhere near his business.

"No, she doesn't fucking know anything. Use your fucking head, Jimmy. She knows her son is dead and that's enough." Adolph had been locked up, and then he was keeping things quiet when he was on parole, but now he was back on union business full time and so Jimmy was with him all day every day, and he was seeing Adolph wasn't the man he had been before he'd been sent up. Jimmy thought it was maybe that prison had changed him, sharpened his edges so that he couldn't turn himself off anymore. Maybe he was just running out of time, running out of patience at seventy-three years old.

Now Adolph was saying, "How we going to get our hands on them?"

"She'll surface again."

"Surface? She a submarine?"

"I mean, she's not going home, she's not working a regular job, so we have to wait for her to show herself. And then we go again."

"What about the other one, the other sister? The drunk?"

"We got guys on that, too."

"I can't have this shit go on and on. I need to wrap this up." Jimmy heard Adolph breathing, stiff gasps that came hard through his teeth so that Jimmy thought he's like some animal, something that chuffs and spits and pulls at the chain at its neck. Adolph turned away from Jimmy and walked a few steps up Frankford Avenue and

Jimmy looked at Cam, so the boy followed at a respectful distance when the two men moved onto the street. Adolph pointed across the street into the cemetery.

"Is this where Big John's buried? Down here?"

"Tell the truth, Adolph, I don't remember. I think Holy Cross, out in Yeadon."

"He built this local. Big John. Him and me and . . ." He made a gesture, a wave of the hand, and Jimmy thought, *You were going to say Patrick Mullen*. Adolph shook his head. "There wasn't anything we couldn't do then. You couldn't put a roof up in this town without we got paid. I remember Big John in a roomful of contractors, telling them how it was going to be. The biggest contractors in the city. Locked the doors and looked them in the eye and told them how it was going to work and what was going to happen if it didn't go our way."

"Those were good days."

"Christ, we made money. The K and A gang, Junior and them guys. Everybody paid. You moved drugs, you stole in this town you paid a tax. The envelopes, the bags of money got passed our way."

"I remember the envelopes."

Adolph stepped close and laid a hand on Jimmy's arm. "It's going to be that way again, Jimmy. We get Patrick off the street, we show Tony we can do what needs to get done, we get it all back."

"I'm with you, Adolph."

"I got news, you're with me whether you're with me or not. This goes to shit, we're going in the same hole, you and me." The man getting a hard look in his eyes, leaning in. Changing on a dime, thought, Jimmy, keeping him off-balance. "You get your hands on one of those girls, you use her to get Patrick Mullen. You get Patrick Mullen, we get to sit at the table. That crazy son of a bitch killed my boy. You bring him in to me and he'll pay for what he did to Rudy. Maybe we kill one while he watches. That one with the red hair thinks she's Marshal Dillon. We'll put an end to all this and get back to work. Make some money for a change."

Afterward Jimmy sat in the passenger seat and Cam got behind the wheel. Cam wore a Flyers jersey under his hoodie and had a butterfly bandage at his right brow from a fight outside a strip joint off Delaware Avenue. He watched Jimmy to know how to feel about the conversation he overheard. "He's pissed. Mr. Wurtz."

"Adolph was born pissed."

Cam lifted his hands off the steering wheel. "But his kid got killed by this Mullen guy, right? I mean . . ."

"It's true, it's true. But . . ." He pointed back downtown and Cam started the car and drove back into the city, the road narrowing, the strip shopping centers giving way to dark storefronts and steel shutters. Jimmy found another cigarette and pulled out a slim gold lighter with "225" engraved on the side. He lit the cigarette and pointed at Cam. "But notice what he mentions first. Union business, right?"

Jimmy looked at Cam out of the corner of his eye. Thought to himself, *This is a moment. How sharp is the kid? Will he get this?* He said, "Adolph's been away, he wants to get the local back. He needs to deal with all this, get Patrick Mullen under control or Tony's going to pass on Adolph, which he half wants to, anyway."

Cam nodded, thinking, watching the road go by. "He built the local, right, though? I mean, that part's true. That's what Marty Wurtz says, anyway."

"Well, sure, Marty is Adolph's grandson. And Marty gets what Adolph leaves him. I mean the kid's loyal, he's a good kid, but how else is he going to see it?"

Cam let a little smile tease at the corner of his mouth. "You think something else, though."

"I think if he gets the local back it's good for us, too."

"Like the fish. The pilot fish, you said."

"There you go. You pay attention. Like the pilot fish. Adolph takes a bite and we all eat."

"But."

"I don't know 'but.' I just think Adolph's from a different day. All that stuff about Big John and a lot of guys been dead for thirty years. You heard him say the K and A gang? You know who they were?"

"I hear guys your age talking about it."

"Guys my age? How old you think I am?" He mugged and made to slap the kid's face and they laughed. "No, but that's it. That K and A, that's Kensington and Allegheny. Adolph Wurtz thinks of the neighborhood in them days. Kensington, Frankford, all this down here.

He thinks about when the people living under the El were white and spoke English." He gestured at the street, because that's where they were, moving south along Frankford Avenue under the El.

"I got white friends down here."

"I'm talking about white people aren't addicted to crack." His voice got quiet. "When everybody came down here to shop. Get the winter clothes for the kids, get the school clothes. When there was jewelry stores and not a Church's Chicken on every corner. When you could read the signs in the store window. When there was a shamrock in all the bar windows. You saw people on the street you knew their names." He was talking to himself, or to somebody who wasn't in the car with them. He came out of it, but his mood was sharp. "Nowadays," he said, and Cam knew better than to make fun of him now. "Nowadays to find three white people sitting still in Frankford you got to go up to Cedar Hill." Meaning the cemetery up at Bustleton Avenue. "That's where it all went. But what the hell, right? We got work to do. We're the little fish. We go where the shark goes."

They sat in silence for a minute, Cam working his mouth so Jimmy could tell he was thinking. Finally Cam said, "Yeah, so."

"What?"

"Those fish, the little fish?"

"The pilot fish?"

Cam nodded, turned a little in his seat, looking at his uncle huddled in the dark. "The shark ever eat them, too?"

# 14

Frannie stood watch in the dark, standing in the shadow next to the entry to a Holiday Inn on the river south of the airport while Sleeper walked the perimeter. When he came up the driveway she stepped out of the shadow and he nodded. He looked at her face and curled his lip.

"What?" she said.

"Nothing. You got that look."

"What look?" But she was conscious now of trying to keep her face neutral. "What?"

"It's your WITSEC look."

"My what, now?"

"Every time Scanlon sent you to do WITSEC you either begged off or got that look."

She thought for a minute. "Yeah, I guess it was no secret I hated working security." She shrugged. "I did it a couple times. It's part of the job."

"But," he said. He waited. She looked at him in his neat suit, his bullet-shaped head under the close-cropped blond hair.

"Yeah, I don't know." There was a long note from the river, a ship moving slowly through the channel at night and lowing like a nervous animal in the dark.

"You know."

"Okay. Okay. I'll tell you. They don't want to be protected."

"They don't?"

"No. A lot of them, anyway. All you're thinking about is how to keep them safe, and all they can think about is how to get back to whatever trouble they were in. And that's not counting the ones that are in trouble because they were crooked. They call old friends, they call their mothers. They call people they were in the life with. The people you're fucking . . . *hiding* them from. They don't ever get it's serious. There are consequences, and if they'd just keep their heads down and their mouths shut they'd already be safe."

Sleeper nodded. "That's not all of them. Some people it's just . . ." He shook his head. "Wrong place, wrong time."

"And we're supposed to bet our lives on that." She looked over at him and he was smiling. "What?"

"So you'd rather just lock up the bad guys."

"Definitely. With fugitives it's just, you know. You find them and throw a net over them. I don't have to wonder who's wrong or right or who's got what coming." She watched a family get out of a battered SUV in the dark. A father carried two sleeping children folded to his sloping shoulders. "I don't want to have to rely on somebody's else's will to live. I don't want to have to trust anyone that much."

"You trust me."

"That's different. I know you."

"You know me?" He smiled again.

"I know enough." She raised a shoulder, let it drop, not liking that they were getting personal. "You know what I mean. Don't you?"

He smiled again, but she thought there was something sad in it. He inclined his head toward the road and said, "I'll find a store."

She nodded, grateful that there was an end to the conversation but feeling (as she so often did) that she had gotten something wrong. Some chance to say or do something that was expected and it had gone by her unrecognized. She raised a hand to his back as he went.

She went up to the room and waited for Sleeper to come back with more food, something the girl might eat. Tina sat in the center of the bed surrounded by Burger King bags and discarded Tastykake cartons, her hands on her belly. She'd barely touched the food, taking a few bites of a hamburger and laying it aside. While they waited,

Frannie picked up the TV remote and flipped through the channels, trying to find something to take the girl's mind off her situation.

"What do you watch, at home?"

"Home? What do you mean, in Kerry?" Tina wrestled with the cap of a water bottle. "*Love/Hate*, do you know it? You don't have it here in the States, I don't think. That's when I could get the TV away from my ma. She was always on *Law & Order*. Or *CSI*, that was her favorite. She fancied the old manky one, Gil Grissom. When I moved up to Blanchardstown in Dublin I didn't have a TV. We'd watch at the pub where we worked sometimes."

She was quiet, Frannie thought, distracted. This was how people in protection were, sometimes. Out of it, dreamy, as if what was happening wasn't real. Though some were furious, demanding, unable to accept the change in their situation.

"How did you meet Patrick?"

Tina smiled at that. "At the Oasis, where me and my friends used to go. He knew the serious boys there, but he was never serious, Patrick. Not then, anyway."

"He's quite a bit older than you, Tina."

"Yeah, but you don't think of that when you're with him, do you? He's so handsome, all my girlfriends would tease me about it. I thought he looked like Johnny Boy. From *Love/Hate*. Aiden Gillen is his real name. He's on *The Wire*, too, playing an American, the *gombeen* politician."

*Gombeen?* Frannie thought she was getting about half

of what the girl said. "And you followed him here? Patrick?"

"He arranged it, said I'd never have to work again. I was waiting tables in Blanchardstown, do you know it? No? Well, if you did you wouldn't ask why come to America. It's not all the Southside pubs and the Guinness Storehouse."

"How did he get out of prison?"

She got up then, slowly, her small hands cushioning her stomach as she pulled herself up and went to the window. She cupped her hands around her face and tried to see out the window into the dark, then reached over and shut off the nearest lamp. The street ended at the Delaware and there were boats moving, and Frannie turned to watch the girl watching the black hulks on the river.

Into the glass Tina said, "What was your ma like?"

"My mother?" Frannie lowered herself to the arm of a chair. "I don't know. She was talented, made these beautiful paintings that she never showed to anyone. She was funny. She was sad, I think. Depressed, maybe. She used to tell us funny stories, but she never laughed at them. She wanted to be an artist. Was an artist, I guess. Her paintings were beautiful." But sad, she almost said, wondering why she trusted this girl enough to tell her things about her life.

"He talks about her. Nora, that was her name? I think he wanted me to be her."

"How did he get out of prison?"

"He had a friend from the union. They were going to kill him in there, in the prison, Patrick said, and he had me call a man from the union who gave me some money. I went down and waited where he told me, and he came walking up the road, just bold as you please." She smiled. "Oh, it was good to see him. We went to New Orleans for a day and a night, and it was like when we first met. I was so happy."

"Then you came home."

The glass had misted over with her breath, and Tina bunched up the sleeve of her hoodie and wiped at the glass. "Yeah, we came here to Philadelphia. But being in the prison, it changed him, I don't know. He got . . . harder. Just angry all the time."

Frannie put her hand on Tina's arm and she flinched so she held up her hands in a placating gesture and the girl relaxed, and Frannie pulled the drapes closed. "It's not a good idea, to be standing at the window."

"Oh, right. I wasn't thinking, I'm sorry." She moved back to the bed.

"It's okay." She smiled at Tina and let a moment go by. She was conscious of the effort to keep her voice neutral as she said, "Tell me about the man he killed in the alley."

Tina got up again, moved to stand in the middle of the room and rocking on her legs as if she was preparing to run. "Am I in trouble? I don't want to get sent back."

"I'm not the police, Tina. Not anymore. I can't pretend I know what will happen, but you're safe here. Tell me your story and we'll decide what to do next, okay?"

The girl was looking at her, pursing her lips, when the door opened and Sleeper came in, his eyes set and his jaw working like he was chewing on something bitter.

"Scanlon."

Tina looked from one to the other. "Who?"

Frannie grabbed her bag and slung it over her shoulder. "We have to go." To Sleeper she said, "How did he find out where we are?"

Tina grabbed her purse and stood ready, gathered around her own swollen middle, and seeing the young woman draw herself up to run, Frannie had another moment of dislocation from her past life. She remembered how many times she and the other Marshals had been the ones on the hunt, ready to grab the felon of the day and take them off to court or to jail. Enjoying the game of it, really, feeling part of the relentless and certain machinery. Now it was all different, and she wasn't sure how to think about herself and what she was doing.

"Let's go, then." Frannie opened the curtains as Sleeper shut off the remaining light. Blue lights pulsed on the wet street and in the trees. Sleeper opened the door and they moved into the hall. Sleeper pointed soundlessly to the exit stairs at the end of the hall and walked toward the elevator without looking back.


At the bottom of the stairs the door to the outside had an alarm on it, and Frannie motioned Tina to crouch out of sight under the lowest flight of stairs while she opened the door to the first floor hallway by inches. The view was of the vending machines, and she heard footsteps on the rough carpet and voices, near in the hallway and echoing from the lobby. She let the handle turn back soundlessly and stepped back beneath the stairs to hold a finger across Tina's mouth as the door burst open and two men moved over their heads, taking the stairs two at a time as they ran up toward the upstairs hallways. She could hear the radios going, human voices turned to a rattling buzz as the men banged through the fire doors. She heard Scanlon's voice, in the hall and a beat later through the radios, as if he were everywhere at once, saying *Third floor, by the elevator.*

Tina spoke quietly around her fingers, her eyes resigned. "Will they kill us?"

Frannie got out her phone and started texting Sleeper. To Tina she said, "No, no. Not those men, they're police. But they'd arrest us. They'd make you tell about Patrick and then they'd deport you. And there are men, other men out there who might kill us, if they can."

"Why are you helping me?"

"I want this over, and I can't do anything from a jail cell. You're going to help me find Patrick and end this feud, or whatever it is." She dropped her phone back in her pocket and got off her knees, awkwardly crouching. The alarm began to blare. There was shouting from the hallways and more movement, people running. Frannie helped Tina stand up, moved through the doors and into a hallway crowded with people. She looked left, back through the moving people, a man carrying a baby, a woman in a business suit with high-heeled shoes under her arm. Scanlon was in the lobby, shouting into a radio. Frannie shepherded Tina along, though the crowd, and then they were through the door and out in the cold.

# 15

Ten minutes later Frannie stopped at a Wawa off MacDade Boulevard and nosed the Mazda in next to a Dumpster. She got hot coffee while Tina wandered the place, picking up candy bars and putting them back. Frannie picked up a fruit cup and handed it to her and she made a face.

"You should be eating better."

"You sound like my ma."

"I don't know anything about being pregnant, but I know you shouldn't be eating junk."

"It's not that. I just eat the fruit I'll be up all night with it."

She remembered Mae when she was pregnant, her body sleek and full and mysteriously changed. She had panicked when her skin darkened with melasma, had brushed layers of primer and powder around her eyes and lips and gobbed handfuls of moisturizing creams onto her swollen belly. Frannie had never been pregnant. The closest had been a false alarm after a drunken night in Atlanta with another Marshal, a married guy from Houston she'd never spoken to again. She must have felt something more than just panic when her period was late, but that was all she could remember now.

They went back the car and sat, watching the few cars going by, watching kids and drunks and people getting off night work wandering into the store.

"Did you always want to be in the police?" Tina worked on an ice cream sandwich, slowly and methodically scalloping the edges with small bites.

Frannie closed her eyes and sank back in the driver's seat. "No. I wanted to be a fighter."

"Oh, he'd have loved that, wouldn't he?"

"I don't know what he thought of it. I never talked to him after I left home."

"Why didn't you? Become a fighter, then?"

Frannie pursed her lips. "I wasn't good enough. There weren't a lot of women fighters then. Christy Martin. Laila Ali, you know, Muhammad's daughter. And it wasn't just you had to be good, you had to fight to *get* a fight. Sue people to try to get onto a card somewhere." She smiled, a sly look. "And I think I didn't want to lose my looks." She tapped her nose at the bridge, the slight swell at the old break.

"Somehow it looks good on you, though."

"Character, that's what the boys always said when they were trying too hard. It gives my face character."

"I could never do it. Fight. You know he talks about it all the time. Took me to see the fights once and Deidre Gogarty was there. You know her? She's from Drogheda. I couldn't watch it, the blood and all that. Makes me flinchy just to see it."

"Everyone's afraid at first. You get hit a few times, you lose that."

Now the girl smiled shyly. "And a lot of them, the women who box, they look, you know. Hard. Masculine, you know?"

"Lesbian? Is that what you're going for?"

"Well, you know, it's just they look tough. Not girly. I didn't mean anything."

"Oh, some are, I guess. Christy Martin left her husband for a woman and got shot for her trouble."

"Jesus."

"Yeah, but she came back from it. Tough as nails. Came back and fought again." Now it was Frannie's turn to smile. "I'll tell you something for nothing, the boys who box?"

"Yeah?"

"Tight as drums. Stomachs hard as marble. And all that training for stamina?" Tina covered her mouth, laughed through her fingers. "You spar with a boy, give him a couple of shots, dance away. If he's game he'll go and go, like the energizer bunny."

They laughed out loud at that, Tina shaking her head. Frannie asked about growing up in Ireland.

The girl grew serious, looked out the window. "My

dad moved us from Kenmare to Blanchardstown and my ma died there. I was thirteen? My dad just . . ." She shrugged. "He lost it. Used to beat us stupid. Finally did a runner. Off to London or somewhere. Anyway, gone, and good riddance. I kipped with my friends, waited tables. The boys were all so serious there. Doing their drug deals, talking like gangsters in the films when they weren't trying to get into your pants. Patrick was funny. I mean, he was serious, too, but he could make me laugh. Always singing some daft song."

Frannie said, "Elvis," before she could stop herself; the memory of him, the singing and his jokes, trying to make her mother laugh. All of it strong in her head and every hour bringing it closer.

"Yeah, God! He buys me these CDs. I'm like, Patrick, do you not like music by anyone under a hundred?"

There was a moment's silence, each thinking their thoughts. Frannie reached behind her into the darkness of the car and touched the bag with the guns. She'd have to make a decision soon about where to go. She needed to sleep, and Tina was running on junk food and fear. A police car pulled into the parking lot and they both stopped to watch. It pulled in slowly, and Frannie started the car and waited until the patrolman got out and wandered into the Wawa before she put the car in gear and headed back out to MacDade Boulevard.

"Where are we going?"

"We'll work something out." Frannie went awkwardly into her pocket and brought out Mae's phone. She'd had it silenced and there were what looked like dozens of calls from Mae's house and Sleeper and Wyatt and numbers she didn't know. She hit callback on Sleeper's number. It answered and there was a pause, and then a voice she didn't know said, "Yes?" and she hung up. She cursed.

"Is something wrong?"

"They're holding my friend, Eric Hansen. Answering his phone and trying to be clever."

"You know their tricks, then?"

"I know them."

"So what do we do?"

It was a good question. She wanted to get Tina safe somewhere, and she wanted to make sure Mae was out of town, but now with Sleeper maybe in custody she wasn't sure how to do that. She needed sleep and a chance to plan and think. She hated being hunted, feeling powerless. She had another moment, another shift in her consciousness like she'd had crouching under the stairs with Tina and in the conference room at the Marshals office. She was on the other side of the game now.

She was running.

# 16

Artie Seward's house was in Mayfair, in an old block of two-story houses fronted with pale and colorless brick, set back from the street behind lawns so small they held not much more than a few tufts of graying grass. The owner of the house where Frannie had brought Lino Camacho had opted for a poured slab instead of even that small square of green. The house and the block had the look of some old concrete fort looming over Robbins Street, and if one of the homeowners had installed a cannon instead of rusting lawn chairs and iron railings it would have not looked out of place.

It said something about Lino that he would risk meeting her here, and she greeted him with a smile and a nod of the head that she hoped carried her appreciation that he could get in serious trouble if anyone from Philly PD got wise to his being near her. She moved quickly off the curb and he followed her up the short flight of concrete stairs and met her at the door, keeping his back to the street.

"Thanks, Lino, I mean it."

"Ah, if I don't do something stupid once in a while I don't feel like a cop, you know?"

She said, "When this gets straightened out—" and he held a hand up, stopping her.

He asked, "How's your sister?"

"Good. Well, okay, considering. She's out in Chester County, with a friend."

"And your father's, uh . . ." He shook his head, unsure what to call Tina. "The girlfriend. How is she?"

"Safe, I hope." She had stashed Tina with Wyatt, at an apartment above his shop not far away on Frankford. "If she does what she's told, she should be okay. I'm taking her out of the city this afternoon. A friend from the Marshals has a place upstate." Her phone buzzed, and she looked at it. "That's her, checking in. I have her and Tina texting me every hour just to make sure everyone's where they should be."

"You must be going nuts."

"Ah, I should just turn them over to the feds and be done with it all."

Lino frowned. "I don't know about that. I was talking to Red Ahearn on the way over here, and he tells me Scanlon wants your head. Something tells me there's a story there."

She nodded. "We had a kid, a failure to appear. Three or four years ago. Twenty-one, twenty-two, a Nigerian kid. We tried to scoop him up at his mother's in Manayunk and he runs."

"Oh, great."

"Yeah, up and down those fucking hills. The kid was like a rabbit, popping up everywhere, running, disappearing. And you've seen Scanlon. Not in the best shape. We had to get the cops involved, some guys from the Fifth, and they were riding Scanlon about the kid getting away from him."

"Makes you crazy, don't it?"

"A couple of the cops finally caught the kid on Green Lane with a pick gun working on the lock on a Tastykake van. Scanlon comes running up, red as the hand of doom. Pukes all over the side of the Suburban. When the cops put him in the back of the RMP, Scanlon reached in and smacked the kid."

"Smart."

"Yeah, he's a charmer. One of the neighbors saw it and complained. I thought he was wrong and told him so. I hate that old school thumper bullshit. He got reprimanded. Five people saw him do it, but he decides I was the one ratted him out."

"Wow, okay. Maybe that explains it. Red Ahearn says he's got his hooks out." He narrowed her eyes. "What was that? 'Red as the hand of doom'?"

"Red as what?"

"You said his face was red as the hand of doom."

"Did I?" Her brows came together. "I didn't notice."

"Just never heard it before. The hand of doom."

"It's just . . . something my mother used to say. Don't know where she got it. Haven't thought about it in years." She shook her head, as if trying to clear it. "Whenever it was cold. Whenever we came in from the outside, if it was snowing or something. Me and my sister. She'd say, you know. *Get inside, you look red as the hand of doom*."

Lino laughed. "I'll remember it." He inclined his head toward the door. "Who we seeing?"

"Artie Seward. He was a roofer, a friend of my father." She shrugged. "He might be able to tell us something. Where Patrick might hide, who he might reach out to."

"What did Tina say?"

"She told us about the apartment they'd been hiding in, a place with rooms for rent down off Aramingo. It's empty. Sleeper reported the location as a tip from an informant so the Marshals will keep an eye on it, but Patrick's got to know it's burned. He won't go back."

"Is Sleeper in trouble?"

"Not so far." The wind picked up and they turned their backs to it, huddled in the gap between the two front doors of the adjoining homes where they stood. "He told me they grabbed him at the motel down on the river, but he told them he'd gotten there three minutes before they had, also looking for me and Tina." She smiled and raised an eyebrow. "He said I'd called him and he was there to get me to turn myself in."

Lino laughed soundlessly. "Nobody lies like a cop. Did they buy it?"

"I'm sure Scanlon doesn't, but I don't know if he can

prove anything." She turned and knocked on Artie Seward's door. "Sleeper's got a spotless record. Or he did, before he started trying to help me stay out of jail." She shrugged, hating that she was a kind of poison now to everyone who tried to help her. She felt wrong, contaminated in some way, but there wasn't time to sort it out.

The door opened and a short, wiry man wearing a denim work shirt over a long-sleeved flannel undershirt stood looking at them, his face tight, and the door held in front of him like a shield. He had battered glasses with thick lenses that made his expression difficult to read. "What do you need?"

"It's me, Mr. Seward. Frannie Mullen."

He lifted his head and a thin smile dimpled the line of his mouth. "Sure, Frannie." He opened the door wider and waved them in. When they were past him in the small living room he looked back out toward the curb, then quickly up and down the length of Robbins Street before he closed and locked the door.

Frannie introduced Lino, and Artie Seward looked at Frannie out of the corner of his eye while he appraised the city detective. The house was small, Frannie saw, but neat, with pictures of children over the stairs and propped on the dining room furniture. The house smelled of wax and disinfectant and there was a white vase shaped like a boot with an arrangement of silk flowers on the dining room table.

"Sorry," Artie said, pointing them to an overstuffed couch the frank purple of a jungle flower. "I wasn't expecting two, you know? Frannie didn't say she'd have company."

She smiled and apologized. "Detective Camacho is trying to find Patrick, Artie." Camacho fished a notebook out of his coat and Artie licked his lips and looked toward the street again. His face seemed to swell slightly, his lips protruding.

"I don't know what I can tell you. I haven't seen Patrick in a long time."

Camacho nodded. "He hasn't called you?"

"Patrick wouldn't call me. Not now."

"Who would he call, do you think?"

Artie looked from Frannie to Camacho and chewed on his lip. She said, "Artie, we don't mean to make you uncomfortable."

"'Uncomfortable,'" he said, his voice flat. "I think you . . ." He trailed off. "Detective, uh—"

"Camacho."

"Right, Camacho." Artie sat back and looked at the ceiling before he spoke again. "I don't know what Miss Mullen told you. I knew Patrick years ago, when we were in the union. We worked together. I worked on the roof, Patrick was, you know . . ." His voice trailed off again. "He wasn't a roof guy."

"He was a roofer, but he didn't work on the roof?"

"I don't know. I was never one of those guys."

"What guys, Mr. Seward?" Camacho smiled.

"No guys. I don't know. I just went to work. I'm retired

now. Look, my wife will be home any minute." He stood up, put his hands in his pockets and took them out again. Frannie saw small white scars and puckered marks fringed with stiff gray hair on the backs of his hands.

Camacho looked at Frannie and she stood up, a hand out. "I'm sorry, Artie. We don't want to put you on the spot. We're just trying to get Patrick off the street before somebody else gets hurt."

Artie Seward moved to stand by the door, turned to avoid their eyes. "Good luck to you, then." He opened the door and stood aside. Frannie let Lino Camacho go outside and exchanged a look with him as the door swung closed. She turned to Artie, who flexed his arms and balled his fists. Frannie let him breathe for a minute, his breath whistling.

"I'm sorry, Artie." He made a motion with his hand, like flicking something from the tips of his fingers. She smiled and said, "You know, I see your hands, they remind me of his hands. You've got those scars, like his do, those little nicks and cuts."

Artie lifted his hands and looked at them and traced a mark with one thick finger. He turned to her. Holding the back of one hand out. "You see this? These pink dots? That's from the kettle, from the hot lugger. Somebody has to work the kettle, pour the tar into the mop cart, haul it up to the roof." He went to a closet under the stairs and pulled out a pair of boots. He dropped them onto the carpet at her feet. "See those boots, that black crap all over them?" His voice was quiet, grave. He was telling her something important. "Your dad have a pair like that at home?"

She shook her head. He said, "My hands. There's a big difference between my hands and your father's hands. I can bet your old man's hands got scars. But they ain't scars from working on a roof."

"I understand, Mr. Seward."

He made a face. "You understand? What do you understand? You understand what it means you bring a cop to my house, Frannie?"

"I'm trying to get Patrick off the street. You were his friend."

"His friend." He nodded. "Is that how you remember it, that I was Patrick Mullen's friend?"

"You were at our house, he talked about you, about the things you did together. He told us stories about things you did . . ." But she trailed off, looking at his face, the set of his mouth.

"You think what, we were drinking buddies?" Artie moved to a table set with pictures of children, a boy in a cap and gown, Artie and his wife with their arms around what must have been a grandchild. Artie touched the frames lightly. She didn't recognize anyone in the photos, and thought about that. What did she know about Artie Seward, other than what Patrick had said about him? Artie said, "I was a roofer thirty-nine years. I went up and down ladders, screwed up my back hauling pots of tar and cartons of tiles. I don't complain about it. I made decent money and I put my kids through Father Judge and my oldest went to Penn State."

He talked to the pictures, and Frannie had the thought the things he was saying out loud were things he'd said over and over but only to himself. "You can look at it a certain way and say the union did right by me. People make me laugh, they think unions are obsolete, meanwhile the workingman is shit out of luck. He gets replaced by a Guatemalan kid making a dollar an hour, his job gets shipped to China. I had a high school diploma and made a good wage and took care of my family, and all my friends who voted for Bush think another tax break for the millionaires is going to bring back their jobs. I say man, you are dreaming.

"But nothing's free, right? So . . ." He took his glasses off and held them up to the light, his face taking on a raw, unprotected look. He got a tissue from a box with a cover crocheted in brown and green, to match the room, and Frannie could picture the woman in the photographs sitting in this room, crochet needle working. While Artie talked he cleaned the lenses of his glasses, first one, then the other. "Maybe I had a choice, I don't know. I do know I was in Petey O'Brian's office on Torresdale Avenue when he tried to hang a punch clock on the wall for us to use, you know, to punch in and out when we came and went. You know who Petey O'Brian was? No? He was a roofing contractor tried to fight it out with Adolph Wurtz. He gets the idea he's going to start having union guys punch in and out. That way maybe guys don't show up at ten o'clock with a beer in each hand and expect to get paid for a full day. Which some guys, they did.

"But, the call goes out to Adolph about Petey and the clock. An hour later, your father shows up, takes a pry bar and pops the punch clock off the wall, says if Petey puts it back up again, Patrick's going to make him eat it." He put his glasses back on, looking up and down the street outside. "You know, the guys still tell that story, about the punch clock. It's funny, I guess, if you weren't there. I *was* there and it scared the shit out of me. And the guys who tell that story, I don't tell the rest of it."

"What's the rest of the story?"

"After Patrick pulled the clock down, he chased Petey O'Brian out into the parking lot and broke his arm." He sighed. "I never seen a guy like that, like Patrick got. Later you'd think, why didn't we do anything? There was a bunch of guys there could have done something, but the look on Patrick, his face. I never saw somebody get that look."

She stood silent for a minute, picturing her father, picturing his face distorted by rage. She'd seen that face. Something inhuman in it, something animal.

Artie said, "That's who those guys were, Adolph and Rudy and Patrick and their guys. The guys with no necks didn't know a tar mop from a tack hammer. And that's just one story, and I know a hundred just like it." Artie cocked his head at her, his white brows knit together. "You really don't know this? These stories? Anyway, whenever they had Patrick doing that shit to people a couple days later they'd come to me. Rudy Wurtz says, *Artie, you were with Patrick last Tuesday night,* I say, *Okay.* I say, *What did we do, me and Patrick?* He says, *You went to see the Phils. You had a couple steaks at Chink's. You had a couple drinks at Walt's. Anybody asks, you know what to say."* His shoulders went up and down.

She made a vague move, a weak shrug, and there was a flare of heat as if someone had touched a lit match to the back of her neck. She said, "I knew they were violent and I knew they were corrupt. I never put it together. I thought you were his friend."

He looked at her. "I wasn't his *friend*, Frances. Jesus. Patrick Mullen didn't have *friends*. I was his alibi."

Frannie felt suddenly sick, as if trying to get close to her father's path through the world she had been irradiated. Poisoned, somehow. She opened and closed her mouth. *Of course*, she wanted to say. How could she think otherwise? That a man like her father could have working buddies, sit in a room like this and watch a ball game? She nodded and moved to the door.

"I know it's not your fault," Artie said, and there was something else in his voice, some edge that hadn't been there before. "I can't imagine what it was like having that as a father. You don't know what normal people are like, do you? Normal families. People who work for a living. You need something, you need a witness or a story to tell your police friends, you just go get it, right? You don't know. Somebody's going to get a rock through his window, somebody's going to get a bullet in his eye. You don't know whose life you're tipping over, do you? 'Cause you don't know what normal's like, do you? You never had a chance."

She grabbed at the doorknob and blundered out into the wind, her coat open and the icy wind scouring her face. She wrestled the car door open and sat breathing hard, a blast of cold air rocking the frame and blowing a long, low note as it set up a vibration in some remote part of the car. There were tears in her eyes that she wanted to believe were from the cold and she thought, *How could I think I could do this?* How could she look under all these rocks and not be wounded by what she found? And what had she done her whole life but hide from the true and certain knowledge of where she had come from?

A shadow fell across her and she started, her hand going to her waist. She blinked to clear her eyes, the figure reaching for the window. She got the Glock clear of the holster as there was a hard rap on the glass and she saw it was Lino Camacho, gesturing for her to roll the window down. She stuck the pistol under her thigh and hit the button, the skin of her face suddenly red and hot, as if she had been slapped. She turned, trying to keep her expression neutral.

He said, "Did he say anything else?"

She cleared her throat. "Artie? No, nothing. He just . . ." She shrugged. "I think he wants to forget he ever knew Patrick." Lino nodded and she said, "Who can blame him?"

"You all right, Frannie?"

She nodded, but wondered if it was true. "Got to go check on the Rose of Tralee."

"Tina?" He raised his eyebrows. "Has she asked you to call her 'mom'?"

She laughed. "Jesus, please. She feels more like the kid sister I never had."

"Seriously, how's she doing?"

"Seriously? I don't know. People in protection, they can get pretty crazy, but she just seems shut down. Maybe she's always like that. He was looking for somebody to manipulate, somebody who'd be dependent on him, in a country she didn't know. With no friends, no family? Anyone would lose it."

"Think she knows where he is?"

"Maybe. I tell you one thing, she's not being honest with me. I can feel that." She lifted her hands. "Look, I'm sorry today didn't work out."

He nodded, and tapped the hood of the car. "No sweat. You need anything, you let me know." He waved as she drove off.

# 17

Marty Wurtz at his father's wake: The hallways of the house full of people whose names he didn't know; his mother's friends from the neighborhood, his grandfather's guys, all big, slow-moving men who drank beer from the bottle and spoke only to each other, except when one of them would grab Marty's arm in a meaty hand like the paw of a bear and whisper how sorry he was about Rudy. Marty's uncles Curt and Gerhart, both of them drunk, arguing about how long it took to drive to Wildwood. His mother sitting on the big green chair in the living room, the chair that used to be his father's chair, her eyes stunned and her head so full of tranquilizers that her mouth hung open, pink and wet. The fighters, mostly young kids, black and Latino kids who had trained with Rudy and Adolph and stood respectfully in knots in the front room looking at the nice things in the house, the big TV and his mother's Hummel na-

tivity set. His fat aunts Lida and Florence spearing pickles and eggs from the platters on the dining room table
and whispering about his dead father's girlfriend, who
he wasn't supposed to know about but had seen waiting
for Rudy in the gym more than once, with the baby who
had the same wiry hair they all had, Marty and Alan
and James.

Marty's brothers were there, Alan back from Los An-
geles, standing out with his tan and blond streaks in his
hair checking his phone every three minutes. James,
named for Jim Braddock with his twenty-six knockouts,
but who had turned into a slight, shy kid who thought
in numbers and read books one after the other when he
wasn't in a classroom at U of P down in the city. His
brothers sat by his mother, James holding her hand absently from the couch that matched the chair and the
drapes and the carpet. Marty got a beer from the kitchen
and walked on through to the deck where Adolph sat in
the cold looking out at the yard that ran down to Po-
quessing Creek and the park beyond, everything washed-
out grays and browns.

Marty stood by his grandfather and waited.

Adolph said, "You know we're looking. Everywhere."

"I thought we had it done. She was this close to me."

"It matters just as much to me we get this guy."

"Let me help."

"You tried. We'll see what happens."

"I want to be there once you've got him. You know
that, right?"

"Jimmy Coonan is handling it. Him and Cam and friends of ours from the local." Adolph closed his eyes. A minute went by, two. A man Marty didn't recognize came to the back door, opened it, saw them there and closed it again. "Marty, what are you in this for? I mean, what do you want?"

"Somebody has to pay. Not just that. I want to put my hands on him. The one who killed my dad."

"I don't mean that. I mean, what do you want long term, if you ever think that way. Guys your age, I don't know what the hell you're talking about half the time. It all sounds like stuff people say in movies and TV shows. Them kids who drive me, Kevin and Eddie Mac, I listen to them sometimes I think they're retarded. I know you're smart, Marty. Your older brother, he can't wait to get back to L.A. and suck more cock, or whatever he does out there. Jimmy, he's a genius needs his mother to tie his shoes. You, you're smart enough to run the business. Tough enough, that's what you want."

"That's what I want. That's all me and Pop ever talked about."

"Then you think about what you need to do now. Things got to get done doesn't mean you have to do them, you understand?"

"I want to. I can get my hands dirty."

"I know that. I'm saying what you do now can cost you what you want in your life. Yeah, it's your father, you're angry. You want to make something happen and be there when it does, but if you ever paid attention to me, pay attention to this." Adolph got up and stood close to Marty. It was a thing he did, a way of not respecting the space people liked around them, the distance from other people. Marty saw it was a small, small thing but it gave his grandfather power. People would do what he said because they couldn't stand how close he came, what it meant that he didn't care. His grandfather, so close Marty could feel his breath on his cheek, said, "Sometimes you got to set things in motion and see how they go. Sometimes you got to trust that when something happens, people will think it's you made it happen."

Marty nodded, smart enough not to talk back to Adolph. But thinking, *Yeah, but when they* see *you do it, then they* know.

Frannie drove north and east, overshooting Frankford Avenue before doubling back toward Wyatt's garage, watching her rearview. She turned a block short of the shop and drove a quick circle to sit in the parking lot of a 7-Eleven across the street and watch the intersection for anyone who looked out of place. She saw delivery trucks lumbering toward 95, the normal traffic of the working day. She called Red Ahearn. He answered on the first ring.

"Frannie." His voice was low.

"Just checking in. I'm sorry I haven't called."

"No, it's just as well." She heard noises in the background, men talking. There was a pause, then his voice again, louder. "That's better. I had to duck out."

"Look, I put you and Lino in a spot and I'm sorry."

"No, not at all. I tell you off the record you're doing the right thing. I don't know what's up with Scanlon but I got to say I never saw anything about the guy that made me like him. You know, back when we were working the union cases, there was a witness disappeared. I never thought Bill did it, but a lot of us never trusted him after that." There was a pause, a sound like a door opening and closing. "Do you have her now? Tina?"

"I'm about to scoop her up. I'm giving her to Eric Hansen. He'll put her in a place he knows in Jersey. Then I'm coming in and we're getting this sorted out, Scanlon or no Scanlon."

"You're moving her? Good, because I know he asked for a court order to cover your phone."

"Son of a bitch. I better move."

She hung up and then texted Wyatt that she was coming in. After one last look up and down the street, she got out of the car, then crossed against the traffic, moving fast.


The streets of northeast Philly were wide and flat and reminded her sometimes of western cities she had seen, not the cramped and airless warrens of the neighborhoods where she'd grown up. She crossed the avenue and kept going to Sackett Street, a short road behind the garage that angled back toward Frankford. She looked into the parked cars, at the blank windows of the houses across the street. A FedEx truck pulled up at a house across Levick Street and a man in a blue uniform hopped out of the truck with a package in his arms and headed for a door near the corner. Frannie reached the lot behind the garage that was enclosed by a chain-link fence topped with razor wire and punched in a code to release the lock.

When she reached the garage she stood unseen at the back of the bays for a minute and watched the men inside work. A big Dayton heater whined, blasting out a stream of hot air and the men laughed and joked and swore at each other. She recognized a short, muscular Latino kid named Mateo who was lightly touching a flame to a piece of sheet metal, and she saw Wyatt and a tall man wearing a kerchief on his head as they stood looking at a motor on a steel table.

Wyatt said, "That's a sweet Panhead, man," and the taller man, who she knew was called Kingfish, said, "I hope you didn't pay nothing for this, Wyatt. It's all cracked, look at this, this is all just ate up with cracks."

"Four thousand."

"Four thousand dollars," Kingfish said, and he put his massive hand on Wyatt's forehead, bowed his own shaggy head and said, "Dear Jesus, watch out for this poor dumb country boy who has eyes but sees not. I am too old to go find another job when this witless hillbilly goes out of business. In your name I pray." And every-body in the shop called out, "Amen."

Mateo raised his goggled eyes and saw Frannie and he smiled shyly and called to Wyatt and he noticed her and came over while the other men called out to her and she waved and asked when she was going to get her bike.

Wyatt walked her out the back door into the pen and they climbed the stairs to the apartment.

"She been good?"

Wyatt shrugged. "Ain't heard a peep from her, so I guess so. Got her fixed up with some groceries from the Acme and Mateo brought her hot soup 'cause he said in Guatemala they believe pregnant women should only eat hot foods."

"That's sure better than the junk she's been eating."

At the top of the stairs Frannie reached a hand toward the door, but Wyatt stopped her and pulled her in and they kissed, once quickly and then again, slowly, giving it something. When they stepped back, he nodded as if she had said something and he thought it true.

They leaned against the railing and looked at each other. He said, "When your friend Sleeper was here, he told me you don't care for this kind of duty. Witness security."

She shook her head. "No. I never have. When I was in the Marshals I always tried to get out of it, to tell the truth."

"Somebody as all-the-time fierce as you? If somebody was after me, I'd sure want you."

"Well, maybe you're prejudiced a little." She laughed quietly. "It's true, though. I hate it."

"Why?"

Frannie looked away, over the scrap yard and the street. "They lie. These people we protect. They're mostly dirty from whatever they've been doing. They call their old friends, they try to sneak away. It's like they can't wait to get themselves killed. And we're supposed to protect them with our lives."

"That does sound like bad duty. There must be some that's innocent, right?"

"Yeah, but you never get to pick. And what do you know about anybody? Who they are really, what they've done?"

"You're slow to trust."

She nodded, still watching the street. He touched her. "Do you trust me?"

She looked his way, then away, opened her mouth and closed it again. "I want to. Wyatt, I do."

"But what?"

"It just comes very slowly for me." And here it was again, a moment to get it right. She looked at him, at his eyes that were like rain clouds, blue shot through with gray. "I called him," she said, very softly and her voice caught in her throat so that she had to let go a long breath before she could say anything else.

He looked at her intensely and answered, his voice as quiet as hers had been. "Who did you call?"

"My father. I've never told anyone. Not Mae, not the police, not anyone." She had to reach out and find his hand with hers. "The night he came and killed her. That was how he knew we were there. There was a list of numbers by the phone and I knew what they were. The bars where he hung out, the union hall. We were never to call, but I knew that he'd be at one of those numbers. So I called and they put him on the phone and I told him we were back and he should . . ." She had to stop and close her eyes. "He should come."

Wyatt took her in his arms, then, and she didn't say anything else for a long time. Finally she said, "So, you see? It's me, me who can't be trusted. He was an animal, a killer, and it was me who let him in."

"You were just a kid, Frannie. You couldn't know."

She shook her head, but her face was desolate. "I'm sorry. I shouldn't have told you that." Her skin was bloodless and she looked stunned. "I don't know what I was thinking."

"Frannie."

She saw the look in his eyes, reading it for pity or contempt, unable to breathe. He started to talk again and she held one hand up, willing the conversation over. "Maybe someday. But not now, okay?"

After a moment he stepped back, and she turned away.

————

When they opened the door Tina scrambled to her feet, shutting her phone and dropping it in her bag. Frannie looked at her, thought about grabbing the phone. "Everything all right?"

"Sure you scared me," the girl said, her eyes too bright. "I'm all jumpy up here alone."

"Who were you talking to?"

"My sister, at home. She's getting married."

Frannie narrowed her eyes, but then her own phone buzzed and she looked at it. "Marshal Hansen's on his way. We need to move." Tina scrambled to put her things back in her bag, then tried to heft it with shaking hands. Wyatt took it from her and waited while Frannie went over what would happen next. "As soon as I see Sleeper's van, we're going downstairs and out to the end of the lot. Don't run, but don't stop moving, okay?" The girl nodded. "You met Sleeper, Tina. He's a Marshal, so he's better equipped than anyone I know to get you someplace safe."

Frannie turned away from Tina and took her pistol from the holster at her waist, worked the slide to see the dull brass glint of the load in the chamber and put it away again.

"Where are we going?"

"I don't know and it's better that way." In fact, Frannie did know—he was taking her to a safe house, the place she'd told Red Ahearn about that the Marshals sometimes used, over in Jersey near Fort Dix.

"Will you come with me?"

"No, but we'll stay in touch. I can do more knowing you're safely out of the area."

Tina nodded, but her face was grim and she looked to Frannie as if she might cry. "You'll stay in touch, then?"

"I absolutely will. Believe me, this is for the best."

"I don't know those others. I don't trust anyone but you."

Frannie's phone buzzed again, and she looked at it, then at Tina. "We'll talk in the car, okay? Let's move."

She saw Sleeper pull up to the curb behind the shop in a blacked-out Chevy van as the three of them made their way down. Frannie tried to take the bag from Wyatt at the bottom of the stairs, but he waved her off. "You need your hands free." She walked ahead, crossing the lot that was crowded with junk from the shop, stacks of rusted bike frames and chrome pipes streaked blue and black. The wind picked up, pushed at the squat trees across Sackett Street and sang in the empty pipes, a sound that reminded Frannie of the organ music at Mother of Divine Grace down in Fishtown, of coming from the cold of Cambria Street into the nave that was like a echoing cavern and the nuns shushing everyone so that they could hear God's voice.

When they reached the gate Wyatt swung it open and Sleeper was opening the side door of the van. Frannie stopped, reflexively touching the holster at her waist, and saw Tina as she looked up and down the road, her eyes wide. She looked back to the street and saw the FedEx truck was still across the street, the windshield opaque with glare. She had time to ask herself, *How long has he been sitting there?* and then the white truck jolted into action, jumping forward across the wide intersection and gathering speed as it came.

"Eric!" She grabbed the collar of Tina's coat and pushed her down against the sidewalk at the same time she shouted to Sleeper and tried to show him the threat, jabbing the air in the direction of the rushing bulk of the white truck, but he was inside the van at the side door and had to pivot to try to see what was coming from across the street. Tina screamed as she went down and rolled on her side, her thin arms gathered around her middle. Frannie pulled her pistol and raised it to the oncoming windshield and saw that the driver looked frozen in place, his hands up as the truck loomed, and in the seconds it took for the truck to close the distance the glare cleared from the windshield and she saw that someone crouched in the open doorway behind the driver, holding something to his head. Wyatt dropped the bag and threw himself across the sidewalk to reach where Tina lay, her teeth bared and eyes squeezed shut.

There was a quiet second, a pause as long as a drawn breath, then a bang and a shriek of metal as the truck punched into the passenger side of the black van and Sleeper was catapulted through the open door onto the curb. The windshield went white and burst outward into a shower of white crystals that rattled onto the hood of the van and the street as Sleeper lay stunned and blinking. Frannie saw the driver of the FedEx truck twisted in his seat, groaning and holding his hands to his bloodied head, and she raised the Glock and pointed into the dark space to the left of his seat and fired a shot. Tina screamed again, and Wyatt threw himself over her and whispered something that Frannie couldn't catch as she pivoted, trying to cover the truck for whoever had held the gun on the driver.

Now there was a roar and a squeal of tires as another car shot down Levick Street and came to a hard stop just behind the van, a beat-up green LTD that Frannie thought had to be thirty years old, the undercarriage pink with rust. It was still rocking on its suspension when the side doors opened and two men stepped out, one on the far side of the Ford carrying a shotgun and the nearer man holding a blocky semiautomatic pistol. She shifted the front sight of her Glock and shot the one with the pistol as he raised it and then again as he staggered. He dropped the pistol and slid down the long door to his knees, empty hands grasping weakly at the slick green metal. She forced herself to move forward, trying to get a clear shot at the man with the shotgun, but he pulled his head down behind the far side of the LTD and disappeared. She looked again at the man down on the street and saw his face change and change again, his large, black eyebrows knitted with concentration as he struggled to understand what had happened to him.

She reached out one hand without taking her eyes from the street and shook Sleeper and she heard him struggle to his feet. She stole a quick look out of the corner of her eye and took in his jacket speckled with bits of broken glass and his face painted with blood from a cut at his hairline. There was a zipping sound as he pulled his pistol clear of its leather holster, a reassuring sound that told her he was still alert and able to act. Now she pointed hard down the side of the van and then slashed at the air with a cupped hand indicating he should make his way around the rear of his van to protect their blind side. From there he could flush anyone in the street around the back of the steaming wreck of the FedEx truck and into her sights. She heard him move, taking quick steps to the rear of the van and sidestepping out into the open, bits of glass dropping out of the folds of his coat to rattle on the street.

She heard noises behind her, running feet and the voices of Mateo and Kingfish and the other men from the shop. Wyatt called to them to get back, to call the cops, and the men shouted questions and banged on the fence. Frannie thought of the risk she had exposed them to and felt sweat forming at the roots of her hair and a tremor that passed from her shoulders down her arms to rattle the gun in her clenched fists. How had they been discovered? Had she been followed? She thought of Tina on the phone when she'd opened the door. Had she called Patrick or somebody else who might have given them up? She should have grabbed the phone away from the girl and gotten some answers. The wind gusted and snatched at her hair and whistled in her ears. She pushed herself to keep moving, closing the distance to the man with the shotgun and whoever else might be hiding behind the wreck.

At the curb she paused and then stepped carefully, feeling her way, dropping slightly to try to see under the car or the van, but she couldn't get low enough to make anything out. There was a garbled shout from the other side of the van and the sound of feet moving in the street and then she heard Sleeper identify himself as a federal agent and tell somebody to drop his weapon. She tensed and drove herself forward, passing where the smashed grill of the FedEx truck hissed and spat green coolant onto the black street, close enough now to the LTD to hear the man she had shot as he shifted and moaned. The driver of the FedEx climbed out from under the dash, his face speckled with glass and blood and his eyes wide. Frannie motioned for him to keep coming and he vaulted to his feet like a sprinter from his blocks and disappeared behind her, running flat out for Frankford Avenue or maybe to find a bridge across the river to Jersey.

A man in a blue tracksuit backed out from behind the truck and almost stumbled into Frannie and they both shouted. She registered him as a blur—the piping on the cheap gym wear, gray hair, and a potbelly, her attention drawn mostly to the big chrome pistol in his hand as he swung it around to point it her way. The long barrel of the gun connected with her temple and she fell back, raising her own gun as there were three quick shots from the other side of the truck. The man made a sound, a breathy, clotted syllable as he expelled the air in his lungs and then folded unnaturally, the pistol spinning away and hitting the ragged asphalt where it discharged with a hollow pop and a white spark. Tina screamed again and Frannie heard a rattle of keys as Kingfish and the men from the shop tried to get the lock open.

"Get them back inside!" She made a sweeping motion over her shoulder, hoping the men would either retreat or grab Tina and Wyatt out of the line of fire and inside until the police came or the shooting was over. Frannie let herself sag against the side of the FedEx truck and lifted to hand to her temple, and when she brought her fingers away she saw them wet with blood from where the man had caught her with the gun barrel, the man now dying at her feet. She saw Wyatt kneeling at the gate, crouched protectively over Tina, who was clearly too terrified to move. She waved again, herding them back toward the shop. "Back inside, Wyatt, now!"

She heard motion, the sound of footsteps on the street and tensed again, the pistol out, her eyes darting as she tried to take in everything in her field of view, assess all possible threats. Sleeper called her name and she leaned around the corner. Her eyes stung from blood and cold sweat and she lifted a hand from the pistol to wipe again at her face. Her vision cleared and she saw Sleeper crouched in the street, his pistol pointed at the LTD where there was at least one more player, the man with the short-barreled shotgun.

As she turned around again the man broke from behind the car, his overcoat flapping open, running hard and straight toward the opposite corner and the shelter of the line of cars, and she thought of a flightless bird flushed from cover. He raised the shotgun over his head as he ran, as if he were a soldier fording a stream in an old war movie, a bald spot showing white at the crown of his head. Sleeper yelled for him to stop, for him to drop the weapon. At the bumper of the first car he came to he stumbled and fell, the long gun tangled in the folds of his wool overcoat. Frannie joined Sleeper, both of them screaming at him to stop moving, to drop the gun, but his eyes were wild with fear and adrenaline and he tore a ragged line in the tail of his coat as he lifted the barrel of the shotgun toward them. His face was slick with sweat and maybe tears, she thought, so she wished there was one more moment to talk with him, because they were going to kill him and it seemed so stupid to her, so meaningless to die in the street like this for nothing she could understand.

She was so focused on the man and the long gun she didn't notice the van until it was on them, the roaring engine and the dark bulk of it filling the street between where she and Sleeper stood near the ancient dull-green LTD and the where the man with the shotgun crouched, one hand on the bumper of a beat-up old Pathfinder with an Eagles pennant on the antenna. The van made a wall in the street between them, Frannie's eyes going immediately to the slightly open side door and a black steel muzzle in the gap. She heard Sleeper scream, "Gun!" as he dropped back behind the car and the rifle in the door opened up, the hard clatter of an AK-47 echoing in the wide street. The gun was close and the roar of it filled her head so that she was instantly deaf. She dropped to her knees and found herself crawling, retreating toward the cover of Sleeper's van where Wyatt and Tina clutched at each other, the girl's hands over her ears. She found Sleeper already there, sheltering behind the black van as bullets punched through the steel and knocked splinters of glass and plastic into the street. She heard muffled sounds through a high whine in her head, car doors slamming and men shouting and then the van's transmission screamed and caught and she leaned out of cover to see the van fishtailing, white smoke curling from the rear wheels, then straightening out to rocket down Sackett Street and slip into the traffic heading down Frankford Avenue toward the center of the city.

She turned to see Sleeper on his feet, his pistol out, and she followed him around the side of the van out into the street again. He went fast toward the Pathfinder and she swung left toward where the first man she had shot had lain by the door of the LTD, but she saw only blood in spattered dots and dark, curling lines like something written in a dead language. The man who had lain there shot through the abdomen—the man she knew she had hit—was gone. The man Sleeper had shot, the man with the chromed, long-barreled pistol, he was missing, too, and she looked across the wide intersection to see Sleeper moving cautiously around the SUV, his gun hand out, his arms rigid. After a minute he looked back at her and lifted his arms. Nothing. All of them, the dead, the wounded, all the men were gone.

For a long moment Frannie was deaf but for the screaming, distorted tones in her head from the machine gun and she screwed up her face at the pain of it. She watched Sleeper come back across the street, seeing his mouth move soundlessly, and she shook her head and lifted one hand to her ear. She turned to see the side of the LTD spattered with dark holes from the shot and the window glass blown in. She put her pistol away, waiting for the roaring in her head to fade, and then she saw Tina climbing to her feet, her mouth open, and the men from the shop pushing through the door and reaching for her and Wyatt, who was still kneeling on the ground.

The whine in her head resolved itself into the howl of a police siren overlaid with the scream of the pregnant girl as Mateo and Kingfish lifted her to her feet. Frannie saw that her front was splattered with blood. Her mind went blank as she ran toward them while Mateo gently pulled her shirt aside, but the girl was screaming and pointing down and it took them all a long moment, a terrible and confused and panicked moment to look away from her and the wide expanse of the white and unmarked skin stretched tight across her belly and down at Wyatt kneeling on the sidewalk, his mouth hanging open and blood pooling at his knees.

# 18

What did she remember? She remembered the screaming coming from everywhere, from the men in their strangled, choking voices, from Tina in her high wail, and from her own burned and empty throat. She remembered holding Wyatt in her arms and his mouth moving soundlessly. She remembered police in their dark coats suddenly everywhere, and ambulances, and faces she knew and many she didn't know, men first shouting at her and then talking quietly, and she saw Sleeper talking to Lino and Red Ahearn and when Scanlon got out of a black Suburban he and Sleeper started screaming at each other, though it was like she was behind a wall of blue glass that stopped all the sound, so it was just their mouths going, their faces distorted by rage, and she remembered Sleeper launching himself at the older man and two uniformed policemen holding him down and cuffing him. She saw Tina put in the back of a police car with her mascara running down her pale skin so that for a moment she had the white and unearthly beauty of a stone angel in a cemetery, her face streaked by rain.

When they took Frannie's gun and cuffed her she went meekly and sat in the open door of a police car and someone snapped her picture and that night it showed up online. The picture captured her looking down, staring into nothing, but what she was actually seeing was one of the tiles in the street, the white and blue letters cut into sharp pieces as if shattered, and the letters spelling out RESURRECT DEAD ON PLANET JUPITER. So sitting there in the cold dark she had pictured it again, how it would be in the yellow light and mist and shrieking wind, all of them waiting there in the endless night, her mother and her aunt and Frank Russo and all the gone and now Wyatt, his blue eyes bright with starlight.


They took her to the Fifteenth District station house up at Harbison Avenue and put her in the lockup, and that's where Mari Rivera found her; silent, staring, her shirt thick with Wyatt's blood. There were a lot of phone conversations, Mari pacing in the hallway between the front desk and the cell in her blues, and talking nonstop for what seemed like a long time. It was after midnight when they unlocked the cell, Mari taking her by the hand and driving her back to the house. She wanted to put Frannie in her bed and sleep with the kids, but Frannie dropped onto the couch and sat unmoving and eventually Mari gave up and went to bed.

In the middle of the night the light went on and Mari came in to the living room. Frannie sat up fast, her hand going to her empty holster, and Mari had to tell her that she'd been calling out in her sleep.

"I'm sorry."

"It's okay. It's just the kids gotta get up."

"Oh, God. The boys. I can't stay here, Mari."

"No, it's okay. You got to rest."

Frannie stood up, blinking and staggered. "Jesus, Mari, if anything happened to those boys I'd never be able to live with it."

Mari put a hand on her arm. "It's okay, Frannie, there's a black-and-white at the curb and that detective from South is outside somewhere, too."

"Camacho."

"So it's okay. We're okay."

After a moment Frannie nodded, let herself sink to the couch again. Mari asked, "Can you sleep again, you think?"

Frannie shook her head. "I don't think so. What time is it?"

"I'll make coffee."

"I'm sorry."

"Stop fucking saying that. If I'm ever in your shoes I'll be at your house and I don't want to have to keep apologizing."

Mari made coffee and they moved into the kitchen.

Frannie lifted the cup, put it down. She said, "I keep seeing them putting him in the bag. The zipper going up, and he's gone. If I didn't see it, it would still be true, I guess."

Mari heaped sugar into her coffee and sipped at it, let Frannie talk.

"I keep thinking there's people I should call. His family. He's got a brother and a sister in Oklahoma. I have to call the guys at the shop, they'll know. I don't have his numbers. I don't know anything about . . ." Then she couldn't talk and Mari held her hand across the table.

Another long silence, Frannie staring into the dark outside the window. She said, "What did he see when he saw me? I mean, what were we? I kept him out, I don't even know why now. What I was afraid of?"

"Frannie, you don't trust nobody. You never did."

"I trust you."

"That's different. We were friends since we were thirteen."

Frannie took a napkin from a dispenser on the table. Mari told her, "We seen each other every kind of way. You seen me scared and lonely and hurt. Pregnant and sick. I seen you beat up and angry and scared. Well, angry, anyway. I don't think anyone's ever seen you scared. You know what I got for you. And you, you did for me and I let you."

Frannie said, "I saw a woman, a therapist.. She said anger and fear are the same thing, the same emotion just run different ways through your brain. Like an optical illusion, you look at it one way and it's a woman sitting at a mirror, then you see it another way it's a skull. Your brain moving back and forth between those things so you're not sure what you're supposed to be seeing."

Mari narrowed her eyes, thinking. "That might be right. I don't know. It's easy to get angry, maybe, hold somebody off. You and me, we need a history with somebody to trust them. You never had the time to make that history with Wyatt."

"Because I pushed him away." She closed her eyes and whispered, as if afraid of being overheard. "I was afraid of what he wanted. That I couldn't give it. I hear people talk about love, I don't know what they're talking about. I think they must be dreaming."

"You can't blame yourself, Frannie. The way things went, your father and mother? Where would you learn about it?"

"I just want to hear him say something. Just one more thing. I thought he was trying to talk. I keep seeing him on that sidewalk. That cold ground. If I had been faster to get to him, maybe he would have said something. If I was two steps closer." She put her hand out, reaching into empty air. "He was looking in my eyes." Mari moved to her and put her arms around her and Frannie held her so tight they both shook with it. "And there was something. He said something. If I could hear it."

Mari whispered, "You know what it was, Frannie. Inside you, you already know."

The next day Mari put the kids on the bus and came into the kitchen, where Frannie sat looking at the woods out the window. After a minute she went to the cabinet over the refrigerator and opened a Tupperware container hiding a half pack of cigarettes. She opened the window a crack and lit two cigarettes and gave one to Frannie.

"These are stale."

"Yeah, I smoke like one a month. I get a bad shift, some damn thing I can't get out of my head." They both leaned to the open window to blow thin streams of smoke into the cold. "I used to think about that thing in that movie, *Men in Black*. They got that thing in that movie where they flash you, you know, in your eyes, and you forget whatever they need you to forget. It had like a dial on it, go back a minute, an hour, a year. Some nights I'd come home I think: get me that flashing thing. And that was just the normal misery. The stuff we think is normal."

Frannie lifted the cigarette. "I guess this is as close as we get."

"You want to go get some things, move in here with me and the boys a few days?"

"I don't know, Mari. I got to face things. And I worry about the boys, if anybody shows up here looking for me. Those guys outside, they can't be there forever. But thanks."

"Ah." Mari lifted a shoulder, the one Frannie knew had a tattoo of a butterfly, tiny and perfect, executed in orange and purple with a blue shadow cast beneath it as if it might lift off. She'd been with Mari when she got it, a place in Chinatown. While Mari got her shoulder done, Frannie held her hand and watched a boy with gauged ears get an elaborate design that ran the length of his arm and looked as if his flesh was pulled away to reveal the shadowed wheels and gears within. As if inside him he were made of metal, held together with rivets and wires. The image had stayed with her. It was a way to see yourself.

Mari said, "I remember that night Jorge went crazy. I thought I was dead." Jorge was the father of her oldest son, Ezequiel. Things between Mari and Jorge had ended badly and one night he had come in through the window of the boys' room with a pistol and a bottle of *pitorro*. Mari had launched herself at him and he had cracked her across the head with the bottle. That night Frannie had swung by the way she did at the end of a shift and seen his car pulled up on the sidewalk. She had made her way silently through the house and found Jorge trying to explain custody law to the terrified kids while Mari held a towel to her bloody head and tried to get up off the floor. Frannie stuck her Glock in his ear and got him into her cuffs then got Mari to her feet and they took him outside, where Mari tased him, the way she told it later, "until she thought of the night as a win."

"Jorge, I haven't thought about him in a while."

"Ah, I hear he got hooked up with a nurse over in Cherry Hill. Got her knocked up, of course."

"Well, good. He can go climb in her windows."

"But what you did that night . . ."

"Ah, it was just . . ." Frannie shrugged.

"Just shit. You saw we were in trouble and you kept coming. That's all that matters. To you and me, that's all that matters."

Sleeper found her at Mari's, sitting by the window where she'd been on and off for two days, in the kitchen that smelled of the *pasteles* Mari's mother had made the night before. He sat in the living room looking uncomfortable, perched on the edge of an overstuffed chair covered in red parrots peeking from behind white begonias. He told her the cops were combing the city for any sign of the blue van or the men who had shot at them, but so far nothing had turned up. The neighbors at the scene had all hidden when the shooting started and the FedEx guy never saw the face of the guy who'd stuck the gun against his temple. There were blood trails, bullet holes, shell casings.

"But no bodies," he said.

"Except one," Frannie said. She got a rag from the sink, absently wiped at the tabletop. "What happened to Tina O'Bannon?" she asked, her voice empty, as if it was all something that had nothing to do with her. Something he had brought from another life.

"Ahearn's got her in protection, offered her a deal if she cooperates. But they'll dump her back in Ireland when they're done with her."

He got up to go, standing at the door and touching his pockets as if he had forgotten something. "What will you do now?"

She shook her head, a gesture that could have meant she didn't know or she couldn't bring herself to answer. It was so quiet they could hear the rhythmic snap of the kitchen clock. He said, "I'm not going anywhere, Frannie. I'll help. I want to help." For a moment she thought he was going to move toward her and she was glad when the moment passed and he stayed where he was.

She asked, "Are you okay? At work?"

"Scanlon wants me out. He might get his wish." He scowled at something outside. "You know, you could just leave. Leave town."

"And Mae? What would I do with her? She can't stay out of town forever. She's got Tansy."

"No. But that's not it, though, is it?

She shook her head. "No. Patrick's still out there. It's not over," she said, and then, "It's not over until he's locked up or dead."

He let a long breath go. "So tell me what to do."

"Stay away." She looked at him, into his face, for the first time since he had come in. "Me and Mae, we're trapped in this. But I won't have anybody else. I can't take that chance. So. Just stay out of it."

He took his keys out. She said, "Sleeper."

He turned to the door and started through it. "Eric," she said, as if saying his given name would change the way he heard her. "Will you do that for me? Will you just stay away?"

On his way out he reached behind him and closed the door without looking back.

Bertie McCullough was laying low: Red Lady 21 instead of Jäger, oxy to keep her mellow, instead of wet, the dope soaked in formaldehyde that gave her visions and let her talk to the ghosts. Keeping things clamped down and quiet, she told Jen. Staying out of the places she usually went, like Cathy's and Mick's, staying off Clearfield and Frankford Avenue and wherever people knew her face. She borrowed a pink hoodie from Jen that covered her PEACE top like Rihanna wore in that picture from Coachella, the one where she's smoking a blunt and partying with Katy Perry. Diante from Cornwall Street up in the Badlands had the keys to an empty garage on Tulip Street and she was hanging out there with Jen and Slim and Slim's cousins and thinking where she should go. Jen said she could go down the Shore to stay with her aunt and Bertie said yeah, but she needed money and where was that coming from? One of Slim's cousins whose name was Eightball hooked up his phone to a set of speakers and they had music but Jen said, "Keep it low, keep it low," and Diante gave Bertie a blunt and as she put it to her lips she knew it wasn't just weed. She frowned at the chemical stink and said, "Is this wet?" and Diante did an exaggerated shrug, like trying to be cute, and Eightball, who was called that not because of dope but because he had one of the old plastic fortune-telling balls, shook it and said, "It is decidedly so," and even Jen laughed. It was what they did, her and Jen and their set, smoked these soaked blunts, and they called it wet, or fry, or water-water, or sherm, the boys making up a thousand names for it because that was part of the fun for them, she knew.

The music was good, familiar, a sound like something old with scratchy sounds like the vinyl records that had been her mother's, but mixed up with something new and she asked Slim what it was and he told her Moby and then she remembered the CD. She was breaking her rule, doing the stick soaked in embalming fluid, but it was hard, the way she was living. Hiding and hoping the cops forgot about her. Not seeing her boys and staying out of the Palmer Burial Ground where Brianna was under a pink stone shaped like a heart, even though it was just down the street at Memphis and Palmer.

Eightball and Jen got up and danced, their long limbs white and their shadows black in the empty space. Bertie began to sweat, and she took off the hoodie and stood on a stack of tires stripped to the steel with her hands on her head and Slim asked, "Why do you hold your head?" and she said, "Just to make sure," and he said, "Sure of what?" And how could she explain it? That the wet dope made her head feel like it was open to all the sounds and spirits moving through the houses and streets and right through the walls and she could catch them if she wanted. But she was waiting, waiting for one special one but the music had to be right. She pointed at the speakers and said, "More beautiful, more beautiful," and Diante poked with his long dark finger, saying the titles of each song and Bertie making a spinning motion with her hand that meant *Keep going* until the right song came on which was "My Weakness," so that the music and the dope were the same, like a slow current circling and grabbing at her heart.

Bertie knew people who got wild smoking wet, got crazy paranoid. Her cousin Danny had been like that, jabbing at the air with a knife in his hand so that nobody wanted to be around him when he was doing it. For Bertie it was different. She tried to explain it to Slim, who stood quiet at the edge of things and watched the dancing. She said, "It's like waves are all around me and the waves are warm and I float, I just float," with her hands up, showing him what it would be like if there was something like water around her. "I can call, like, *souls* to me, the spirits of everybody from my life." He was watching her, Slim, in a way that she noticed and she wasn't sure if he wanted to get on her or if it was something else, because sometimes he looked at Diante, too, as if trying to catch his eye.

Diante reached up and gave her another stick, the bitter reek not as bad the second time. Somebody's phone rang and Diante went outside through the door that was just an old piece of rotting plywood, talking and looking at her over his shoulder, saying "Yeah, Marty, yeah." "Yeah, Marty, yeah," louder, and Jen took it up and laughed,

"Yeah, Marty, yeah," until Slim looked at her hard and shook his head and she made her pissed-off girl face and waved her hands saying, *Whatever, fucker.* There was an old calendar on the wall and when the door opened the pages rattled and flipped, the women in the pictures replaced with different people she knew, her mother and her husband and her brother and everyone who was gone from her life. Dead or run off or hiding or in prison. And then there *she* was, the small girl with white blond hair like her father, hiding behind the tall black columns of tires and the metal boxes that stood empty, all the tools and things long gone, stolen away by Diante and his cousins. This was Brianna, her girl, her beautiful dead child, but tonight she was standing in the corners and not coming to her, even though Bertie held her hands out and reached for her.

There was something going on now, Eightball and Slim looking at Diante and all of them looking at her standing there on the low circle of black wheels and Slim asked Diante, "Is that enough? Did she get enough?" and Eightball shrugged and laughed like he did and said, "Outlook good," and they looked at Jen who shook her head and said, "Do whatever you think, man, just leave me out of it." Then "Flower" came on, and Slim stepped to the tower of wheels and she thought he might start singing, joining the beautiful sound of the black girls but he had a knife in his hands. Brianna peeked out and then put her hands on her eyes so she wouldn't see, and Slim held his hand out to coax her down to the ground but she was afraid, not of dying but of the pain of dying and would have explained it if she could. Brianna began to dart around the room, then, and Slim flapped his hand and said, "Come on, come on down, now, girl, let's get this done," and Brianna was running in circles around them, faster and faster and it made Bertie dizzy and she stepped back off the tires and went down hard against a pile of wheels and rims that made a noise like thunder and screaming.

That was it, then. The beautiful party was over and Brianna was gone but for a lingering scent, her little-baby smell of powder and juice and soap. Jen giggled through the hand she'd clamped over her mouth. The boys stood like posts, hands at their sides, their skin slick and bright like they were cutouts that let light in from the other world.

Bertie ran. She ran though her arms and legs seemed to be disconnected from her body, held only by thin strings that bent and twisted as she moved. She pushed Eightball as she ran and he went over, his arms out, catching Diante so that they both went down and then she banged into the piece of wet plywood that was the door so that it gave way and slapped down into the street and somebody yelled that they were calling the cops and people need to sleep. She turned left and followed the tiny white blur that shimmered in and out of her vision, moving too fast, though she sobbed and called to the spirit to wait, to slow down. When she looked behind her the boys were coming, running hard, mouths open and calling to each other.

At Memphis she didn't stop but ran hard, hitting the fence and reaching up, catching her hoodie as she went. She pulled herself hard, kicking at the green fence and her breath coming in wet sobs and when she flipped down into the dark grass on the other side she could feel that she'd torn her shirt and the skin beneath it. She got up and kept moving, limping now, biting the meat of her dirty palm to keep from screaming. Behind her the boys came on, rattling the fence as they climbed, and she pulled the shredded hoodie off and threw it away.

Palmer Burial Ground was a dark square behind the trees and fences, the ground humped in waves, the stones jutting at every crazy angle and some of them ringed with iron fences that slowed her down but she kept going toward the far corner where Brianna lay and she thought if she was going to die it would be all right as long as she was with her baby. Behind her the boys called, telling each other to spread out, telling her to slow down and talk, just talk with them.

She reached the brick walkway that cut through the middle and came up short when there was a man there, a black shape that drew a long breath and lit a cigarette and so she stopped, her chest heaving, her face stung by cuts and grass and sticks woven into her hair.

————

Patrick Mullen sat on a low stone and watched them come. The woman he'd seen around the neighborhood and the boys who were just shapes under the dark trees. The street far away was full of sulfurous yellow light but the cemetery was dark except for small electric votives with flickering crimson lights and plastic crosses that glowed with dim luminescence and showed only a word or a fragment of a date.

The woman looked from his face to the darkness where the young men stood and then knelt by a stone shaped like a heart. There were flattened silver balloons still tied in a nest of string and stuffed animals that might have been bears or rabbits or mice, so worn by rain and wind that they looked like they had been worried by dogs.

Patrick waved his hands over the sunken earth and said to her, "I don't know about this. About leaving these things. It's all over the place now. It used to be just flowers, but now it's candy and toys and everything else."

"It makes me feel better. Like I can still do something."

"But you can't." He got up and walked along the path. The boys were close now, their shaved white heads like knobs of bone in the dark. He pointed to each in the dark. "I used to love this. To fight like this. Mess a guy up. They only called me when that was it, when there was nothing to talk about but just the beating to do. I didn't even have to be drunk. Though mostly I was."

One of the boys said, "If we all just go at him," so

Patrick lunged at him. He hit the boy low, around the body, which the boy thought meant that he had some advantage over the old man and pounded on his back and his head with the heel of his fist while the other two came close and made gestures with their open hands, maybe looking for a purchase, a place to grab on. Patrick made his move then, driving up, lifting the boy off his feet and slamming him down on a flat stone like a tabletop. The boy's head hit the grass but his back thumped down on the old granite. There was a long moment before he coughed out a ragged breath and rolled onto the ground, suddenly as useless as if he were dead.

Bertie watched them fight for a minute in the dark and then retreated to sit by Brianna's stone. When it was over and the boys rolled in the dirt or lay motionless he came and sat by her and she saw his chest heaved and his face was wet with tears.

She was shaking, her head bent. "I'm afraid it will hurt. What doesn't hurt? I heard a guy say he got his throat cut and never even knew it until later. The knife was that sharp. He lived. Got stitches and he lived."

"I don't know," he said. "It's all terrible. From what I've seen. What's your name?"

She started at his sudden movement, but he settled next to her on his knees, groaning with the effort. She said, "I'm Bertie McCullough. I won't tell," but she was crying so hard she could barely form the words.

"Bertie. Tell or don't tell. It's nothing to me." There were lights now from a police car coming up Belgrade. He closed his eyes. "I'm doing what I have to do for her, then it doesn't matter what happens to me." He asked, "Do you pray?"

"I do. I do." Her voice was shrill, her eyes streaming. "I pray to stop! I pray to be good."

He pulled himself up. "Pray for me," he said, and limped away into the dark.

The cop had them all down on the sidewalk and the boys were in handcuffs and she was sitting with her back to a tree. The detective she knew came by, Lino Camacho, passing Slim and Diante and Eightball down on the ground with their hands tight against their backs and then outside where Jen was fighting a cop trying to get her into the back of a squad car, saying, "I didn't do shit, what'd I do?"

Lino shook his head at Jen, that way the cops did like they were sad about something, "Yeah, Jennifer. You tell that story. You stick with that story when the judge asks you about how you brought your best friend to these boys to get cut up."

It took Bertie a while to get what had happened, that it was Jen who had given her up to the boys who knew Marty Wurtz. That they were getting her high, working themselves up to cutting her because somebody was afraid she was going to talk about what she'd seen when those guys had tried to snatch Patrick Mullen's daughter Frannie off the street down by the Pour House on Clearfield street. Lino had to explain it a few times, telling her he had been looking all over for her and he was glad she was safe and wasn't it better if she told her story? That if she told what she saw he'd be able to protect her and her family.

She was quiet, watching, sitting in the old cemetery. Slim was yelling things about her and about the cops and trying to blink away the blood in his eyes from Patrick beating him and his friends. Eightball moaned on the ground and asked for somebody to help him up. Across Tulip Street she saw Patrick standing in a shadowed doorway across Memphis, illuminated only by the blue and red strobes of the police car lights. He stood motionless, his silhouette appearing and disappearing in the pulsing light. She saw his head dip and then a flare of light near his face as he lit another cigarette. What had he said? That he was doing it for somebody. For *her*, he had said. And that then it wouldn't matter what happened to him. Lino looked from Bertie to Brianna's pink heart and crossed himself. The red lights played across the trees and houses and the canted old stones around her in the cemetery, and she saw what she had never seen before, that just there, a few feet from where they had buried Brianna, was the grave of Nora Mullen.

Frannie sat on the edge of the bed in a bra and panties and Mari's mother, Teresa, came in and gave her the clothes she'd washed. "The shirt had to go," she said, and handed Frannie one of Mari's black tank tops. When she was dressed she stood by the door, but Teresa took her hand and made her sit by the *boveda*, a low table just off the kitchen that was like an altar covered with polished shells, flowers, a dried starfish, photographs with curled edges of people that must have been grandparents and aunts and uncles. Glass-eyed dolls in bright dresses with lips painted pink and purple. Teresa lit the candles, poured a glass of rum, talked to the orishas on Frannie's behalf. Mari came in from her shift, began to say something when she saw the two of them with heads bowed and held a finger to her own lips. She hovered while her mother murmured prayers in Spanish. Frannie caught a few words she knew, names of saints and spirits, *santos* and *orishas* and the virgin mother. Mari took off her gun and put it in the gun safe in the hall, took off her belt and poured herself a shot from the bottle of Don Q.

Teresa lifted one of the tall glass cylinders and lit the wick. She said, "It ain't enough you burn the candles. You got to read the flame. My aunt Mapita, she knew all the ways. If it burns clean that's one thing, if it sizzles or sparks that's something else."

Frannie heard Mari click her tongue. "Is that the black, *Mai*? Why the black, why not the white?"

Her mother looked at her and lifted her eyebrows, an expression Frannie knew from her own mother that said, *Who's in charge here?* Teresa asked her daughter, "You want to do this? You the expert?"

"No, *Mai*, Jesus. Just saying . . . why the black?" Her voice trailing off under her mother's hard stare.

Frannie looked from the mother to the daughter. "What does it mean?"

Teresa covered Frannie's pale hand with her own. "The white is to keep evil away."

"I don't want that?"

"No." The woman sat back, her dark hair coming undone, the ends showing red. "The white is so evil don't find you, like, let the spirits pass by the house. I know you since you were thirteen, running around *al garete* in the street, like a runaway, and fighting everyone. Girls, boys, you don't care. You're not going to run, *mija*. You're going to fight. So, not the white. The black. That's the color to destroy the evil, to get the power over it." She took the shot glass from Mari's hands and threw back the rum and then smacked her lips. She winked. "The black, *mija*. So you fight the devil, and you win."

# 19

At the gym on Lemon Street Jimmy Coonan and Cam stood in the dark and waited for the word from Adolph Wurtz. Adolph sat with his back to them looking at the window, at the place where there would be a view out to the street if all the windows weren't painted over. Jimmy let a sigh go, rattled the keys in his pocket. He'd wanted a drink, almost stopped to get one before he came back up from seeing his Polish girl down in Bridesburg.

Adolph didn't turn around. "What'd he say?"

"Tony?"

"Tony. What did he say? How did he sound?" Inside the club it was dark except for the lights in Adolph's office, a square of light in the black expanse of the empty gym. Outside the office the two kids Kevin and Eddie Mac in tracksuits sitting in the dark on chairs against the wall, Kevin squinting at the tiny screen of a phone and Eddie watching Jimmy and Cam as if they might do something.

"Fine, I don't know. I asked could we talk to him and he said sure. There wasn't a conversation."

The place had been built as a church, still had stained-glass windows high up on the walls, though most of them had been painted over. Adolph's office had been the apse, and the sacristy had become the locker room, which for a long time had seemed right to Jimmy Coonan. On the walls were posters of the fighters Adolph had trained, including a bright red poster featuring Rudy in his prime, gloves up, one dark eye squinting.

Rudy had been something then, twenty years ago. Jimmy remembered Adolph working him, the kid snapping punches at the bag with his ankles tethered by a two-foot band to teach him to keep his feet under him, each punch landing with a sound like a gunshot and the rattle of the chains holding the bag and a hissing breath through Rudy's clenched teeth so it was like Rudy was a machine that ran on steam and sweat. He'd gotten older, they all had, but he'd kept the bulk in his shoulders, Rudy, and it was impossible to imagine Patrick Mullen getting the best of him. Jimmy hadn't seen Rudy's body yet, but he'd heard from Kevin and Eddie Mac, the two kids who'd been with Adolph that morning, that it had been bad. Rudy bled out so that his skin was blue and white and cold as stone, left out in the street for everybody in Port Richmond to see.

Now Adolph wanted somebody to pay, and for Jimmy

it was a long walk across the black space, Adolph with a look screwed onto his face, that thing he did, moving his lips like he was chewing his own teeth. Jimmy knew it was Adolph working himself up.

"Who else was there?"

"The usual bunch. Joey Pep. Chuckie, Harry Buono. That fat Angelo Santaguida."

"They seem okay?"

"I don't know, Adolph. I can't tell with them guys. Good or bad they look the same at me, out of the corners of their eyes."

"You don't know why I'm asking, you make me drag it out of you?"

"I know, Adolph, I just couldn't tell, okay? Tony's the one, anyway, right? Them other guys do what he says. I figure he wants it to be over, one way or the other. He didn't say he was happy or unhappy, but what would he say? It would be better we got Patrick Mullen in a hole, right?"

The door opened across the old church and they all turned to look: Adolph, Jimmy, Cam, and the two tall boys. Eddie Mac sat up straight in his chair and Kevin put his phone inside his jacket and left his hand there. There was a moment, the door open, the cold wind pushing at the corners of the old posters on the walls, a figure framed in the door, somebody getting the layout and the feel of the room. Eddie Mac stood up but didn't move from in front of the chair.

The first figure stepped in and then another came

through and moved into the light. Tony Buck, white haired, big across the middle, wearing a white jacket and cap and glasses that made his eyes look bigger, so that he seemed to be staring intently at everyone in the room. Kevin stood up then and Eddie Mac carried a chair from the wall so the old man could sit. Adolph got up, too, and crossed to shake Tony's hand and then retreated back behind the desk. Jimmy Coonan heard Tony Buck sigh when he sat down and watched the large eyes go around the room, looking at the posters, the empty ring, the heavy bags swaying on their chains. Harry Buono followed him and stood behind him at his shoulder and behind him were two young guys Jimmy didn't know who stood in the dark beyond the circle of light from Adolph's desk lamp.

Tony looked at the poster of Rudy. "I'm sorry what happened to Rudy. He was a good kid."

"Thanks, Tony. We got the flowers. His mother appreciated it."

"Too many guys, young guys. I don't know. This business we all lost friends, children. You have to ask if it's worth it, all the pain of it."

"His mother's heartbroken. His kids."

"That why I say, for what, Adolph? Is it worth it that kind of pain?"

Adolph nodded. "Are you asking me like a question with no answer, like what are you going to do? Or do you mean me, Tony? Us, right now?"

"I'm saying, do you know what you're doing is worth what it costs? You know that to be true?"

"You don't have to ask that, Tony."

"I'm asking."

Jimmy looked at Cam out of the corner of his eye without moving and Cam raised his eyebrows. The old men, maybe the same age: Tony slow and fat, the breathing they could hear ten feet away, and Adolph, still hard, compact. Both of them showing power like they were lit from within. Tony cold and remote, slow, his voice a quiet rumble like the grinding of rocks under a mountain, and Adolph hot, a taut wire vibrating. Adolph said, "I gave my life to this local. Big John brought me into this thing and him and me and a couple of other guys built it up from nothing. From an idea. Yeah, we got help from you guys, from Passyunk Avenue, and we did things for that help, and we paid for it. And when the feds took an interest we stood up and took our lumps."

Harry Buono spoke for the first time. "Five years," he said.

"That's right, Harry. Five years I did, and never asked for anything. Never talked to nobody, Tony, which I shouldn't have to say. Marion. Atlanta." Adolph stood up again, but stayed behind the desk. "And now Rudy's dead. My boy. There's not one thing I haven't done to earn this local. I got this Patrick Mullen situation now and I'm going to handle that like I always handled everything and I don't ask you to do nothing but let it happen."

Tony nodded. "You been like a soldier, Adolph." He got up then, and Adolph walked around the desk and Tony took his hand. "I'm going to say good night. You talk with Harry here, okay?"

"Sure, Tony." Adolph looked at Jimmy Coonan and Jimmy raised one shoulder. Who knew what to think?

One of the young Italian kids got the door and went out with Tony, leaving Harry standing in the gym. He sat in the chair and took out a cigarette. He held out the pack and offered it around but Adolph shook his head and the rest of them stood still. Harry said, "Where you stand right now? Today. With the Patrick Mullen thing."

Adolph looked at Jimmy, who said, "We got guys at the houses of the two girls, the one was a cop and the other one, the drunk. They show up there we'll pick them up."

"That's it?" Jimmy looked at him, and Harry went on. "What about the girlfriend?"

"She's locked up."

"We know where?"

He shook his head. "FBI has her, what we heard."

Harry nodded, thinking. He let a long stream of cigarette smoke go. "That thing up in the Northeast, that was you idiots, right?"

Jimmy looked at Adolph out of the corner of his eye, watching him tighten up. Jimmy said, "We had good information, we took a shot."

"Information how?"

Adolph shook his head. "I got friends. A guy, feeds me information when I need it."

"Who?"

"You don't need to know. I start talking about it, the source will dry up."

Harry nodded. "We'll see. You know when you hear from me, you're hearing from Tony Buck, right? My mouth moves, it's Tony's voice coming out."

Jimmy looked at Adolph, who nodded and said, "Yeah."

"Then you tell me 'no,' you're telling Tony 'no.'" He looked from Adolph to Jimmy to the kids. "You took a shot, you said."

Jimmy said, "It went wrong, but we cleaned it up. No bodies, no mess, nobody got arrested. Nobody got nothing. Like it never happened."

"Yeah, maybe. But here's Tony Buck's problem. Every time you try and miss, every time Patrick Mullen or his daughter go on the news, that's a story about the local, and all that history, and Tony and the rest of us see our faces on the news. That's not happening again."

They all nodded. Harry said, "So, you don't want to tell me who your source is, that's fine if he does what we need him to. We're doing this one more time." He held up an index finger, crooked and knotty. "Once. You think you grab the daughter and you get Patrick, fine. You do what you have to do. I don't care how it gets done. You're so proud of all the shit you done, Adolph, all the money you made off the union? All that time you did in Atlanta, those five years we spent putting the feds to sleep. They got that bullshit trustee and they think they run the local now, but it's Tony's local and it's Tony's call who gets what.

"Them old days you're so proud of, you fucking guys were on the news every week, and the feds had to step up and everybody went to jail." He held a finger to his lips and lowered his voice. "But now it's all quiet, you get that? Tony's not going to jail. I'm not going to jail. You know who you remind me of? All this talk about how you built the local, how it all should come to you? Hoffa. Jimmy Hoffa, he did time for union bullshit, too. And he came out and he's giving interviews and he's saying he's getting the union back. You know what happened to Jimmy Hoffa? You know where he is now?" He looked at them, each in turn, Adolph and Jimmy and the young guys. "Yeah," he said. "Me neither."

# 20

It had rained the last night at Mari's and the rain had frozen as it fell so that the streets and cars were glazed with silver crystals and people walked with exaggerated care, lifting and dropping each foot, thinking about each step before they made it. Frannie had lost her gloves somewhere between the crime scene and the lockup and Mari's house and her hands were raw from scraping the ice off the Audi with no gloves. She turned on the radio just long enough to hear that snow was coming and then turned it back off so she could try to think about what to do next.

When she got home her house was dark and cold, and she turned up the heater and kept her coat on, carrying in the black duffel with her pistols and the broken-down Winchester shotgun Sleeper had given her the night she went to find Tina at the hospital. The cops had kept the Glock she'd been carrying on Levick Street and she didn't know when she would see it again. She double-locked the doors and then dragged the trashcan in front of the refrigerator and dumped everything except a jar of pickles and couple of cans of diet Coke. She opened one and walked back into the front room and spun the dial on her gun safe. Working by the slanting orange light coming through the front windows she pulled out a long-barreled Colt automatic and laid it on the carpet next to the small Glock 27. She found the boxes of .40 and .45 ammunition and loaded the guns and the extra magazines, feeling more power as she pushed in each bright shell, thinking of Teresa and the candles. When the guns were loaded she hefted them, feeling the difference between the guns empty and the guns ready to work, and she hiked the leg of her jeans and strapped on the ankle rig. She assembled the Winchester and loaded it with squat black shotgun shells from the box Sleeper had left her. *Fight the devil*, she thought. *Fight the devil and win.* She rocked back on the carpet to lean against the couch and sipped at the can, the shotgun across her knees, and after a minute she fell asleep.

She woke with a start, disoriented, the cold white sun lower, flaring before it dropped behind the walls of the old prison. She gripped the shotgun hard and looked hard around her for a moment before she saw her phone vibrating on the floor where she had left it, the screen bright in the darkening room. It was a 610 number she didn't know.

"Frannie Mullen."

The voice on the other end was uncertain. "Frannie, it's, uh, Giselle? Mae's friend?" Frannie could hear something in the background, a voice rising and falling, and something dropped inside her.

"Sure, Giselle, what's up?"

"Oh, I don't mean to bother, I'm just not sure, you know . . ."

"It's okay, really. How's Mae?"

"Oh, not good, really. I thought there was nothing in the house. I mean, I don't really drink myself, I just didn't think of everywhere there might be alcohol, and there was some wine I forgot about in a box in the basement." The woman running on, and Frannie felt her face go hot.

"Of course. I understand. It's not your fault, Giselle."

"I was gone at work and she was home alone." She heard the voice in the background get louder. *"Is that her?"* Mae's voice, from another room. *"Is that my sister?"*

To the woman Frannie said, "It's okay, Giselle, I'm on my way. I'll come get her, just don't let her leave the house."

"I'll do my best." The woman's voice uncertain. "I would, uh . . ." There was a muted crash and long and terrible laugh from somewhere else in the house, as if Mae had become a spirit, a poltergeist floating from room to room knocking pictures out of square and tipping glasses onto the floor. "If I were you? I would hurry."

———

Jimmy sat next to Adolph, who was behind the wheel of the Navigator parked on Bainbridge Street and watching the front of a coffee shop across Seventh. The sun was going down but the intersection was bright with lights from houses and shops and streetlights with haloes of icy fog.

"Who we looking for?"

"Shut up." Adolph looked at his watch. After a minute or two a black Crown Vic appeared, moving slowly along Seventh, whoever it was looking for a place to park, maybe, and Adolph pulled a black bag onto his lap and picked up his phone. He looked at the display and then rocked on his thin haunches to stick it in the pocket of his coat. Jimmy saw a gray-haired man in a neat suit come up the street the way the Crown Vic had gone, picking his way carefully along the iced-over street.

Adolph handed the bag to Jimmy. "Get out your phone."

Jimmy fished it out of his pocket and put it on the dash, and Adolph pointed at it. "In a minute I'm going to buzz you. You get out of the car and stand on the street, got it?"

"You want him to see me."

"I want you to do what I tell you. What I told you a hundred times already."

"Okay."

Adolph got out and slammed the door. He walked fast, like he always did, sure-footed on the glazed asphalt, crossing the street without looking behind him and going into the bright coffee shop. Jimmy watched him greet a neatly dressed man with gray hair and an expensive haircut, the man shaking hands and smiling, making some joke and pointing to a table in the back. Adolph jerked his head toward a table by the window and after a moment the guy followed, frowning, not liking that but going along. Because, Jimmy knew, when it was Adolph you went along. Jimmy opened the bag on the seat, glancing away for a minute and then back, watching the guy's reactions to Adolph talking. The guy listened, his eyebrows coming together, looking more and more unhappy about whatever Adolph was saying. Glancing at the street, not liking being out in front, not liking whatever Adolph was telling him. The guy's shoulders going up and down, the head going back and forth.

Jimmy knew the conversation even if he didn't know the guy or the situation. Adolph had a piece of the guy's business, or a hold on the guy. The Crown Vic said cop to Jimmy, so it was maybe a cop who owed money or a favor and now the money or the favor was due, and it was more than the cop could stand. Somebody who thought he was going to manage Adolph, hold him off. Pay later, or pay less, and Jimmy said to himself, *You are dreaming, pal.* Jimmy knew Adolph and knew how it went when Adolph wanted something, how it always went, which was Adolph's way.

The guy was shaking his head no, forming the words that Jimmy could see from across the street, and he pushed back in his chair. Adolph put his hand on the guy's arm and the guy's face went dead, as if somebody had stuck a gun in his ribs. The guy's head dropped and Adolph must have been explaining how it was going to be because for a minute the man didn't move, just listened to the voice telling him what was at stake, what the guy could lose. How bad it could go. After a minute the guy's face lifted, and now his pink skin had gone white and his eyes had gotten wide and he was looking around him, a little frantic, trying to keep it together but right there, at the edge of coming apart. Jimmy was fascinated by those moments when people turned back into animals, and here was this guy, this well-dressed and professional guy with his nice haircut and neat goatee and there was that *thing* coming out from behind his eyes, that presence that was inside us and only made itself known when things got as bad as they could be. The part of us that was left over from when we tore at each other with teeth and claws and only stopped when we tasted blood.

When the guy finally stood up, pointing at Adolph and saying something he thought was going to make a difference, his teeth bared, Adolph stuck a hand in his coat and the man shook his head, thinking maybe Adolph was going for a gun and doing that thing cops did when they were in the hot seat, that dismissive thing, lips pursed and a wave of the hand to remind you if you didn't know that they were untouchable. In the car the phone on the dash buzzed and Jimmy went into the bag.

Jimmy got out of the Navigator and stood on the street

and when the guy walked to the door Adolph said something and the guy stopped and Adolph got up slowly, taking his time, and put his arm around the guy, who went rigid. Adolph leaned in to the man and pointed across the street and the guy followed the line of Adolph's arm to where Jimmy stood under a streetlight and pointing a big digital camera. Jimmy found the button and pushed it, listening to the satisfying click it made, holding the button down so that it fired over and over again, the motor whirring and the shutter snapping fast. Through the lens Jimmy saw the cop bigger, his eyes wide and white, could make out the hairs in his gray goatee. The cop looked at Jimmy and then back at Adolph, who was holding up the phone now, showing him how he'd used it to record the conversation, pushing a button and holding it up to the cop's ear.

Adolph put the phone away and through the camera Jimmy watched the cop shut down, the last fight in him extinguished. He backed up against the cold stone wall and Adolph whispered quietly, one arm on the man's wrist and the other in his pocket. There was a word for it, Jimmy thought, and it came to him: *intimate*. The way Adolph leaned into the man's collar, whispering into his ear, touching his sleeve, almost seductive or sexual. The cop, who thought he had some power or some say or some distance from the thing, now getting that he was under Adolph's thumb, maybe finding he had been there all along. After a minute Adolph stood back, nodding, and then reaching out to close the cop's coat and straighten his tie for him, the cop holding himself rigid and waiting for it to be over. Jimmy thought of a kid on the first day of school, suffering his mother to smooth his hair and send him out to join the other kids at the bus stop.

Jimmy lowered the camera and Adolph nodded at him across the street, and Jimmy got back in the car and reached across to the driver's side and started it to get the heater going. Adolph came across the street toward the car and the cop stood where he was, leaning against the brick wall of the coffee shop and looking at nothing. The car door slamming made a hard pop that echoed in the quiet street and the cop came upright as if he'd heard a shot and then he moved away across Bainbridge toward his car, shuffling his feet, trying to keep his purchase on the ice. Jimmy felt almost bad for the guy, watching him go. He said, "What do you want me to do with the pictures?" but Adolph was starting the car and said, "It's good, driving. Instead of letting Kenny do it. Feels good. I forgot how easy it handles for a truck."

Frannie drove west, squinting into the last of the sun and trying to be aware of anyone who might be trailing behind her while she negotiated the sluggish river of traffic carrying her out Lancaster Avenue to the end of the Main Line. A couple of times she saw a bike three or four car lengths back carrying a rider who looked so much like Wyatt she had to force herself to stop staring into the rearview and once she had to jam on the brakes to avoid climbing the bumper of the car ahead. A bright ribbon of hot blood crawled the back of her neck, something that was guilt and shame and grief that she knew would be there in her forever, in her blood and her skin, a physical manifestation that would flare up whenever she thought of him, the way a burn scar feels the heat first, as if remembering the fire that made it.

Her phone rang, and she tried to read the numbers and drive. She wondered if she should let it ring, then finally hit the answer button. "Hello?"

"Frannie."

"Agent Ahearn."

"Good, it's you. I wasn't sure I had the right number."

"Well, I dumped my old phone after we talked last time. How did you reach me?"

"Detective Camacho gave it to me. I hope that's all right."

"No, it's fine. I'm glad you called. I got rid of the old phone so fast I lost almost all my numbers."

"Good. You're keeping safe?"

"Doing my best." She told him about having to move Mae but didn't tell him why. "I'm heading back to the city, but we won't stay. I'll work out a plan and get her safe." She was aware of her own voice, of trying to sound like she actually was on top of everything, had figured the angles and would act decisively.

"If you need a place to go, though, you call me and we'll work it out, right?"

"Thanks."

After the call ended, Marty stole looks from the passenger seat into the back of the van where Ahearn sat with the Stingray unit balanced on the seat next to him. Cam Coonan made a turn south onto Kelly Drive and joined a line of traffic inching along the river.

"Why didn't you keep her talking?"

Ahearn watched the display. "It doesn't matter."

"Why don't it matter?"

Ahearn sighed. "It's technical. You want to know how the machine works?"

Marty lifted his legs to turn in the seat to look at him, blinking, his shaved head looming. Ahearn said, "It's not like a tap, like on TV. It's picking up the signal. The unit fools her phone into thinking it's connected to a cell tower." He tapped the display, conscious of not trying to look at the two shotguns loosely wrapped in a green blanket on the floor at his feet, the black stocks and gray parkerized barrels visible to anyone who might look through the window. Any cop who might stop a van sitting too long in the wrong place.

"Where is she now?"

"I don't know. It doesn't have that long a range. But I know she's coming from the Main Line, so we're not more than a mile from where she's crossing the river, and we'll pick her up."

"Then what?"

"Then you call your grandfather and I'm out of it."

"We'll see you're out of it."

"Your grandfather doesn't want me around for that part."

"I don't think you get to say what he wants." Cam pulled into a turnout on the river side of the drive and they sat and watched the traffic coming out of the city, starting and stopping, people worried about the ice and the coming snow. The line of taillights flared red, a cab stopped short and a man in a Volvo laid on his horn.

Ahearn flinched from the horn sounding. He said, "You want me sitting here when you grab them? Maybe I get seen, maybe show up on a traffic camera or a cop's dash cam. Then what? You burn me, what's that buy you? I can do you and your grandfather a lot more good right where I am. On the inside, looking out."

"Yeah, or maybe you should be thinking about how to make sure it all goes as good as it can go. Maybe use that giant police brain of yours to tell me how we get them off the street with no drama."

There was a banging from the back of the van and Ahearn shook his head vigorously, as if denying he'd heard the noise. Marty said, "Shut up back there, you hear me?"

Ahearn pointed obliquely back at the source of the

noise. "Listen to me. That's a mistake. I did what Adolph asked. I got her here. But driving her around is a mistake." He stole a look. The girl was tied at the ankles and her hands were cuffed together. There was a piece of slick brown tape over her mouth and her eyes were wild. She screamed behind the tape and tried to move, but could only bang her head against the carpeted floor of the van.

Marty said, "What if we use her? Get her out where they can see her, they got to do what we say."

"Christ, no. You going to keep ahold of her *and* take control of the Mullens *and* disarm the other one, the one they're meeting? You'd need five more guys. You open that door and put her on her feet she'll be fighting you the whole time."

"Yeah, you got a point." Marty looked at him. "See, you can be a help when you want to be."

Ahearn spoke quietly, as if to himself. "I just want this fucking nightmare to be over."

"Well, you help us scoop 'em all up, you get your wish."

"And what then? Where are you going to take them?"

The line of cars stopped and started and at the curb the Volvo driver hit the horn again. Twice, three times, and the guy's face twisted behind the windshield, screaming something nobody could hear. Ahearn shook his head and spoke softly, "What are you so angry about, Volvo man? What do you need?"

Marty reached over in front of Cam and hit the horn and Ahearn jumped. Under her tape, Tina tried to scream again. Marty said, "Maybe he just needs to make noise.

Tell everybody's he's here. Tell everybody they should all do what he says." He hit the horn again and turned to look down at Red Ahearn. "Maybe everybody should do what the man with the horn says, and stop asking fucking questions."

# 21

Frannie reached Giselle's house after dark, a development out in Chester County called Harriton Estates where half-built faux farmhouses loomed on wide plots of wilted brown grass cut by a broad asphalt lane that was cracked and showing weeds. She stopped the car and looked back the way she had come, sitting for a full minute. No one else pulled in, no white vans or low-slung Harleys, and she got out into a cold wind that almost pulled the car door from her hands. She squinted against the cold glare and climbed the humped lawn toward the house.

Giselle pulled open the door as she reached it, her skin crimson and her smile lopsided and guilty. She was a small woman wearing a kelly green sweater and good makeup that rendered her face with a precise geometry, one of Mae's wealthy friends from before her life went off the rails. "I'm sorry," she whispered.

Frannie shook her head. "No, I'm sorry, really. She's been under so much strain. It was a lot to take on and I'm just . . ." Frannie shrugged. "I'll take her." She had almost said, *I'll take her home,* but that wasn't possible, was it? She hadn't thought about more than coming to get Mae, to relieve her overwhelmed friend. Where would they go now?

Mae's bags were packed and standing in the entryway, Frannie wondering if Mae or Giselle had done the packing. The woman went on, still whispering. "She's upstairs. She's much calmer." Frannie noticed a shard of white crockery on the good stone of the entryway and drew a sharp breath, but Giselle put her hand on Frannie's arm. "I know she feels terrible."

"She always does." Frannie surprising herself with the uncharitable edge to her voice. So she said, "She's lost a lot. Dealt with a lot this last couple of years." After a minute of wondering at her own capacity for annoyance she nodded and went upstairs.


Mae sat on the edge of the bed in her bright red coat, picking at a bandage in the palm of her left hand. Her eyes were pink and swollen and her head swayed slightly with a tremor, as if an unseen hand pushed rhythmically at the back of her neck. She said, "I called my sponsor. I called Sunrise House. They'll take me back if you can drive me there."

"Mae—"

"Please don't. Please don't start, Frannie." She dropped

her head and held up her bandaged hand, as if her sister had raised a fist to her. "Just get me out of here. I'm coming out of my skin."

Frannie took a cautious step into the room, moving crabwise along the wall to lean against a cherry armoire, her arms crossed, aware of trying to seem supportive, of trying to project a calm she didn't feel. She spoke softly. "I'll take you. Out of here. We'll go. I just don't think we can go to . . ." She trailed off, trying not to use the word rehab, anything that might sound like a reproach. "We shouldn't go anywhere you're known. Anywhere they might expect."

Mae stopped rocking, looked at her sister. "Anywhere I'm known?"

"Right. Patrick, his people, whoever these guys are. We have to stay away from anywhere they might expect us to be."

Mae looked over at a framed picture on the nightstand, a picture of Giselle and her family. Two boys with wide shoulders, a gray-haired man, all of them smiling under black trees, a pile of bright orange leaves at their feet. She lifted a finger to touch each face in turn, then captured the sleeve of her coat in her hand and wiped off the smudge she had left on the glass. "Where they might expect us to be," she said, her voice empty. "Where they might expect us to be."

Frannie reached a hand out, very slowly, fingers hanging, the way someone might reach out to touch an unfamiliar housecat. "Mae," she said.

"Where would they expect us to be? Where *do* you expect to find the Mullens? What's our habitat?" She bared her teeth, a twisting of the mouth that was meant to look like a smile. "Rehab. Maybe a hospital, when things get bad?" Frannie touched her sister, closed her hand slowly on Mae's thin arm through the coat. Mae said, "Prison. That's a good bet, you're looking for a Mullen. Or the graveyard."

Frannie sat next to her sister, then, putting her arms around her, a gesture so unfamiliar that they both stiffened for a minute until Mae let a long breath go and gathered her sister's arm in both of hers. Frannie remembered something then with a clarity so sharp it dissolved the room around her: She and Mae, small as lambs, huddled in the space between a bed and the dresser under a tent made from a pink blanket, and from downstairs the sounds of their mother and father, of screaming and splintering wood, and a wild howling as if the house itself were being consumed by an animal. Mae saying, then in the house they'd grown up in and now, in the strange room with the wind hissing in the dead grass outside the window and the clouds going by the moon, blue and black. Mae with her small voice. *Don't let me go,* she'd said, and said again now. "Please, please, please. Don't let me die."

It began to snow harder as they drove back toward Philadelphia, the wide and luminous flakes making white streaks against the black as they broke around the car. It made Frannie think of being in a spaceship, the two of them, of moving through black space and numberless stars.

Where could they go? A hotel would get them out of the weather, but she couldn't leave Mae there to go out and look for Patrick and she was tired of hiding. She needed somewhere safe, somewhere where Mae would have somebody who could handle whatever came up while Frannie went out and did what she needed to do. Mari would take her, but Frannie wouldn't put her in that position again. She picked up her cell phone and looked at it and made a noise of frustration.

Mae watched her. "What?"

"This cell phone. When we dumped the old ones I lost my numbers and now I'm trying to remember some of them."

Mae fished in her bag. "Is it one I'd have?"

"Mae."

"What?"

"I told you to dump the phone."

"I did. As soon as you told me to I went to the store and got a new one."

"Then how did you keep your numbers?"

"The kid at the store pulled the little card out of it and put it in the new phone." She held it up, paging through her contacts. "See? Whose number did you need?"

"The card? The SIM card? Jesus, Mae, that's how the

phone is tracked. Moving the SIM card is like you never got rid of the old phone."

"I didn't know that! You didn't say anything like that!"

Frannie hit the brakes and the car began to fishtail, the sound of the antilock system like gravel under the tires. She lifted her foot and let the car coast, looking up and down the road for a place to pull over. They were on Spring Mill Road heading toward the river in a sluggish line of cars. She saw a turnoff and slipped out of the flow of traffic to stop short on a short driveway that led downhill toward a broad expanse of grass that might have been a park or a golf course. The car stopped hard, slid and stopped again. Mae grabbed the phone out of Frannie's hands and jumped out of the car.

"Mae!" She watched through the open door as her sister climbed over a split-rail fence and ran down into a field, the air thick with snow. Frannie switched off the car and got out into the silence and Mae stopped, a tall figure with black hair and a red coat facing away toward the trees.

Frannie walked down through the thick flakes and stood by her sister. The headlights made a ribbon of bright light over their heads, a space filled with suspended flakes of snow lit yellow so they looked like sparks from a distant fire. Mae held up the phone in one red hand. "If we didn't do anything, would they come? Would they follow the signal or whatever and come to us?"

"I don't know. Maybe."

"What would you do if they came?"

"Fight them. I'm sure as shit tired of running away."

"Could you beat him? Patrick?"

"I don't know. Probably not. He's got a lot of people with him."

The snow fell harder and Frannie could hear it, a rushing whisper as it came, settling on the grass and the trees and their coats and in their hair. Mae pulled her arm back and threw the phone hard and it disappeared into the field. The snow on the grass at their feet glowed dully, as if lit from within.

Mae took Frannie's hand, cold and wet as a stick. "We're no good at life, are we? You and me?"

"No, I guess we're not."

"But I realized this, you know? This much about myself, sitting on my little pathetic stack of luggage at Giselle's house."

"What?"

"I still want to be alive. I don't want to die, and I sure don't want to drink myself to death or let somebody kill me for things I didn't do."

"No." Mae turned to look at her and smiled, her teeth clicking in the cold. Frannie said, "That's good, Mae. That's *good*. I mean it." She turned and nodded her head back at the car. "We should go, though."

They started moving, their breath making white clouds of steam. Mae asked, "Where to? Where can we go?"

"I don't know. Somewhere. We'll find the right place."

"And then what?"

"And then we'll call them. We'll make them come to us and we'll end it." They reached the edge of the field, struggled up the low hill in the deepening snow. Frannie crossed the fence and reached out for her sister. They stopped for a moment at the car, shaking the snow out of their hair and looking toward the blue glare beyond the trees that was the city under the snow. They got into the car and slammed the doors, and Frannie eased back into the traffic heading toward the expressway and the bridge over the Schuylkill. Back among the cars behind her she saw a single headlight, weaving in and out of the line of snowbound traffic. A motorcycle.

Frannie said "shit" under her breath, then lifted her phone and dialed one of the few numbers she'd memorized. When the call connected to his voicemail she said, "Eric. Call me," and then dropped the phone on the console.

They were silent for a while, the trees along the river thinning as they got closer to town, Frannie pushing the Audi, weaving in and out of the lines, using the shoulders and watching the rearview more than was safe. They came around a long curve and passed under a railroad bridge and there was the city suddenly looming in the dark, the tops of the buildings lost in clouds and halos of snow encircling the streetlights. Across the river on Kelly Drive an ambulance moved in a shower of red and blue. The sisters watched it go and Mae said, "Teach me how to fight."

The museum sat on the crest of a small hill and a man and two small girls were sledding on the front steps under lights that stained the whirling snow a chemical yellow. The girls were small and sleek in bright parkas and shot down fast while Frannie and Mae watched from the top of the stairs, Mae wincing with motherly empathy as their tiny plastic sleds dropped down and spun away into the dark space at the bottom of the stone steps. It was something the neighborhood people did, Frannie knew, had seen the families coming out of the Fairmount neighborhoods on snowy days to pack the snow into ramps over the stairs. The two little girls worked fast, as if on a deadline, jumping up and towing the blue plastic toboggans to the top to make another run, and another. When one of the girls passed close to them her face was set, focused, not the face of a child at play but of someone working methodically at a task. Their father shot his arms into the air at the end of every run.

Frannie had a sense of competition, a score being kept, and she watched Mae counting the completed runs, her face screwed up in concentration. She asked her sister, "Who do you want to win?"

Mae said, "Whoever can't."

Inside the museum was dark and quiet, and there were Christmas trees along the stairway leading up to the statue of Diana. They waited, Frannie scanning every face while Mae fidgeted.

"I can't stand not having a phone."

"We'll get you one tomorrow."

"Okay. I just want to call Tansy."

Frannie handed her phone to Mae, who took it and stepped away toward a side gallery. "Stay where I can see you."

Frannie heard her sister's voice as a series of chirps, distorted by distance and the echoes off the stone walls, and she was struck again by how Mae could always sound cheerful and busy and full of good news when she spoke to her daughter. Her absences rendered as adventures, full of surprises and detours and chance meetings with exotic characters. She saw Mae lift her hand as she whispered into the phone, making a broad sweep in front of a painting as she described it and in the same instant Frannie recognized it as another Homer, like the painting from the therapist's office. This one showed two men hanging on a line above gray waves, one unconscious and the other obscured by a red rag.

Frannie had been to a seminar run for cops by a woman, an art historian, who showed them sixteenth- and seventeenth-century paintings and told them to describe what they saw. It was supposed to help them assess a scene or think about how to describe a suspect to somebody else who might have to find that suspect or pick him out of a crowd. She told them to avoid words like "obviously," or "clearly," because nothing was obvious or clear. Frannie was paired with a thick-necked captain from the NYPD, the two of them tasked with examining a seventeenth-century painting of a men in black armor restraining a muscled giant. Samson captured by the Philistines, the woman said. She asked them to strip away everything they knew about the story, the biblical setting, and tell her what they saw. The captain squinted for a minute, then muttered out of the side of his mouth. "Someone's getting their ass beat."

Frannie watched Mae and the painting on the wall and wondered what she should be seeing. What she was missing. She tried to back it all up in her head to when she'd been running on the parkway on the bottom of the hill below the museum, fifty yards from where she sat at that moment, and the van had come for her. But that wasn't the start of it, not really. There was a difference, she knew, between the way she had seen things and the way they had happened. The first thing wasn't the men trying to grab her. It was whatever had made her father decide he had to get out of Pollock and come back. Her father had broken out of prison, and he had killed Rudy Wurtz, and then the men had tried to take her, once on the Parkway and again in Port Richmond.

Ahearn had told her that Patrick was coming for her and Mae. Shown her the journals, the crazy talk about murder. But Patrick went for Rudy Wurtz first. And why had he broken out of prison to begin with? Somebody tried to kill him, Ahearn said. But the one story undermined the other, didn't it? Was he a lunatic with no agenda but murder, or a man fighting for his life?

Mae walked back from the side gallery and handed the phone to Frannie, who was watching an older couple come in out of the snow. "God, this place is spooky, isn't it?"

"I thought it would be full of people." Frannie felt it, too. In the car the museum had seemed like a good idea, but now they were here it was too empty and dark, a maze of echoing chambers and stone caverns.

Mae sat on a step. "Do you remember Mom bringing us here?"

"Sure. Here, the river, the park. Chinatown. Anything to get out of the house and away from Patrick."

"It wasn't just that, I think. She wanted us to know art, I think. For us to have an appreciation for it."

"It didn't take. Not for me, anyway."

"Oh, maybe it did, in some way. I think sometimes it was something else, too. Something she wanted us to know about her."

"What do you mean?"

"This last time in Sunrise House one of the therapists asked me whether there was a history of depression in the family. I began to wonder if Mom was, you know, if she was depressed."

"Jesus, could you blame her?"

"No, of course not. Living with the abuse, the drinking? It would have broken anybody."

"So, what's your point?"

"I don't know. Just wondering if it was more than just Patrick and the crazy way we lived. I mean, do you remember her happy, really? Ever?"

"I don't remember any of us being happy."

"I guess."

Frannie shook her head. "Where are you going with this?"

"Do I have to be going somewhere? I'm just trying to know them, how they were. I mean, like it or not they're where we came from. I know you want to think you're just, you know . . . *You*, but we grew up in the house with the two of them." She reached up from the step and took her sister's hand. "They're in your head, Frannie. They're in your memories. Not just mine."

The phone buzzed in Frannie's hands and she looked at it. "Sleeper's here."

"Why do you call him that?"

"It's a story. You should ask him to tell you."

"He likes you, you know."

"I know. I don't want to think about it now."

Frannie stood up and put her hand out to help Mae from the step. Mae said, "I'm so sorry about Wyatt."

"I know."

"I just didn't want you to think, you know, with everything, with falling off the wagon, with being so afraid all the time, that I wasn't thinking about you. About you losing him."

Frannie looked up the long flight of stairs at the statue

of Diana, the lithe young woman with the bow and the empty stare. "I don't know what I lost."

Mae asked her, "Is that a better way to think of it? Does that make it easier for you?"

"No. It's worse, I think. I'll never know." Mae nodded, tears standing out in her eyes. Frannie squeezed her hand. "We should go."

# 22

They moved out the front door, through the stone columns and across the plaza that was cut into squares to look down at the Eakins Oval and the statue of Washington. The girls with their sleds were gone and the street was quiet but for the cars headed to the expressway and down the wide parkway that led into the heart of the city. Sleeper was standing by his car, his Challenger, his hand in his coat and the door open.

Frannie put a hand up and they started down the steps, Frannie conscious of shielding Mae with her body, not liking the gigantic scale of the space and forcing herself to think of it as good to be out in the open where it would be more difficult for anyone to try anything. At the bottom of the stairs they began to pick up the pace and Frannie heard the deep mechanical rattle of a motorcycle engine idling. She slowed and gripped Mae's arm tighter and her sister almost slipped on the icy step and made a noise in her throat that might have been a stifled word or just a frightened sound, the call of a startled bird. They froze there, Frannie trying to see around the corner to where Spring Garden Street and Kelly Drive split, trying to remember the geography of the place.

Sleeper saw them stop and went into alert, backing up against the car and swinging his head left and right. There were too many cars coming and going, sliding around the circle, pausing, jockeying for position. It was too much to watch and hard to fix on anything as meaningful. He shook his head and just waved his arm hard. Anything they did was better than staying where they were. Frannie bent her head to Mae's ear. "Run."

They loped awkwardly down the steps, Sleeper waving them on, his hand out. They had reached the bottom of the stairs where the lights were fewer and the trees threw shadows over the street and created cover for anyone who might be standing in the dark. Frannie heard the motorcycle engine revving in the dark, but she couldn't see its source and tried to concentrate on crossing the long expanse of dark pavement to Sleeper's car.

They were there, standing at the car, Mae with one hand on the car door and Sleeper turned for that second to watch the sisters when the man stepped out of the shadow of an oak and they all heard the sound of a shotgun, the clack-clack of the slide that anybody who'd ever carried a gun would know. The sound froze Frannie and Sleeper and their reaction stopped Mae, who looked from one to the other, unsure what to do.

"Hold up."

A man's voice, another man, not the one who had racked the slide but another man with an identical gun a few paces behind and to the right of the first man. Frannie turned, slowly, and saw them clearly for the first time. They were both young, one taller and with close-cropped black hair, the other with a hoodie on, a pink hoodie with a Phillies logo and the broad shoulders of somebody who worked out every day. A fighter.

The one with the hoodie and the shotgun said, "I know you got guns, but there's nothing you can do here, right?" His friend stood rock still in the dark. It was hard to make out much, but the ends of the shotguns looked huge. Black holes rimmed with steel that were impossible to look away from. "If everybody just relaxes it would be better. It's not the coward move, right? It's the smart move. You could get one of us, maybe, if you were fast, but we'd definitely pull the trigger, both of us, and that splatter from the gun, you know what that would do." His voice was calm for somebody so young holding a shotgun in a public place. Frannie knew he wasn't a scared, desperate kid. He was somebody who'd been in the life, had maybe grown up in it.

"All you got to do now is put your hands on the car, right?" Frannie saw Mae's eyes, which had gone dull. She was conscious of her hands as soon as the kid had spoken, of their position in space, one on her sister and the other on the door of Sleeper's car. "We can't stay here all night, people. Let's go." He moved forward, then, bringing the gun out of the dark and closing the distance so that he was maybe twenty feet away, standing at the edge of the shadow so that the shotgun was plain but his features were still obscured. "Come on, man. One hand, then the other hand, and it's done. Can't nothing stop it now. Nothing you can think of, and nothing you can say."

There was more movement in the dark and another sound, a snap that Frannie also recognized, the sound of a pistol being cocked. She heard the kid with the hoodie draw a breath and saw a figure behind him, a taller man with wild hair and dark glasses on who had materialized next to the kid with the hoodie.

"The fuck," the kid with the hoodie said, and a hand reached out of the dark and took the shotgun slowly, slowly out of his hands. There was a big chrome pistol against the side of the kid's head, she saw, and he seemed suddenly paralyzed.

The figure holding the pistol spoke quietly, his voice deep and Frannie, thought, familiar. "Relax, now. Just give it up," and the other kid, the taller kid with the shaved head, pivoted the gun, but the man with the deep voice and the big pistol said, "Come on, now, son. You got no move."

He didn't. The man with the pistol had positioned himself on the far side of the kid with the hoodie and in the moment the tall kid took to make up his mind what he should do about the changing situation Sleeper came off the car and put his pistol against the side of his face and it was over. Sleeper got him down and was putting the cuffs on him when the third man, the man who had come out of the darkness pushed the kid with the hoodie down onto his knees and stepped forward and it was Wyatt.

Frannie sucked in a breath and her sister held her as she sagged to her knees. A pain grew up in her chest and Frannie blinked and grabbed at the air, and Mae could only keep her from falling into the street. Sleeper grabbed the other kid by the hair and forced him down and they all watched Frannie's face as the man came to put his hand on Frannie's arm and helped her to her feet.

"I'm sorry, I know," he said, in a rougher version of Wyatt's gentle drawl. "We didn't look nothing alike when we was kids, but the older we got . . ." He shrugged. "Our sister says our mama couldn't say which was which now, if we knew where she was to ask her."

Frannie slowly got her breath back. "My God," she said, and dropped her head and blinked. "I thought it was him."

In the light she could see he was taller than Wyatt had been, bigger in the shoulders, maybe, and his hair longer. He wore a jean jacket and over it Bandido colors, a black vest with patches in red and yellow. He stuck the pistol behind his back and put his hands in his pockets.

She shook her head, trying to smile. Frannie said, "No, I'm just embarrassed."

Mae said, "It's been a hard week."

The man said, "I'm Wyatt's brother, Dalton. I should have made myself known before now." He apologized to Frannie and Mae.

Frannie said, "You know us? Who we are?" She was still trying to process it all.

"When he was hiding that girl Wyatt called me, told me you all was in a spot. I'm the kind, I been real, uh, *watchful* in my life, as a rule." His gaze was direct, but his voice quiet. Frannie had the sense of a man who was more comfortable in shadow. It was impossible not to contrast him with Wyatt and his easy, disarming way. "I don't come at things direct as some do, maybe. I followed you all to this place and was going to try to introduce myself when I come on this here, these boys standing in the trees. I thought I'd maybe try to make myself of use." He pushed his glasses up and had the same steel blue eyes as his brother, but set deeper, she thought.

Frannie could feel Mae shaking. Her sister said, "Thank you, thank you." She held out her hand and touched Dalton's arm. "I was so scared." She stole glances at the two figures on the ground, in handcuffs now, and the guns they'd been carrying. "Look at them, they're children, for Christ's sake."

"Yeah, sometimes they're the most dangerous ones, the young ones."

The kid at Sleeper's feet, the one with the hoodie said, "You made a mistake, mister."

Dalton said, "I know, son. It won't be the last one." To Sleeper he said, "There's a van down around the side." He inclined his head around the corner toward the dark back lot. "I think there's another one in there."

They got the kids, now in handcuffs, up on their feet. Frannie picked up the nearest shotgun, a short-barreled twelve gauge with a plastic stock, and flipped it over to check the shell latch. She worked the shells out one at a time and jacked the last shell from the chamber and put the shells in her pockets and laid the gun in the trunk. While she worked she looked over her shoulder at Mae. "Go to my place. It's only a couple blocks away. It gets you off the street till we can get this mess cleaned up." Sleeper handed her the other shotgun and she emptied that one and then reloaded it. When she couldn't get another shell into the magazine she jacked a round into the chamber.

She turned to Dalton and he held up a hand. "I'll stay with her. You go on."

Sleeper handed Dalton the keys and pointed the two kids down into the dark side lot of the museum. "Let's go see if your friend wants to play." Dalton started the car and pulled out into the empty parkway, Mae at his side.

Sleeper watched the car disappear into the dark, then looked at Frannie. "You trust him?"

"He could have watched it all happen. He's Wyatt's brother. I have nothing else to go on." She turned and pointed the shotgun at the kid with the hoodie. "What's your name?"

"Fuck you."

"Yeah, I thought you looked familiar." Sleeper handed her the boy's wallet and she opened it with one hand, holding the shotgun up with the other. "Martin Wurtz. Huh. Your grandfather know you're out getting up to shit? Or did he put you up to this?"

The kid spit. Frannie said, "Nice." She pointed into the dark. "Let's go."

The van was in a driveway by the side entrance, parked next to a Dumpster and facing out toward the street. The museum loomed in fog that rose from the river and dimmed the green glow from the sparse light poles. Sleeper got Marty Wurtz and Cam Coonan in front of him and pointed Frannie into the boxwood and arborvitae closer to the wall. He spoke quietly to Marty and Cam. "Talk to your friend in the van. Tell him to open the window and stick his hands out."

Frannie moved slowly through the dark under the trees, keeping out of sight as best she could, trying to keep up with Sleeper and keep an eye on the windows of the van for any sign of who might be inside.

Martin Wurtz said, "Yeah, I don't think he's doing that."

The three of them were about forty feet from the van, which sat quiet and blank under the dull lights. "You'll talk to him, if you don't want him to get hurt."

Marty stepped forward, his hands up and the handcuffs catching the light. "Hey, fuckhead! You hear me in there?" He pointed over his shoulder at Sleeper. "Shoot this motherfucker right here."

There was a pop and a bright flash from inside the van and the side window blew out. Sleeper yelled *"Gun!"* and threw himself down and Cam Coonan did the same, his cuffed hands breaking his fall.

Martin Wurtz didn't flinch, but pointed toward Frannie. "There's another one over in the bushes." There were more shots, louder now with the windows of the van blown out. Frannie could hear the rounds snapping through the brush over her head and threw herself flat behind a rock, the heavy shotgun banging off the stone as she fell. She watched Sleeper return fire and lifted the barrel of the shotgun, trying to get a line of sight on the van. Cam Coonan lay flat, his eyes wide as bullets struck the ground around him, muttering under his breath and holding himself rigid.

Martin Wurtz looked from Sleeper on the ground to Frannie writhing behind the rock in the trees and then sprinted for the front door of the van. Sleeper cursed and yelled for him to stop, but he had reached the front door when there was another loud pop from inside the van and Marty dropped, his face hitting the asphalt, his lifeless body crumpled over his own cuffed hands as if he were hiding something. Sleeper opened up again and Frannie aimed at the window where she had seen the flash and fired the twelve gauge, feeling the hard jolt of the recoil in her shoulder. She rolled awkwardly to work the slide without leaving cover and fired again while Sleeper walked rounds across the expanse of the van, putting a series of holes at even spaces from the driver's door to the rear bumper.

There was a moment of silence, then a woman's scream. Frannie and Sleeper met each other's eyes, then Frannie jumped up and ran for the van. There was a coughing noise and the van engine sputtered to life. Frannie had almost reached the back of the van when it jerked forward at the same instant Frannie saw Tina O'Bannon pull herself up into the rear window, her hands cuffed and a piece of tape hanging from her mouth. There were bits of glass in her hair and blood ran from a cut at her temple. Their eyes met, then the van surged forward, muscled the Dumpster aside with a metallic groan, and disappeared around the back of the lot toward Kelly Drive.

Frannie began running toward her car, Sleeper waving after her. She called, "He's got Tina!"

"I've got to stay with this one!" He pointed at the prone Cam.

"Call it in!"

"Who's behind the wheel?"

Frannie hit her jeans pockets for her keys as she ran, hearing Sleeper telling the Philadelphia police dispatcher that there was a late-model Chevy van heading east into the city with a kidnap victim in handcuffs. She got the Audi open and jumped in, bracing the shotgun against the opposite door while she cranked the ignition. The van shot across the Kelly Drive and Pennsylvania Avenue and she followed, fishing in her pockets for more shells for the twelve gauge as she drove.

The van fishtailed in a wide arc onto Twenty-fifth, narrowly missing a blue tour bus and forcing a red BMW up onto the curb where it sideswiped a fire hydrant that peeled a bright sheet of metal from the rear quarter panel from the car as it passed. Her phone rang and she answered it.

Sleeper said, "The cops have it. What's he doing?" Ahead of her the driver of the van cut the wheel hard at Fairmount to head east. The van's wheels spun and caught just as it connected with a parked Camry. The driver gunned the motor, leaving a trail of shattered plastic and chrome. She hit the speaker icon on her phone and threw it onto the console, trying to drive and pull shotgun shells from her pockets to spill on the seat next to her.

"He's having trouble holding the road in that thing!" She had to scream over the racing engine. "He's going to kill himself and Tina before the cops can get in on this."

"Can you bump him?"

"If I can get close enough."

"Who's driving? Is it Patrick at the wheel?"

"I can't get eyes on him."

They were a block from her apartment, the walls of the old Eastern State Penitentiary looming in the icy fog. As they came even with Twenty-fourth Street, the van lights flashed and a blue-striped PECO truck materialized from the side street, amber light bar glowing. Frannie pumped the brakes and cut right as the two-ton truck slid across the intersection, horn blaring as its wide rear end lost its grip on the ice and slid in a wide arc, clipping the back of the van.

Frannie smacked the wheel and screamed to herself as the van spun hard and smacked into a black Prius, crumpling it against the curb and the sign pole behind it and overturning a bright yellow newspaper box onto the sidewalk. She stood on the brakes and was out of the car before it stopped. She sprinted the last of the block to cross Twenty-fourth Street, pulling the pistol from her hip as she ran, the shotgun forgotten in the car. A man in an orange vest and hardhat was getting out of the truck, cursing and rubbing his arm. She pointed at him and screamed for him to get back in the cab. He reared back, startled at the sight of Frannie's wild look and the Colt in her hands and scrambled to get back in the truck.

She stopped, closer than was probably safe and watched the Chevy as it steamed and rattled, the engine still running raggedly. Thin blue smoke issued from the shattered hood and she could smell oil and battery acid. She pointed the gun, moving in a tight arc from the front to the rear of the van, unsure where a threat might come from and desperate to know if Tina was hurt, even if she no longer understood what their connection was, even if she was furious at herself, at her vulnerability, her concern for this confused and manipulated and directionless girl who had caused her so much trouble and pain.

The back door banged open, shards of smoked glass stuck to the window molding that dangled like a jagged tail. Frannie went still, trying to take in the scene and follow her training. To keep aware of the big picture, not get tunnel vision and be ready for threats from any direction. She saw two legs descend to the asphalt and then Tina O'Bannon came out, her arms extended. Behind her was Red Ahearn with a gun to her head. His face was streaked with blood and sweat and a piece of dark glass stuck to his cheek. His eyes looked unfocused and he limped as he spun Tina around to stand between him and Frannie.

He said, "I never fired my weapon. Not once in twenty-five years. All those hours at the range and I couldn't remember shit." He blinked and looked around himself. "Ah, Christ. I did a lot of good, you know? Twenty-five years. Got some bad people off the street. And it all ends like this, for this stupidity."

Frannie sighted down the barrel at him, shocked to see the man she'd trusted holding a hostage in the street, unable to think what to do next. She had expected to see strutting Adolph, or her father, frightened and diminished and ready to die. She could barely bring herself to speak.

"Red," she said. "Put the gun down. I don't . . ." She stopped. "Whatever happened, we can work it out. You know, Red, you've been here. Before. You've been where I am now. It's never as bad as it looks in this moment. You know something? You can tell it in court. Somebody put you up to this? Got something on you? Was it Patrick?"

"Your father?" He laughed. They could hear sirens now down Fairmount Avenue and see red and blue lights pulsing in the distant fog. "Your father. If he had just done what the fuck he was told, you know?" He pushed Tina out in front of him and she hunched into herself, shaking, her eyes full of tears, her body all protruding belly over stick-thin legs.

"Tell me, Agent Ahearn. Red."

"You know, I called him, to tell him what happened to Marty. Only I laid it on you. You and that other idiot. Eric Hansen."

"Who did you call? I don't understand."

"I called Adolph Wurtz. You really have no idea what's going on, do you?"

"No, I don't. Tell me. What about Adolph? Is he the one who tried to grab me and Mae? To get at Patrick?"

He drew himself up. "Fuck Patrick Mullen. I don't know why I bothered bringing him into this. That worthless animal. I hope he cuts your throat." He jerked his pistol up and put it to his temple and before Frannie could draw a breath to scream there was a pop and his body went rigid and dropped onto the black ice and was still.

# 23

Tina collapsed, her eyes rolling back in her head. Frannie fought panic as she picked her up from the frozen street and ran awkwardly toward her own apartment, just across the square from where the van had lost the road. She knew she shouldn't have moved the girl but her mind was racing and it seemed as good a course as any to get her out of the cold, to wait indoors for an ambulance to take her to the hospital.

Mae and Dalton stood at her door, watching the flashing lights and hearing the sirens. Dalton took Tina from her arms and they got her inside. She became more alert as they were wrapping her in blankets on Frannie's overstuffed couch.

"I'm all right, really. Just rattled, you know. I keep seeing the man and the gun and all that blood." Mae looked at Frannie, who said an ambulance was just a couple of minutes out and they'd get her checked out. Tina asked for a glass of water and Mae ran to the kitchen.

Frannie said, "I shouldn't have taken her off the street before they got there, but it's so damn cold out there. I had no way to keep her warm."

Dalton nodded. "You did right. They can find her here same as on the street."

She found her phone in a pocket stuffed with shotgun shells, called Sleeper and told him about the last conversation with Ahearn.

"I don't get it."

"I think I'm beginning to. You need to get Adolph Wurtz picked up right now. He knows his grandson is dead and he thinks we killed him. You and me."

"I'm on it. I'll be there in two minutes."

Tina said something to Mae, who sat by her head. Mae said, "She'd like your phone."

Frannie handed it to Tina, who nodded her thanks. "He got it, Ahearn, when he took me. I just want to call my sister. I want her to know I'm al right. I was on the phone with her at the safe house when Agent Ahearn came in and grabbed me. She'd think I'm dead."

The ambulance came across the square and Dalton went outside to flag it down. Mae and Frannie listened to Tina talking, reassuring her sister that she was okay and that she was with friends, describing Mae and Frannie but breaking down as she spoke. The ambulance crew came in as she was crying and they got Tina onto a stretcher.

When they were closing the doors Dalton held up his hand. "I'll go with her." He looked at Mae and Frannie. "My brother did what he did to protect that girl. I guess I'll want to see it through."

As the ambulance pulled away, Sleeper jogged across the square from the crash scene where Ahearn lay dead. He came holding his own phone up, telling Frannie, "We got the kid who was with Marty Wurtz on his way down to court to get processed. And I got FBI, Marshals, and Philly PD looking for Adolph Wurtz."

Frannie nodded, thoughtful. "Guess he got that call from Ahearn and hit the road. Think he'll come here?"

Sleeper lifted his shoulders. "I'd say, not if he was smart, but . . ."

"Yeah."

"We'll get RMPs out front here and get you two out of town till we pick him up. I think the rest of this is going to go fast."

Frannie got her phone out. "He tracked my phone. Not Scanlon, Ahearn. Working for Adolph? I can't put it all together."

"It's not the first time that kind of shit has happened. The Winter Hill Gang in Boston? Whitey Bulger had his own personal FBI guy who took Bulger's tips and made cases, clearing out the competition and fingering witnesses."

"He said something, that first day. That Bill Scanlon had lost a witness in protection when they were trying to prosecute Adolph Wurtz." She looked across the square at the flashing lights in the fog, hearing the voices and static from the police radios echo across the hollow from the stone walls of the old prison. "I figured it was Scanlon who was selling us out. All this time."

Mae walked back into the house and they followed. From the front door Sleeper said, "Sometimes that's how it is. It's right in front of you and you can't see it." Frannie picked up the glass that Tina had been drinking from and walked back into the dining room, a tiny space leading to the galley kitchen. She was trying to clear her head, but could still feel the weight of Tina in her arms as she shook and moaned and her eyelids flickered. She was trying not to picture how Ahearn looked, sprawled and dead in the street, his body sliding slowly, almost imperceptibly downhill toward the river on a thin layer of ice, when her father stepped into the dining room with a knife in his right hand and Frannie hit him.

She had no windup and the punch didn't have much in it, but he bounced off the door frame and she threw her body against his, driving into his upper arm and hitting his wrist so that he dropped the knife, and then hooking her arms under his leg and dumping him onto the ground, all of it so fast that it was only when he went down that she registered that she'd cracked her nose against the doorjamb. Patrick rolled, trying to get up, his right arm useless, and she kicked him in the ribs, the steel-toed CAT boot connecting solidly with his ribs. He made a noise then, something between a moan and a snarl and turned in on himself, clutching at his wounded side.

Frannie reached down to where he lay half under the dining room table and grabbed his shoulder to spin him onto his back. She drove a fist into his cheek, raised it again and snapped down wildly, finding the outside of his eye socket. Her knuckles flared with pain, and she wasn't defending herself, wasn't thinking at all, but was punishing him. She was a machine, an engine, like the boy in the tattoo shop with the design on his arm of the skin flayed away and the pistons and gears beneath as her arm went up and down, laying open cuts on his brows and his chin and his lips. She realized she was screaming, calling him liar and killer and motherfucker and there was spit and blood on her own lips and dripping down onto her hands, mingling with his blood and sweat.

Finally she stopped and fell back, heaving, and became aware of Sleeper standing in the doorway. She crawled across the floor and took his handcuffs from his belt and hit the ground again and jerked Patrick's arms up so that he roared with pain and she snapped the cuffs on him. She went into her holster and yanked the Colt loose.

Sleeper took a step and she pointed the gun at him. She screamed "Get out!" and wheeled to put the small black pistol to Patrick's temple.

"Open your eyes." She smacked him with the gun. "Open your eyes, you piece of shit." He finally did, though the right eye was swollen almost shut and he blinked to bring her into focus. "You know I'm going to kill you, right? You know you can't be alive in this world for one more minute. I couldn't stand it. I couldn't stand it."

"Frances," he said. "I know it. I knew it since I saw your face when you found me with your mother dead." His voice had gotten raspier, thinner, as if over the years in prison he'd been hollowed out and all that was left was hard shell. To hear his voice was to remember him from before, when she was young, the screaming and swearing but also the singing, the drunken sweetness of him crooning to her mother, dead Nora who never smiled, who made pictures of herself drowning. "That look in your eye, you have it still. I knew it would be something I'd pay for forever, putting that look in your eye."

"And Mae, do you know her? What she's been through? How she lives?" She sniffed, realizing she was crying, the tears now mixing with the blood. "No, you couldn't know. You wouldn't. But you'd come all this way, wouldn't you, to do what? To kill us? To do what you couldn't do then?"

Eric Hansen moved slowly, with great care, dropping to his knees, getting closer. She pivoted to keep Patrick's body between them. He held up his hands to show himself harmless. "Frannie," he said, something in his voice she'd never heard before. A softness she hadn't heard from anyone except Wyatt.

She shook her head. "If you're going to stay, you have to sit still and watch. I had one thing to do in my life. I know it now. I have to end this." She put one hand over Patrick's eyes. "Some people are born for one thing, and this is the thing I was born to do. To stop this."

She pulled the hammer back on the pistol. Patrick reached up, very slowly, and lifted her hand from his eyes. He blinked away the blood. He said softly, "I killed her. I did that."

"And I called you. I was the one who told you we had come home. I could never tell anybody. I was that ashamed. So it doesn't matter what happens to me. I was too stupid to know what you were, how terrible a thing you were. I called you, and you came to kill us."

"Yes, you called me. And I came. But not to kill her. To stop her."

"To stop her leaving you."

"No, Frances, no." His voice was soft, a whisper. "To stop her killing you."

She pushed the pistol hard against his temple, screwing it against his flesh so that he winced. "What? What the fuck did you say to me? What the fuck lie is that?"

"She left me a note, when she ran with you. She said what she'd do. She told me. I thought you would all be dead and I'd never see you again. But then you called me from the house and I came. You fell asleep, you and Mae. She waited until you were asleep. When I came in she was pouring gasoline down the stairs."

"She loved us. Even now you lie to me? Even now?"

"She did love you, but she was sick, Frannie. I thought I'd die with this, I thought I'd die, but I knew that you had to know. She poured gasoline in the house and was waiting there for you girls to be asleep when I came home. Because you called me. I loved you all."

She lifted the pistol and brought it down on his forehead, Sleeper jumping involuntarily when it connected, afraid the hammer would drop and the pistol would fire. Patrick moaned. "Oh my Lord Jesus." He put a hand on the new cut on his head. "She was sick, she was a sick woman and I was too drunk and stupid and angry to know how sick, Frances. She wanted to be an artist, but I wouldn't allow it. I wouldn't see her happy."

Frannie held the barrel of the pistol against his head and screamed, a long sound of anguish and rage and horror, her finger tensed on the trigger.

Patrick closed his eyes again. "I just had to tell you that it was calling me saved you. You and poor Mae. I tried to stop her, Nora, and she fought me. She was possessed with it, she wanted to die that much. Setting the house on fire." He reached up slowly, slowly again and touched her hand, the one that held the gun against her head. "You can do it. You can end me and it will all be all right. You know it now that you were the *good* one. I think for all you were just tiny you knew. You knew what she was and what I was." He nodded, smiling, tears running down the sides of his face. "Go, go ahead."

From the doorway Mae said, "Frannie."

She looked up then, at her sister, and at Sleeper, who was looking at her in a way he never had before, as if seeing her for the first time. He nodded at her, and they all watched, motionless as she lifted the gun away from Patrick's head and handed it over, her limbs shaking so badly that Sleeper had to take her bloody hand in both of his and gently pry it open. He slowly eased the hammer down and Frannie sat up and fell back against the wall, sobbing. Mae crossed the room and knelt and hugged her and they cried together.

Frannie, barely able to speak, asked her sister, "Is it true?" Her voice was thin, unrecognizable even to herself, her vocal cords like taut wires in her throat. She could feel the weight of the water behind her streaming eyes and she felt broken and sick.

Mae said, "She painted herself dead. She painted herself in the water, dead, and us there with her."

Patrick put his cuffed hands out to Sleeper, who helped him up into a chair. Patrick said, "I had to come back. They tried to kill me in Atlanta. That FBI man came to Pollock and told me they had threatened to kill my girls if I ever talked about them, Adolph and Rudy. They'd put those boys in prison onto killing me, he said. He told me what to do, who to talk to. Gave me a few dollars. So I could come home and put a stop to it if I could."

Sleeper said, "So you killed Rudy."

Patrick nodded. "I did. I would have killed them all."

"The FBI agent? What was his name?"

"He never said, but I knew who he was. Ahearn."

Sleeper looked at Frannie. "Red Ahearn."

Patrick shook his head again. "Yeah, that was him. I knew he was in Adolph's pocket somehow. It was why Adolph got so little time, I think. They made a witness disappear. Made it look like the case was weak. I knew Adolph had some kind of thing going with the feds. He wasn't smart enough to be that lucky. I still don't know how it all worked. But I do know what's it's like, to be in

with Adolph Wurtz. Sooner or later he wants everything, every little thing. Whatever you said you'd never
do, you do it, and still he wants more. So that agent, that
Ahearn, he knew his only way was to let me out and kill
them, kill them all. He called me again not an hour ago,
on Tina's phone. To tell me Adolph would be here. So I
came. I thought I'd find him here and kill him."

Sleeper got his phone out and went into the other
room, talking to somebody in the U.S. Attorney's office.
Frannie and Mae leaned back against the wall, holding
each other, and Patrick sat in a chair, his head bowed.

"He showed me something, Ahearn. A diary or something he said you wrote, about how you wanted us
dead."

Patrick raised his cuffed hands and touched his bleeding head. With his eyes down he said, "I didn't keep a
diary, but I did write. There was a program in prison,
something to help us deal with anger. They wanted us
to write, to write letters to people we wronged. I wrote
letters to you both, but I was afraid to send them. A
letter to your mother. Asking her why she did what she
did. Asking her to forgive me." He looked at her. "He
showed them to you? Ahearn did?"

She thought back to the first day. The conference room,
the copied sections of text. She shook her head. "He
showed me phrases, words. He said I shouldn't read it. It
was just enough to make you look crazy. Dangerous, to
me and Mae."

Patrick smiled, "It wouldn't have taken much, would

it?" He took a cloth from his pocket and tilted his head back, trying to stop the blood. Looking at the ceiling he said, "He must have been some desperate. Ahearn. Trying to keep Wurtz happy, hoping I'd make his problems go away. Trying to keep you and me apart." He looked at his daughter. "What did he hope? That I'd do the work and kill them all. And then what?"

She met his eyes. "And then I'd kill you."

From the other room they heard Sleeper spelling the names for someone. Adolph Wurtz and Red Ahearn. Marty and Patrick and Rudy. Bertie McCullough. The missing and the dead.

Frannie said, "I don't know what this changes."

He shook his head, wincing. "Nothing, I suppose. I just had to tell you what I knew."

"It was still you. Who ruined our lives. If she went crazy, it was you driving her there."

"Listen, you can't blame Tina for this. For any of this."

"I knew she was lying to me."

"She had to. I told her to. If she had told you the truth, would you have believed her?"

Mae answered. "No. That you had come to protect us? No. Not in a million years."

"I tried to call you. I did call you."

Frannie said, "Calls from the prison. I wouldn't take them. Wouldn't ever, no matter what happened."

He said, "I had to try."

Frannie felt pain in her head and the dull ache of her bones, her thoughts scrambled and erratic. And these things she thought she'd known about her mother and father? She wondered if this was what it was like to be tortured, to be stretched and broken on a rack. She said, "I still don't know what to believe."

He nodded, then touched his jaw with his cuffed hands. "You can fight. Where'd you learn all that?"

"The Police Athletic League. The old gym on East Clearfield. Cas taught me some."

"Cas Brodzinski." He smiled. "I fought at his place. He must have been some old when he taught you."

"I wore him out, I think. Too angry. No patience."

"He'd have seen that before. I was the same."

There was a shout from the front room and a crashing sound, as if the front door had been kicked off its hinges. Frannie jumped to her feet, knocking Mae off balance so that she had to clutch at the wall to keep from falling. There was a series of quick banging sounds, like the furniture was being pushed against the walls, fast, and Frannie had the crazy thought that someone was making space for a fight, or a dance. Patrick lifted his cuffed hands, swearing. "The keys, the *keys*," he whispered, but Sleeper had them. Along with her gun. Patrick searched the room wildly with his eyes and Frannie had taken two steps toward the living room when there was a shot, and they all froze.

Sleeper stumbled in through the doorway into the dining room, but his face was twisted and white with pain and Adolph had his collar in one dark fist. There was blood on Sleeper's white shirt, a stain that grew as Frannie watched, sickened. Adolph's other hand held the black Colt Frannie had handed over to Sleeper. Adolph's hair was rucked into tangles and his eyes were wild and glazed pink. His sleeve was torn at the elbow, showing the hard red muscles of his arm. He pushed Sleeper's face into the wall and then slid him down until his head connected with a low buffet table. His passage left a smear of red along the white plaster that made Frannie's breath catch in her throat.

Adolph lifted the gun and pointed it at each of them, Frannie and Mae and then Patrick, who leaned out of the chair, half standing.

"Which of you killed my Martin?" he asked, taking a step toward Patrick. "Was it you, you old prick?"

Patrick jutted his chin out like a man looking for a fight in a bar. "I'd have done, if I could. Like I did his father. Like I'll do you, in a minute." He pulled his hands apart hard, rattling the links of chain between his wrists. "Put that gun down, you Kraut fuck, and fight me. I'll end your line right here."

Adolph said, "We'll see." He pushed a chair over crossing the room and grabbed Frannie by the hair. "We'll see what ends." She pulled back, hard, and grabbed at the gun but he leveled it at Mae. "Be still," he said, and cocked the hammer of the pistol. Mae dropped to her knees next to Frannie, her eyes blurred and red, trying to grab at her sister's hands and pull her away but Adolph kicked her, hard, and she screamed and fell back on the rug. Adolph narrowed his eyes. "She looks like our Nora, that one. Doesn't she? Our lovely, lonely girl?"

Patrick took a step forward and Adolph jerked down on Frannie's arm, driving her to her knees. "Tell her something, Patrick. To take into the next world." Mae rolled to her knees, retched and moaned.

"You stupid old bastard. I'd have kept my mouth shut. Didn't I all that time?"

"You know who keeps their mouths shut?" Adolph's red eyes flared. "The dead." He pressed the Colt's barrel into the hollow under Frannie's chin. Mae pushed herself up and drove Patrick's knife into Adolph's stomach, screaming as she went, and he drew a sharp breath and reared back, punching down on her forehead so that she dropped motionless at his feet. Frannie grabbed his gun hand and twisted it, breaking his index finger, the sound plain as a dry twig snapped over a stone. Adolph bellowed his pain and rage and slapped at her head, losing the gun. Patrick launched himself across the room, catching Adolph under the chin with the chain of his cuffs and driving his white head back with such force the drywall tore and then shattered, showering both men with a cloud of gritty silver dust.

The two of them rolled, Adolph's hard biceps working as he punched savagely at Patrick's middle, her father twisting to get Adolph down so that the three links of silver chain between the handcuffs bit hard into the flesh of Adolph's neck. Patrick pulled himself up and bore down, screaming, and a jet of black blood sprayed from Adolph's throat to paint Patrick's face and neck. Sleeper, skin slick and white and his face empty, rolled onto the floor and grabbed at Adolph's left hand as it closed on the gun where he had dropped it. Sleeper pulled weakly, his hands shaking and wet. Adolph grabbed blindly and caught his thumb under the trigger and yanked the gun away. Frannie saw the barrel of the pistol moving and shielded Mae with her body, hearing Adolph's choked sob and Patrick's animal grunt as the men grappled and slammed at each other. The gun popped once, twice, making yellow-white sparks that glowed and vanished, and then the room was still.

# 24

The weather was hotter than she'd have thought, though on the drive down from the airport in Tulsa the ground looked as flat and brown as she had imagined it would be. A crowd was gathering near the crest of a low rise, the ground sloping away toward the stone gate. There was an open square of dark earth under a tent, and Dalton and Kingfish and Mateo and three other men Frannie didn't know hefted the casket from the back of the hearse and laid it gently on the bier. Tina perched uncomfortably on the edge of a folding chair, her belly pressing against an old blue maternity dress she'd borrowed from Mae. Frannie bent over to her and whispered.

"How are you holding up?"

Tina stole glances at the coffin and then looked into her hands. Frannie looked at Mae, who shook her head and grimaced. Frannie said, "It's not your fault."

Tina's voice was thin. Drops fell from her averted eyes and spotted the dress. "Oh, isn't it? Really? If I'd stayed home in Blanchardstown and waited tables, would this all still have happened?"

Mae said, "You can't think like that. You can't." She looked at Frannie, who shrugged. Mae pointed at the top of Tina's head and made a face at her sister, mouthed, *Say something*.

Frannie closed her eyes for a moment, thinking, then opened them and kneeled down so she could see Tina's red face. She said, "Too much happened. Too many did wrong for you to carry the weight just because you're alive and other people are dead." She reached over and took Tina's small hand. "We'll learn something, right?" She looked up at Mae. "We'll try to be better at life."

Tina rubbed at her red eyes with the back of her hand and sighed. Frannie tried to remember what it was like to be that lost, that bereft, and thought of being at her mother's funeral in the cold and snow of Holy Cross. Remembered not just the pure aching sadness but the sense of abandonment and uncertainty. Where would they go, her and Mae? Who would they be? Frannie let herself feel that it must be something like that for Tina.

Mae stretched, groaning, one hand on her bruised ribs. She fanned herself with one hand. "I never thought it would be hot, did you?"

"No, I never thought about it. Who knows what Oklahoma's like?"

Tina said, "It is hot, right? I'm glad it's not just me."

Mae said, "I don't know why I thought it would be as cold as home."

"I'm all right, I shouldn't complain. I appreciate your carting me all the way here, and me peeing every fifteen minutes."

Mae squeezed the girl's hand. "God, I remember that. If I left the house when I was pregnant with Tansy I'd make a map in my head of all the public bathrooms in a ten-mile radius." She looked at Frannie. "How's the nose?"

Frannie shrugged, went into her purse and got a bottle, spilled two tablets into her hand. Tina said, "God, how can you do that, take the pills without water? I'd choke."

"I got in the habit after the ACL surgery. That was some pain. I couldn't be bothered to look for a glass." She gingerly touched the tip of her nose. "How's it look?"

Her sister batted her hand away from her face. "Don't touch. The makeup mostly covers it. It's just a little swollen."

"How about the eyes?"

"Ah, a little bruising. Almost gone."

Frannie reached out a hand to Mae's middle. "How's your ribs?"

"Better." She smiled. "Christ, we're like roller derby girls. All taped up and bruised."

Tina produced a smile under her streaked makeup. "It's okay to have some scars, right? What was it you said? It gives us character."

"Well, we're Mullens." Frannie put her arm around Mae, who winced, but hugged her back, tight, and put her hand on Tina's thin shoulder. "This is what Mullens look like."

It could have been much worse. Frannie thought of the minutes after the gunshots in the small room, the cops running in from the street, Lino Camacho with his shaved head shouting into a radio, the paramedics advancing from body to body, each more bruised and bloody than the last.

At the hospital they told her that her nose was broken (again) and she was forgotten on a gurney in the hallway near the X-ray department. Khandi found her, the trauma nurse with the Purple Heart, and got her a pair of scrubs. She slipped into a bathroom and changed, leaving her ruined blouse and blood-spattered jeans in a trash barrel marked with a hazardous waste symbol. In her new, accidental disguise she moved through the rooms, watching them work on Mae and Sleeper and Adolph, listening to the shouted orders and watching nurses and techs moving in and out of the curtained partitions.

She had seen them bring Sleeper in just ahead of her, a small woman in a blue jumpsuit crouched over his chest and working even as the gurney moved, nurses and doctors and technicians shouting numbers to each other. She watched them work until as long as she could stand and was grateful when Khandi saw her and shooed her out, giving Frannie a deep nod that she took as a promise he would live. She stood motionless in a corner of another room and was the last one with Adolph's body. She pulled down the sheet and saw the slack and empty look, his eyes half open and the terrible wound at his throat partially hidden by a square of gauze, as if he'd been torn at by some wild creature and left to die. She had to restrain the impulse to touch his blue-white skin. When she stepped out of the room she glanced down a long corridor full of police and reporters and other people who might have been the Wurtz family or just the people waiting in any emergency room for bad news or for good, everyone the same.

At the end of the corridor she saw a figure moving slowly, a man. He held one arm held close against his side. He had on a doctor's coat over jeans and a green scrub top and when he reached the end of the hall he turned and looked at her. She could have grabbed a uniformed policeman—there was one a few steps away, or a security guard. If she turned her head slightly she could catch Lino's eye and with one hand point down the corridor. He was hurt, she knew, bleeding from the bullet that had gone through the flesh at his hip. His face was the bloodless gray of stone and he breathed though his mouth, his eyes clouded by pain. When he caught her eye he stopped and leaned against the wall and they stood, staring at each other. The moment passed and then he drew himself up and kept walking and disappeared around the far corner and was gone. At the place where he'd been standing there was a dark star, the faint, crimson print of his hand.

She went in and sat by Mae, holding her unconscious sister's hand and watching her eyes move beneath their fine white lids. "Tell me I did the right thing," she whispered, though she couldn't say who exactly she was talking to. "Tell me how to let go of all this. Please, please," she said. "Tell me what to do."

She'd woken in a private room with no memory of having left her sister's side. There was a doctor she didn't know standing over her and behind him, Scanlon, standing by the window and looking intently at whatever was going on outside. The doctor had a file in his hands and looked at her without speaking for a few minutes. He made a few notes with a pen, his hand moving so fast she couldn't imagine he was leaving legible marks behind.

He said he was worried about her, about her history with boxing and the fights in the last week, her having lost consciousness. He asked, "Do you know what CTE is?" and she shook her head. "Chronic traumatic encephalopathy." She looked over his shoulder at Scanlon, wishing him out of the room. The doctor said, "It's something we see in football players, hockey players. Boxers, like you."

"I haven't really boxed in years."

"Unfortunately, it doesn't take much to do real damage. And these episodes in the last week? These fights?"

She thought about what to say. Scanlon stood unmoving at the window, his gaze averted, as if giving her privacy. "That wasn't boxing," she said. "Those fights. There was nothing I could do about those situations."

The doctor went on, his voice gentle. "People who get repeated brain trauma, they can have loss of motor coordination, memory. Personality changes. There's a lot of new research on this. And one of the things we see in CTE is increased aggression. People have trouble keeping control in tense situations. It's something to be cautious about."

"I didn't want to get into those . . ." She groped for a word, her face hot, feeling herself getting angry that she had to explain herself, especially in front of Scanlon. "Situations," she said again. "What happened. I didn't go looking for those fights."

"But they found you?" He closed the file. "I'd like to see you again, in a few weeks. CTE can be serious, Ms. Mullen. There are things we can do, therapies, but mostly, by the time we see symptoms, the damage is done."


When he left she glared across the room at Scanlon, waiting for him to speak. He didn't seem to be in a hurry. When he finally turned away from the window he looked at her quickly, and then down at his shoes. He said, "I don't understand what happened. To Red Ahearn. I don't know how I could have missed that." He swallowed. "All of that. I knew him, Jesus. Twenty years." He looked at her again and then away. She didn't know how to handle him this way, used to his sputtering anger and hard judgment. He turned to look out the window again. "Out there, the news people, the reporters. They want to know what happened and I don't have one goddamned thing to tell them." Frannie wondered about his life. She knew he had a wife, kids, but didn't know much more. He said, "I thought we were friends. He was giving up witnesses, getting people killed. It makes me think what else I got wrong."

He cleared his throat and stood waiting. She understood this was an apology, little as it was. She thought to say something harsh, to send him on his way. She said, "Yeah, well. There's a lot of that going around."

He worked his mouth, maybe angry again. "I was maybe wrong about you. I don't know, I guess. I guess I don't understand how you come from that, from growing up with that? But then go our way?" She had to think about what he was talking about, who the objects of his vague sentence might be. "To grow up in a house where nobody knows right from wrong and then become a cop? I couldn't see it."

She made a noise in her throat, something that must have sounded like the warning growl of a dog. He held up a hand. "I know. I know how that sounds. My old man was a cop. So I knew everything there was about how to be law enforcement. I thought, anyway. My wife?

We're in counseling. My wife says that's one way to look at it, that my old man was a cop and so I know how to be a cop. She says, another way to look at it is that my old man was a judgmental prick. So, you know."

Frannie wanted him to stop talking, to leave. She rubbed at her swollen face and felt her bones under her fingers. She wasn't ready for this much new reality. She couldn't get a grip on anything and wanted to walk out of the hospital and go somewhere where nobody knew her, to sit someplace quiet and think and get everything straight in her mind. Who was wrong and who was right, who she loved and hated. She wondered if this was what it was like to have amnesia, maybe. To have people telling you your own life story while you tried it out in your mind to see if it seemed it could be true.

Scanlon took a step toward the door, then stopped. He said, "You were a boxer?"

"When I was young. Still do the training."

He jerked a blunt thumb at his chest, "Football. Temple. What he said, the doctor?" He pointed through the door. "It's nothing to fool with. A friend of mine knew that guy who was a coach for the Bears. He was a great guy, a sharp kid and he just got destroyed by it. Brain trauma from getting concussions when he was playing ball in college. It took years to show up, but then depression, drugs, and he just . . . came apart. When he finally killed himself his brain was eaten up, they said. By the damage over the years." He pulled something out of his pocket, a folded piece of paper that he looked down at and then laid on the table next to her bed. At the door he shrugged and said, "But what the hell do I know?"

She waited until she heard his footsteps fade in the hallway before she picked up the paper. She turned it in her hands and saw it was a picture of a car, a distorted, bluish mage that looked like it had been pulled from a surveillance camera in a parking lot. It took her a minute to recognize the road in front of the hospital, the walkway crossing Thirty-fourth Street from the parking lot. A man and a woman were in the front seat of the car. The man had his head turned and his face was in shadow, and if she hadn't seen him in the same outfit – the white coat, the bloodied scrub top - she wouldn't have been able to say who exactly it was. The image of the woman driving the car was sharper, but it wasn't until Frannie pictured her standing in front of a bar on Clearfield with a cigarette in her hand that she could remember Bertie McCullough's name.

At the cemetery in Oklahoma, Frannie stepped away to the shade of a bur oak and made a call. Khandi answered on the first ring.

"How's the patient?"

"Good. As far as I can tell. He doesn't say much, does he?"

"Not much."

"Is that why you all call him Sleeper?"

"No, but you should ask him to tell the story. How do you think he's doing?"

She ran down his vital stats, told Frannie he seemed past any real danger. "The bullet missed his lung, but you know it's not just the path of the bullet, it's the shock wave from something going twelve hundred feet per second hitting you in the chest."

"Tell me he's going to be okay." Frannie was surprised by her own reaction, her breathing suddenly constricted, the air harder to find.

"I don't make promises like that, Frannie. He's stable, he's conscious. The rest is up to God."

"I'm sorry. I just can't lose anyone else. You know?"

"I do. If that was in my power this world would be a different place." Khandi's voice changed. "He wants to get out of here, I can tell you that. What does he like?"

"Sorry?"

"What does he like to do? Does he like magazines? Books?"

"You know, I have no idea."

"His parents are here every day. I guess I can ask them."

"Parents? Jesus, he has parents? What are they like?"

"Hey, I thought this guy was your friend."

"Well, 'friend' might not be the right word."

"Oh, yeah? What would you say is the right word?" Frannie could hear repressed laughter in the nurse's voice. When she didn't answer, Khandi said, "Well, maybe you need to think on that and get back to me."

At the graveside Dalton stepped toward the women and introduced Wyatt's sister, Berenice. She hugged Frannie tight, smelling like vanilla perfume and cigarettes.

"I saw your picture in the paper, but you're much prettier in person," she said, "Wyatt told us about you, that red hair. Look at it."

Frannie held out a hand. "Thank you, for letting us come."

Berenice patted her hand. She was tall, like her brothers, with the same wheat-colored hair and pale blue eyes. "Letting you come? It couldn't have been no other way. My brother would have wanted you here. We all do."

Mae admired the cowboy boots she wore under her black dress, inlaid with white crosses and designs the green of faded copper. She struck a pose. "These are Dan Post. We'll take you shopping before you go home."

Dalton pointed along the slope. "There's the Guthries, down there. Woody's family, though they scattered his ashes in Coney Island, New York, I heard." There was a line of motorcycles leading down through the gates and extending out of sight into the trees. A state trooper was parked at the intersection and directed traffic.

"Look at them all."

Men were walking up the rise, many of them wearing biker colors. There were police in uniform and a couple of long black limousines stuck in the line of bikes. A woman Frannie recognized from a TV show about Chicago detectives laughed with guys in Bandido colors while two California Highway Patrol officers in green jackets looked on. "Look at them all," Frannie said again. "I forgot that he knew so many people."

"He made a lot of bikes for people. Rich people from Hollywood, poor shitkickers from nowhere. He was a good old boy, too. One of them California Highway Patrol boys got clipped by a semi, snapped his spine. Wyatt built him a three-wheeler, a trike with all hand controls out of an old Electraglide like the cops ride. Put a box for the wheelchair on the back. Didn't charge him a thing."

Frannie looked at Dalton, cleared eyed. "I think Wyatt deserved better than he got from me."

Dalton nodded. "I knew my brother about as well as anybody, I guess. We grew up together, building bikes out of junk we got from Rath's down in Tecumseh. I was away in prison some, but we always kept in touch." He looked at the casket, then away up the hill. "He made his mistakes, too. The way we grew up put a darkness in us, in all of us. Wyatt tell you about Pell Carver?"

Frannie nodded. "Your father. He told me some. He told me you fought him, trying to protect Wyatt and your sister."

"Yeah, but I wasn't always around. A lot of bad things happened. Berenice, well, I know she took up with a lot of men who treated her wrong, and she still drinks to fall asleep. Wyatt when he was young, he was a hellraiser. But he had a good heart, and I think he picked you because he knew you would show him a good way. There was something straight and right in you and he knew it was what he wanted to be around."

"What about you, Dalton? What do you want to be around?"

He looked at her directly, his eyes touched with the same fire as his brother's had been, so that for a moment she felt disconnected from the earth. He said, "I don't know, rightly. I been going one way a long time, but I see how Wyatt got clear of it and I wonder." She looked down to break the connection, and he put his hand out and touched her arm. At his wrist was a tattoo; a red diamond enclosing a number and symbol, "1%." He said, "I spent so much time angry. The thing of it is, I'm not sure I know how to be any other way."

She smiled. "Well, you figure that out, you have to come tell me." She scanned the crowd, wondered if Patrick was out there, somewhere, watching. "I sure would like to know."


Jimmy Coonan sat at Curran-Fromhold Correctional Facility in Northeast Philadelphia, in a steel chair in a row of steel chairs bolted to a stone wall, waiting for his name to be called. When the guard came and got him he followed her down a short hallway to a row of cubicles faced with glass. The guard was a young African American woman, wide in the hips and with complicated braids. Jimmy said, "Ain't that hair a problem? I mean, the guys ever grab for it?" She showed him to his chair, pointing wordlessly, and he sat and waited, wanting a cigarette. After about five minutes Cam came in wearing an orange jumpsuit and handcuffs and sat down on the other side of the glass.

"They still do the orange here? I thought it was the red now."

"Nah, that's upstate."

"I guess. How's it going? You got everything?"

Cam shrugged. "I guess. It's just intake. They'll move me out to Graterford after we plead."

Jimmy looked back down the hall. "It's not bad, Curran. I was in last they had me in the overflow, the gym at Holmesburg, around the corner on Torresdale. Now that was a hole, that place. Which they ain't cleaned it since Willie Sutton was in."

"Nah, it's okay. It ain't bad."

"What's Bobby D say?"

"Well, that's the thing."

"What's the thing?"

Cam lifted his cuffed hands to scratch at his beard. "He's trying for Coercion, 2906, instead of Kidnapping, 2903. You know, saying we didn't plan, me and Marty. Or reconnoiter. We didn't send no ransom demand. If that was all there was to it."

"But it ain't."

"No."

Jimmy frowned. "I see your problem."

"Yeah. Ongoing criminal conspiracy, the act committed while in the perpetration of a felony. Plus was I paid to be there, which the no-show job could be seen as. All aggravating factors, Bobby D says."

Jimmy sat for a minute, thinking. Seeing the bind his nephew was in, and how it would go. "Who they want you to give up?"

"Well, there's my question. Who was giving the orders?"

"Adolph and Rudy and Marty are gone." His uncle stared into space, thinking. After a minute, he lifted a corner of his mouth. "Jimmy Hoffa."

Cam waggled his eyebrows. "Those guidos from Passyunk Avenue. What do I owe those people?"

Jimmy laughed. He moved close to the glass and talked out of the side of his mouth. "I knew you was smart. Give 'em up. Harry Buono and Tony Buck and every one of those Italian pricks who took money for work that we did."

"It's a big decision, Jimmy. I go into Witness Protection, I can't ever come back."

"About that I can't say, kid. You got to make your own call. But I say, why let all the weight fall on you?"

Cam leaned forward. "But I need to hear it's okay from you, Jimmy. I'm not doing nothing gets you in a spot."

Jimmy shook his head. "Those Italian boys come for me, they better know what they're doing. Anyway, they get lucky, I got a spot all picked out at Holy Cross out in Yeadon with my pop and my uncles and all the other Coonans."

Cam's eyes clouded, and Jimmy could see the kid was trying to hold it together. "You'll say good-bye to my sister? I mean, we didn't talk much she moved out to Cherry Hill, but if I disappear?"

Jimmy nodded. "I'll do what needs to get done." He waved a dismissive hand. "You know, all this shit was done, anyway. Adolph, the local, it's all over a long time ago. I think I knew it for a while, I just didn't want to know it. Anyway you're what, twenty-one?"

Cam had to think. "Twenty-three, next June."

"Yeah, see, go make your own thing. What would you get, doing what you're told? Working for guys like Adolph? You might as well be working in a factory." The woman came back and they stood up. Cam raised a hand and Jimmy leaned in. He said, "Don't be the fish, kid. Be the shark."

# 25

The gym was a converted garage, oil spots on the floor and hot for June, even with the big fans going in the corner, a roar that Frannie had to shout over as they moved in the ring. Tina watched intently, eyes going back and forth between the two women as Mari, shorter but hard-muscled and broader across the shoulders, moved inside Frannie's reach and tapped her once, twice on the leather pads of her headgear, laughing as she landed light shots to Frannie's cheeks, her forehead. Frannie blinked away sweat, working her head and feeling her coarse hair trapped in spikes at the headband. When the two women stepped apart Mari's head was dripping onto the mat, wet as if she'd run it under a faucet.

There was a big screen TV in the corner and they'd steal glances at it, at two women in an Olympic ring in London, looking small and bright and hard as painted sticks, one in blue and one in red. The space beyond them was black and they stood each other off with stiff-armed jabs or fell into exhausted clinches, arms tangled and chests heaving.

Tansy ran across the wide space after Mari's boys, who were smacking the heavy bag, trying to rattle the chain with their small brown fists. Mari threw up her gloved hands in victory and the boys ran over to watch and they called her champ and made rushing, whistling noises to evoke the roaring crowd on the TV. Mari climbed out of the ring and kissed Zeke on the top of the head and took the sleeping baby from Tina and cooed to her in Spanish, calling her *muñeca* and *cariña*. Mae hugged Tansy and climbed awkwardly through the ropes and then stood chin out while Frannie tugged the straps on her sister's headgear and when she was satisfied she tapped her fist against the forehead padding, Mae squinting uncertainly and hunching her shoulders together and her daughter watching, fascinated.

Frannie took Mae's gloved hands in hers and held them up. "You've got height, so use that." She modeled a stance for her sister, holding her arms out and down, then grabbed Mae's gloves and put them against her own head. "You're punching down, which is better, and I have to get inside your reach to land one, right?" Tansy and Zeke stood in imitation of the women, fists up at their chins, eyes narrowed. Mari jiggled the baby, whispered fiercely, "Get her, Mae. Whup that *blanquita* ass."

The sisters turned and threw their gloved fists, Mae

giving off small involuntary whooping noises when she connected.

"There you go," Frannie said. "You can hit, you're not going to hurt me, okay? But you gotta move your feet, too." She turned and pivoted, pulling back to point to her feet. "Did you see how Mari did, like dancing? You love to dance. Dance here, too." She put her gloves up, pushed at Mae's head and Mae swung hard, her black hair whipping with the effort, and Frannie sidestepped it and tapped her on the temple. They stopped for a minute, Mae slumping, her mouth open, and her sister smiled and shook off her glove.

Frannie put her white hand flat on Mae's heaving chest. "You're okay. You're doing okay."

"Man." Mae opened her mouth wider around the guard, wheezing and rubbing her chest. "I'm going to keep doing this, I need a better sports bra."

Tina laughed from the ropes. "That's where we beat out you top-heavy girls, yeah?" She thrust out her own small chest, curled her arms in a bodybuilder's pose. "Sure, it's the sleek girl wins out in the ring."

Frannie said, "Best workout I know, boxing. But you got to breathe, to remember to breathe." Mae put her hands on her knees and tried to slow her ragged breaths, the air whistling in her teeth. Frannie moved in and hugged her around the shoulder. "You're doing good."

"It's hard. I mean, I knew it was hard, but it's really hard."

"People think fighting is about punching. It's about stamina. Moving and breathing. You'll learn. It's a long game." Mae looked at her and Frannie held up a fist. "They beat on you, they hurt you, yeah, but they wear down and then they beat themselves. You got to keep moving, keep breathing. Then you live long enough to win."

The noise picked up from the television and they turned to watch, Frannie and Mae, Mari cradling the baby and pointing for the boys and Tansy. Tina said, "It's Katie, from Bray." On the screen the women in red and blue stood back from each other and the crowd sang in the echoing space, something beautiful and other-worldly, and then the announcer was calling the winner. The woman in red dropped to her knees and threw up her arms and beamed, crying. Her face bruised and slick with sweat, she punched the air and danced in victory, and when someone handed her a flag she ran circles as the crowd sang and screamed, the silk spread from her shoulders like wings.